OUT OF BODY, INTO MIND
A METAPHYSICAL ADVENTURE

To Order Call
NEW LEAF 1-800-326-2665
MOVING BOOKS 1-800-777-6683

Also by the author:

Beyond   Skepticism

The Search for Nina Fletcher

OUT OF BODY, INTO MIND

A METAPHYSICAL ADVENTURE

BY

STEPHEN HAWLEY MARTIN

The Oaklea Press
Richmond, Virginia

FIRST EDITION
First Printing, 1995

**Preliminary Library of Congress Cataloging-in-Publi-
cation Data**

Martin, Stephen Hawley, 1944-
    Beyond Skepticism: All the Way to Enlightenment /
Stephen Hawley Martin

ISBN 0-9646601-6-4

I. Title.

1 2 3 4 5 6 7 8 9 0

Dedication

For Sophie, Hawley and Hannah Grace.
May you each find and accomplish
your purpose.

FOREWORD

I met the woman you will come to know as Claire DuMond in the East Lodge of Linekin Bay Resort near Booth Bay Harbor, Maine. It was the last week of July and I had recently quit my job as president of an advertising agency. My entire family was there, including my grown daughter from my first marriage, my elderly mother, my wife and my son, Hawley, then a toddler. My wife's relatives were among our party, too, more than a dozen of them. Her brother had flown in from California, an uncle from Texas and some cousins from Switzerland. We'd pretty much taken over the lounge in East Lodge with its big fireplace and shabby stuffed furniture. The lights were low but the room was loud and gay. A crackling fire fought back the evening chill. Children and adults occupied themselves in Trivial Pursuit or Pictionary. It seemed odd among so much family in a place so far away to meet another Richmonder I hadn't met before. She was a good 20 years older than I, and other than the city of her residence we had no connection whatsoever. Yet it was one of those first encounters where I felt I'd known the person all my life. She sat by the fire. I pulled up a chair. After a few minutes I found myself explaining I'd left the ad game because the timing was good, the agency had been sold and would be merged with another, and I'd always had an urge to write.

"I've become convinced," I said, with a frankness reserved for someone I supposed I'd never see again, "that each of us has a purpose, and if we aren't directing our efforts toward the fulfillment of it, we feel disconnected. Life becomes a burden. We begin snapping at the kids."

"I've no doubt," she said. "What sort of books do you intend to write?"

"I have a mystery outlined already, and the first three chapters written. I'm thinking it will be the first in a series."

"A protagonist who just can't seem to stay out of trouble?"

"Precisely," I said. Her smile seemed a bit patronizing so I added, "Of course I eventually plan to write books that are much more profound."

"If your destiny is to write something profound, why not do it now?"

"Mysteries seem a good place to start. After I'm known, developed a following, I'll have an audience for the heavy stuff."

She held me with the hazel-green eyes of a younger woman. "You realize of course that things will not work out as you expect."

"Why not?"

"Because things never work out the way we plan."

"I've noticed," I said dryly.

"Fate has things work in a way you never could have imagined, just to let you know you aren't the one who is in control."

"Who is this fellow, Fate?" I said.

She smiled. "You'll be successful, I'm absolutely certain of it. Just remember to stay flexible."

I thought: *How could she possibly know if I'm going to be successful?*

"You see, you're going to write my story," she added. "*It* will make you famous."

I suddenly felt ill at ease.

"You'll change my name, of course."

"You're serious, aren't you?"

"Absolutely."

"But why me?" By then I knew she'd been a journalist. "Why not write it yourself?"

"I don't want the publicity. And I've had a feeling you'd walk into my life."

"What makes your story so astounding it would make you, and will make me, famous?"

"And hounded by talk show hosts?"

"And hounded by talk show hosts."

"The secret of life."

"Excuse me?"

"My story contains the secret of life."

Sure it does, I thought. But I must confess I was intrigued enough to buy a tape recorder in Booth Bay the next morning.

On Thursday, it rained. All my companions including my wife and daughter, headed to Freeport to join the throng of lemmings while I spent the day in East Lodge by the fire, transfixed by what I had heard.

And so the story you are about to read is Claire DuMond's, not mine. I've honored her wish and changed the names to protect the innocent. I've edited out the chit chat, tightened the prose, organized all of it into sentences, paragraphs and chapters. But alas, I can take no more credit than a midwife for revealing the secret she had kept to herself until that day in Maine.

S. H. M.
May, 1995

Out of Body, Into Mind

*Before it incarnates, each soul
enters into a sacred contract
with the Universe to accomplish
certain things. It enters into this
commitment in the fullness of its
being. Whatever the task that your
soul has agreed to, all of the
experiences of your life serve to
awaken within you the memory of
that contract, and to prepare you
to fulfill it.*

From *The Seat of the Soul*
by Gary Zukav

Out of Body, Into Mind

May, 1952

1

The news so upset me I almost didn't sleep after talking to the doctor from Baltimore. There was nothing more they could do and were sending Papa home on the morning train.

I'd been standing on the worn cement platform for half an hour when at last it appeared out of the darkness, slowing as it approached and jerking to a stop, a hiss and a spray of steam. Passengers streamed out, ladies in hats, men in narrow ties. Porters in red caps pushed hand trucks and stepped lively. Needing to find the sleeper, I weaved through the mass of humanity, past three coaches before I spotted the nurse. She stood on the steps craning her neck and looking as though whomever was supposed to meet her was late.

I raised my voice over the din. "Over here," I said. "I'm Claire DuMond. You're looking for me, right?"

Her eyes swung my way; took me in from top to bottom. No doubt I was not what she had been expecting. Women my age and of my breeding in the South were supposed to be meek and mild. I was anything but. The truth was, I was a rebel and my appearance showed it. I was tall and I dressed in a way I considered smart, suits and dresses with sharp angles and bright colors. No little Bo Peep outfits for me.

"Pleased to meet you, Miss DuMond," she said. "We'll need a couple of porters to get your daddy off the train."

I saw one who wasn't occupied, flagged him down, hailed another. I motioned for them to follow. The nurse led all three of us on board. I lifted my hand to cover my mouth. Nothing could have prepared me for how small and frail, how spindly Papa looked, like one of the hollow-eyed survivors of Dachau I'd seen in news reels at the end of the war. Since eleven the night before I'd been trying to submerge a thought. Now it broke the surface: *He was going to die.*

How could he? He'd been so healthy.

The porters lowered the stretcher to the platform. Everyone, the nurse, porters, Papa, all of us--moved toward the exit. The nurse said, "Ain't come to since we found him outside the emergency room--lyin' facedown, unconscious." She looked down with affection and patted his hand. "Picked the best hospital in Baltimore, he did--Johns Hopkins. May be in a coma, but he ain't dumb."

We entered the enormous main hall of Broad Street Station. The sounds of footfalls bounced off marble walls and the domed ceiling 50 feet up. They echoed inside me and tears welled. I did my best to hold them back. Emotions made a person real but the place to show them was not in public. *Lord, please don't let the flood gates open here.* I always so felt sorry for people who lost control, but looking at Papa--the tears started coming. I couldn't hold them but I must.

I must think of something else--of anything, of my dresses in the closet, pretty dresses and tailored suits, autumn tones. My typewriter needing a new ribbon, how I hated to change it, hated to get my hands smudged. My goal of getting off the Woman's Page, and--Jeff. How he'd proposed marriage the night before after he walked me

from his car, the sent of honeysuckle in the air. I'd
shivered and he'd rubbed my shoulders. Dear Jeff. How
comical he'd looked as he went down on bended knee, his
flat top needing a trim. What was I going to say? I had to
tell him something. There must be a way to keep my
options open, a way not to hurt him. He'd asked me
several times, and now he expected an answer. He'd
made that clear. A simple yes or no.

I straightened my back and held my head up,
trudged on and realized the tears had receded, that the
crisis had passed. I would not become an object of pity.

"If Johns Hopkins is so good," I said, "why don't
they know what's wrong with him? Best minds in
medicine, and all."

"Every now and then one comes along that baffles
the best of them. Besides, your daddy ain't no spring
chicken."

"Just last week we played three sets of tennis--
singles," I said. "Papa was in top form. I was ready to
drop and he still had plenty in reserve."

We moved through a doorway into the shade of the
portico. The porters pushed the stretcher to an ambulance
with its back to the curb, its doors open to a dark hole.
Two men dressed in white lifted Papa in.

"If you don't mind my asking, Miss, how old is
your father?"

"Let me see. Late sixties, I guess."

A knowing look transformed the nurse's face.

The insolence, I thought. Late sixties may have
seemed old in those days, but this nurse had not seen
Papa before. What could she possibly know? He easily
could have passed for 40 or 45. People were shocked
when they learned I was his daughter. "Someone doesn't
just go from being able to play three sets of singles--" I
said, then held my tongue. Anger wasn't going to make
him well.

"Why don't you ride in back with him? I'll sit up
front."

I peered inside. Papa lay on his back, his eyes

14

open in a hollow stare. An attendant stood by, his hand on the handle. His face asked the question.

I glanced at the nurse.

"His condition ain't changed in three days, Miss. He'll be all right." She nodded toward the opening. "We'll see you at Stuart Circle."

I hiked up my skirt. The attendant held my hand and I stepped onto the running board. The odor of rubbing alcohol and iodine hit me as I situated myself on the bench. The doors slammed shut, the ambulance shimmied. We were on our way with a jerk and a shudder.

Papa looked like a zombie in the shadows, gaunt and gray, eyes wide open, staring into space. I leaned over him.

"Papa, can you hear me?"

His lips moved but no sound came out. This time I spoke French. "It's me, Papa. Please try to speak."

His lips moved--still no sound. Then barely audible, "Angelique?"

"It's me, Papa. Claire. You're home."

The words came pouring forth from him in French. "Oh, Angelique, it is you, just as I've dreamed you would come for me at the end and we would be together for all eternity. It has been 50 long years my dear but good years, years the others had not, except Jean-Luc of course, and I would gladly make the sacrifice again, but now the time has come . . . seven o'clock, the eighth of May . . ."

"Papa, it's Claire," I said, but he was back in his trance.

What names had he spoken? Angelique? I didn't know an Angelique. And Jean-Luc? I didn't know a Jean-Luc either.

I held on as the ambulance bumped and swayed. Light filtered through two small windows and flickered on Papa's stone-like face. At last we stopped. I heard the front doors slam. Then the rear doors swung open. The attendants took hold of the stretcher and pulled it out. We were at the emergency entrance. The air felt cool after that

15

ride, and I was glad to see Dr. Martin, my father's golfing partner and physician.

"Sorry I couldn't meet the train, Claire," he said. "Other patients to attend to. Don't you worry--your father's in good hands."

I climbed down. Dr. Martin and I walked beside Papa as they wheeled him down a long, narrow corridor with two-tone walls, pea green above, dark green below. It felt as though a belt were fastened around my chest so tight that I could hardly breathe. "I don't understand, Dr. Martin. The doctors at Johns Hopkins ran all kinds of tests. Don't they know what's wrong?"

"Think they're hot stuff up there in Baltimore--damn Yankees. Don't know beans when it comes down to it. Don't worry, Claire. We'll find out--have him good as new in no time. Your father's strong as a bull."

I drew in air. "He spoke to me," I said.

"He spoke?" Dr. Martin moved his hand in front of Papa's eyes. "Paul," he said in a loud voice. "Can you hear me, Paul?"

We stopped in front of an elevator door, bumped and scratched. An orderly pushed the call button.

"I think I should rephrase that," I said. "He wasn't talking to me. He was talking to someone named Angelique."

Dr. Martin's brow wrinkled. "Delirious?"

"He spoke French. Said something about 50 years. That he was going to join her on the eighth of May."

The doors slid open. The elevator car seemed deep.

"Look, Claire, if he was able to speak--even if he was delirious--it's a good sign." Dr. Martin shrugged. "At least he's not brain dead."

Brain dead?

Dr. Martin gave my arm a squeeze. "I'm going to take him upstairs now and examine him. I'll know more this afternoon. Give me a call or stop by. And for goodness sake, try not to worry."

Dr. Martin, the orderlies, the stretcher with Papa

16

on it moved onto the elevator. The door closed and I was left staring at two glass port holes in a field of beige.

I tried to take hold of myself as I walked down the hallway. He'd been so healthy and robust. He could beat me at tennis. He could beat Jeff at tennis. Was he really going to die? The idea of no more Papa was like the idea of death without an afterlife. I did not believe there was an afterlife then but I couldn't imagine ceasing to exist. How could you imagine nothing? How could I imagine life without Papa?

I exhaled--tried to push away these thoughts along with the air from my lungs. It would be better to think of something else. Something pleasant. Like the dogwoods, bright white dogwoods against an azure sky. Dark trunks sprouting from the yellow-green lawn of the median dividing Monument Avenue. Azalea bushes with red, magenta, and hot pink blossoms lining walkways and framing windows of imposing nineteenth century homes.

God. How could I enjoy the beauty of nature when Papa was about to--

Tires squealed on cobblestones. My gaze came to rest on the J. E. B. Stuart statue encircled by a wrought iron fence. He faced north on a prancing horse. Defiant in the face of the invading Yankees.

Why did I think of Jeff? He wasn't the enemy and the two of us were not at war. Only on occasion, perhaps, and it wasn't his fault. Not really. He was a man and in those days I had a running battle with men. I wasn't where I wanted to be, not by a ways, but I was trying, trying to become the person I knew I could. Men kept blocking me. How could I strive toward goals, how could I unfold? How could I *become* if I was stuck in a kitchen? I hated to cook. Hated darning socks.

I looked at my watch. I was five minutes late.

I parked the Ford in the lot by the newspaper, walked west on Grace Street through the lunchtime crowd, the men in hats, women in small round ones. Little veils. I hurried past a bookstore and a millinery, passed through the door, and breathed in the odor of bacon, pastrami and cheeseburgers. Jeff adjusted his wire-rimmed glasses and waved at me from a booth halfway back. His flat-top still needed a trim, creating a comic look at odds with his solemn expression.

We came together. He put his hands on my arms. "How is he, Claire?"

"Oh God, Jeff, I don't know if I can bear it," I said. "Dr. Martin said not to worry, but I can't help it. He's unconscious. Eyes open and unconscious." I wiped my cheek. "He did speak--delirious. Nothing made any sense. He was talking to someone named Angelique, saying that everyone was dead. Everyone but him. I wonder if he meant her, too? He said he'd had 50 good years--that he'd join them on the eighth of May. Oh, Jeff, I think he meant he's going to die."

Wrinkles in Jeff's brow grew deep. "Where would your father have been 50 years ago?"

"Where he grew up, I suppose. French North Africa. Algeria, I think."

We sat down and a waitress appeared, her pencil poised over a pad. "What'll it be? Meatloaf's good."

"Burger, rare. Fries," Jeff said.

"Whatever," I said. "An egg salad on toast."

She nodded and left.

Jeff seemed to study me. "Did your father ever say anything about what happened when he was young that might give us a clue?"

"Who knows?" I said. "I doubt it matters, anyway. Truth is, he never talked about growing up. Algiers either. I guess it was Algiers. Maybe it was Casablanca. You know, I must have asked him half a dozen times. Always changed the subject . . . seems strange now that I think about it. As though he didn't want me to know. Do you suppose? Maybe he just didn't want to talk about it. Wonder why?"

"And today he talked about having 50 years while all the others were dead? Odd."

"I haven't the slightest idea what that was all

18

about. Just some wild dream, probably."

Jeff removed his glasses and inspected the lenses. "How old would he have been 50 years ago?"

"I'm not sure. Eighteen, I guess. Fifty years. How could anyone remember that far back? What difference could it make?"

"Obviously, it's on his mind. What do you suppose it was?"

The hollow-eyed survivors of Dachau came marching toward me. "I don't know, Jeff. Anyway, could it matter? How could it have anything to do with him being in a coma?"

Jeff replaced his glasses and blinked. "It's an odd feeling. I'd have sworn he was from somewhere other than North Africa. Maybe farther down. More like French Equatorial Africa. Someplace where the local people are more primitive. Where witch doctors still exist. You see, one night--you were late getting home and I was with him alone--we talked about medicine men. He had a kind of fascination with them, you see. Said he used to dabble in magic himself when he was young, but not since he became a Christian. He said the Bible talks about powers and principalities, says to leave magic alone because it's evil. Your father quoted Scripture about it."

"Are you serious?" I said. "Magic? I may be confused right now, Jeff, but I find that difficult to believe. I realize my father is something of a religious nut. Thank goodness he doesn't try to force his beliefs on me. But magic? The two things are incompatible."

"That's what I was saying, don't you see? I'm telling you, Claire, we talked about how a witch doctor can give someone the Evil Eye, and they'll drop dead on the spot." Jeff let his hand flop on the table. "Now, you and I know there's no such thing as an Evil Eye, but primitive people don't. It's got to be their beliefs that cause them to die."

Papa often surprised me with what he thought, but this was too much. "I don't see what that would have to do with his condition now, anyway, no matter where he

19

grew up or what he did when he was young. He certainly doesn't practice magic now. He certainly doesn't believe in, in . . . what did you call it? An Evil Eye?" I shook my head. "His family was from France, Jeff. That's hardly a primitive culture. Not then. Certainly not now."

"Maybe not, but I'm telling you he told me he once dabbled in magic. His very words. Don't you see, Claire? There must be a connection. Magic. Fifty years. The others dead. Yes. It may well have something to do with this mysterious illness." Jeff looked at the ceiling. "Let me give you an example that's close to home: Thomas Jefferson and John Adams--both died on July 4, 1826, exactly 50 years to the day after the Declaration of Independence. They were fierce rivals--both in their eighties, the second and third presidents of the United States. Do you think that was a coincidence?"

"I'm not following you, Jeff. Are you saying magic caused that? Some witch doctor gave Jefferson the Evil Eye? At Monticello? Come on."

"Of course not."

"What then? Are you saying they *planned* their own deaths?"

"Maybe not planned, but at the very least I think they held death at bay so they could see that special day. The mind's a powerful thing."

"Uh-huh. So, what you're saying is, you think my father's illness is in his head--is that it?"

He shrugged. "You said the doctors can't figure out what's wrong. It's possible, I guess. Jefferson and Adams died 50 years after a big event."

"An illness brought on by something that happened 50 years ago. It hardly seems possible," I said. "No. I can't accept that."

"It could be, Claire. My intuition says so, and you know my intuition. It's probably connected with a specific date. Like Washington and Adams and the Fourth of July."

"You really think so don't you, Jeff."

"I really do."

"I suppose anything is possible," I said.

"Why else would he have fallen ill so suddenly? The doctors can't find a reason."

"Fifty years ago. That would be 1902. He did say a date. What was it? May eighth? May 8, 1902. May eighth is next Thursday, that's not much time." I began sliding out of the booth.

"Wait a minute, please." Jeff held up a hand. "Have you forgotten why we're here?"

I remembered, but darn it, we'd made the date before the call from Baltimore. Before I'd learned Papa had collapsed outside the emergency room.

Jeff took a breath. Pain was evident in his eyes. "I thought you'd have an answer. You said you would, but now I see this is the wrong time. Still . . . you did promise you'd let me know today."

"Jeff, Jeff. Dear Jeff. I know what I said, but that was before, before Papa . . . I'm sorry, Jeff, I really am, but you're right, this *is* the wrong time. It's all wrong. I can't think about it now. Papa's in a coma. That's all I can think about. I've got to do something to help him, don't you see?"

"But it's in the doctors' hands now, Claire. What can you do?"

"I don't know, but I can't sit here and ring my hands." I stood. "I'm sorry, Jeff, but we'll have to talk about this later."

Needing a place to think, I went to the newsroom. Most of my co-workers would be at lunch. Only two men sat at their desks, pounding on their Underwoods hunt and peck fashion. It looked as though Alexander O'Malley, the managing editor, was out, too. His office was empty except for the usual clutter as was the woman's corner--the area relegated to female reporters. It was a commentary on the times that all four of us worked exclusively on the Woman's Page.

I tried to think about Papa and what I should do, but my mind kept coming back to my struggle to break out

21

of the society column and recipes and into real reporting. Only the morning before I'd confronted O'Malley about it. Even in my current state the sight of his office caused the memory to flood to mind.

I'd been letting my courage build for weeks-- actually ire was more the word. Papa said everyone had a path they were meant to follow. If I paid attention to my inner voice, and prayed, I'd find mine. I hoped he was right. I wasn't sure about praying, but I believed I had to move in the direction of becoming the person I knew I could be. Otherwise I'd end up nothing more than a façade, and I didn't want that to happen--to end up bitter, unhappy, wondering what might have been.

There I'd been the day before, having these thoughts. I'd taken my hands off the typewriter, clenched my fists and stood. My destiny was to become a reporter, not to sit in a stuffy news room all day pretending life was one long tea party to be reported on with a bunch of superlatives about what all the ladies had worn on any particular day. It was time to take the plunge.

I made my way through the smoke and the racket of typewriters and teletype machines, my high-heels wobbling every time a spike hit a cigarette butt, but not my resolve. I tapped on the glass. O'Malley looked up from a desk that resembled Dresden after the fire bombing. His brows lifted. He gestured for me to come in.

"What is it, Miss DuMond?"

"I'd like to discuss something with you, Mr. O'Malley."

He pulled the cigar from his mouth and picked a flake of tobacco from the end of his tongue. "Uh-huh. Shoot."

"I've been writing engagement announcements, wedding announcements, that sort of thing for the past several days."

"And a mighty fine job of it, too," he said. "A mighty fine job."

"Mr. O'Malley, what does it take to get off the Woman's Page?"

22

"Why would you want to do that?"

"This is a waste of my talent, Mr. O'Malley. I've got a nose for real news, not the stuff we dish out to the old biddies who spend their time with the Woman's Page. I want to prove it. Put me out on the street. Let me show what I can do."

He let out a low whistle. "I don't know, Miss DuMond. There's a rash of weddings coming up."

"Can I ask you something, Mr. O'Malley? Do you call the men around here *Mr.* Jones and *Mr.* Smith and *Mr.* Brown?"

"Do I address them as mister? Hadn't thought about it. No, guess not--what difference does it make?"

"Then please don't address me as Miss."

"No? What should I call you? Mrs.? You're not married, are you?"

"DuMond. Just call me DuMond, same as you call the men Jones and Smith and Brown."

He rolled his eyes. "Whatever you say, Miss Du-- I mean, whatever you say . . . DuMond."

"Now. How about an assignment? A chance to prove my worth? There must be something."

O'Malley picked up a stack of papers and looked through them. His brow wrinkled. He was dying to get rid of me.

"Not much here, I'm afraid. . . . Wait, check that. Here's something. This'll get you out of the office."

"What is it?"

"This is Garden Week, right?"

"Indeed it is." How could I forget? We'd just turned out an entire special section that was so boring it would have put Dolly Madison to sleep.

He tapped the paper. "The Dooley Mansion. There was nothing on it. I want a story on it for Friday's edition. Supposed to be the most spectacular gardens within 200 miles. Take a photographer. That cub--what's her name? The one who does the society stuff. Lydia Blankenship."

I shook my head. "You amaze me, Mr. O'Malley."

"Really?"

"I wasn't just looking for a way out of the office, I was looking for something closer to crime and corruption. Don't you have a murder trial?"

Mr. O'Malley straightened the papers and placed them on the only spot where wood showed through. "That sort of thing can be pretty gruesome, DuMond. Leave it to the men, okay?" He tapped the desk with his palms, a gesture I took to mean the audience he'd granted was over.

"What if I proved it to you?"

"Prove what . . . DuMond?"

"Prove I can compete with the men? Suppose I go out and get a story on my own? Scoop the *News Leader?*"

"First bring me one on the Dooley place, Maymont they call it. I'm telling you I need it." He paused, then shrugged. "Of course, what you do in your spare time is up to you."

I left with as much poise and dignity as I could muster. I even had the presence of mind not to let the door slam although I felt like flinging it hard and watching the glass shatter. After I calmed down I found Lydia Blankenship and drove out to the Dooley Mansion. Wrote a story that afternoon full of the usual superlatives describing the most fabulous gardens within 200 miles. Plopped it in O'Malley's in-basket at about seven that night.

That had only been yesterday, but it seemed ages ago because of the telephone call. Now I was back at my desk. Instead of anger I felt a churning sensation inside. I couldn't just sit there. Maybe Jeff was right. Whatever happened 50 years ago was causing Papa's condition. The more I thought about it, it did seem strange I didn't know where he grew up. How many people didn't know where their father was born and raised? It was odd, all right. How could I find out?

I was a reporter, wasn't I? Reporters dug up information. They started by asking questions, went straight to an expert and didn't beat around.

Who'd known my father longer than anyone? Who

was the expert?

That sick, nostalgic sensation took hold, the one that always came whenever I thought of my mother. She'd know, she'd have to. But how could I get in touch? Papa had told me she'd gone back to Corsica, the island where she was born. According to Papa she'd been homesick and had chosen her homeland over us. I knew her maiden name, Bonifacio, but I didn't know what town she was from. Anyway, she'd probably remarried. There was no way to begin to track her down, no place to begin.

I stared at the telephone next to my black Royal typewriter, then at my message pad. My eyes came to rest on my address book. A thought struck me. Of course, my father's partner, Timothy Calvert. I picked up the book, turned to C. In a moment I had the long distance operator on the line.

"Claire! Haven't heard your voice in ages." He sounded far away. "I'll bet you're all grown up."

It had been a long time--since before the war. Lord, I still had braces then.

"How's your father?" he asked.

I told him about Papa's condition, the coma, and as much as I could remember of the words he had spoken. I concluded with Jeff's theory that something may have happened long ago to cause the illness.

"I can't believe something that happened 50 years ago could cause a problem now," Mr. Calvert said. "Seems awfully far-fetched." There was a pause. "Maybe he did know something was coming on him, though. It would make sense--probably he'd been diagnosed with it. Have you talked to his doctor?"

"Yes, of course. Dr. Martin wasn't aware of anything. Why would it make sense, Mr. Calvert?"

"Well, if he knew he was going to get sick, that would explain why he wanted to sell his share of the business."

"Sell his share?"

"Gave him a check for it on Tuesday. Said he was going to deposit it in a trust."

25

Something inside me went click. Papa *must* have known.

"When did it hit him?" Mr. Calvert said.

"They admitted him to Johns Hopkins Hospital Wednesday afternoon."

"Uh-huh. You'd better contact your father's lawyer immediately to confirm the transaction took place. The deposit to the trust?"

"I will," I said. "But first, can you tell me where Papa grew up? I know it sounds crazy of me to ask. I've always thought it was Algeria or Tunis, or maybe Morocco, but now that I try to put my finger on it, I can't recall he ever said exactly."

Mr. Calvert spoke slowly. "He came to America from that part of the world. Knew a great deal about it and had contacts there in shipping, import-export, that sort of thing, although I can't say for certain he was actually born there. Never told me where his roots were. Seemed odd at the time, too, because I asked him, and he changed the subject. Maybe it was my imagination, of course." Another pause. "Marseilles, maybe. I remember thinking that at the time. Knew one or two customs officials there, but not well. More like he corresponded with them. Corsica, perhaps. Knew a great deal about Corsica. French is the official language. Maybe that was it. It's in that part of the world--on the Mediterranean shipping routes."

"My mother was Corsican," I said.

"So she was. Then he spent some time in Corsica at least. Met there, I think."

"Mr. Calvert, do you know what town in Corsica my mother is from? Maybe she would know where Papa was born."

"Well, let me see. It was either Calvi or Ajaccio, wasn't it? Ajaccio. Ajaccio. No, that's Napoleon. Knew I thought of it for some reason. I'd try Calvi. It definitely wasn't Ajaccio."

"Thank you, Mr. Calvert. I may call you back if something else occurs to me."

"No problem," he said. "I'll do the same."

I glanced around the newsroom and saw I still had it mostly to myself. O'Malley's office was empty.

Should I do it? Should I make an overseas call from the newspaper? Well, I had to do something. I picked up the receiver and dialed zero. The long distance operator picked up.

"I need to make an overseas call. To Calvi, Corsica, to a party named Camille Bonifacio."

The Richmond operator called New York and the three of us talked. Then New York called Paris, Paris called Marseilles and Marseilles called Calvi. It sounded as though I had my ear to a pipe with water running through it. I shouted into the mouthpiece in French. "The telephone number of Camille Bonifacio in Calvi, please." A pause. "I am sorry, madame, I have no such listing."

"Do you have a listing for DuMond? Madame Paul DuMond or Madame Camille DuMond?"

Another pause. "There are six DuMonds, but no Paul and no Camille."

Reluctantly, I rang off.

Next, I dialed my father's lawyer, a local number, which was welcome after all those operators. I didn't go into detail about my father's condition, only enough to say he was in the hospital and unable to communicate.

"I'm so very sorry. You have my deepest condolences," he said. "But yes, the money came into the trust yesterday, Wednesday, from a bank in Baltimore. Ultimately, you will be the beneficiary of it. It is regretful that your father is ill, but if it's any consolation, everything is in order--his will, the trust. In the event something should happen, and let's pray it doesn't, at least there won't be any complications with his estate. Everything goes to you."

"Mr. Coventry, do you have any idea where my father was born? I know it's an odd question, coming from his daughter."

"Where he was born? Let me see." There was a pause. "I can tell you he was an American citizen.

27

Entered the country at the Port of Baltimore. Was naturalized here in Richmond, but there's nothing here to tell me where he was born."

"How can I find out?"

"You might look through his papers. Perhaps there's an old passport or a birth certificate."

"Thank you, Mr. Coventry. I'll do that."

I looked up from my desk. Two more reporters had returned from lunch, but O'Malley's office was still empty. I needed to go home--to do some digging--and I felt compelled to do it right away.

Would O'Malley miss me?

2

I flicked the gearshift into neutral and pulled up the hand brake. Thank goodness I'd finished the story on Maymont yesterday afternoon. I doubted O'Malley had worked his way down that far in the pile of copy on his desk for tomorrow's edition. He'd probably assume I was still working on it. Wouldn't miss me for at least another hour--I hoped.

Bright sunlight made me squint as I hurried across the backyard toward the red brick Tudor. Normally I'd have stopped to relish the dogwoods scattered throughout our three-quarter acre lot. They were at their peak, lush pink and white with little green leaves just beginning to show. The enormous azalea bushes were also in bloom, a vibrant shade of violet but I hardly paused, pushed open the back door and headed straight to Papa's den.

It was a cozy room--perhaps 12 by 12--with an oriental, a window that overlooked the river, a leather wing back, fireplace, built-in bookshelves from the ceiling to the floor. Surely something here would tell me where he'd grown up and maybe, just maybe, what had

29

happened so long ago to cause his condition. The question was where to begin.

My glance rested on the old roll-top desk. I plopped down in the swivel chair and pushed open the top. Papers were piled up, receipts, canceled checks stuffed in cubbyholes. My mind worked as I searched. I became convinced he must have known something was about to happen. It was prudent to have one's will in order. I'd have been surprised if Papa hadn't. But sell his interest in a business he'd been a partner in for 30 years? Put the money in a trust so that all his affairs would be in order? Jeff must have been right. A specific date was coming. Papa had mentioned May 8. Was that it?

I opened a drawer. More canceled checks. More receipts.

I tugged on the one beneath it, but it wouldn't budge. I felt a tingle, the tug of intuition. Something important was inside.

I looked in the other drawers for a key, pulled everything out, sifted through and tossed one piece of paper after another on the floor.

Why wouldn't he want people to know where he grew up?

Even if he knew something was about to happen to him. Why wouldn't he say? What difference could it make?

It was odd, very odd, and there had to be a reason.

Maybe he'd done something he was ashamed of. Or, maybe he'd been afraid someone might interfere.

Was he afraid I might interfere?

If I were going to die, I'd *want* someone to. Why wouldn't he?

Unless . . . could interfering be dangerous?

No key anywhere. Nothing in the cubbyholes or the slots.

Okay. So maybe what I was doing was dangerous. I couldn't just stand by and let him die. I had to try.

I went to the kitchen, found a knife, returned and sawed hard.

I stood and blew hair from my face, placed my hands on my hips. No way was I going to cut through that lock.

What a mess--papers everywhere.

Something important was in there, I could *feel* it. A dead bolt wasn't going to stop me. I went to the pantry and found Papa's tools. A crowbar.

In about three minutes the drawer was broken and splintered, the contents in my hand, a black satin box. Inside was a heart-shaped gold locket on a braided gold chain, and inside the locket a photograph--an old one, turn-of-the-century judging from the faded sepia tones. The young woman it depicted was a beauty by any generation's standard--long dark hair tied up in back, high cheekbones, lips curved in a Mona Lisa smile. She was exotic, not entirely Caucasian, not northern European, anyway. Perhaps she was Slavic, or part Indian or Polynesian. Maybe Negro.

Why had Papa put her in a locked drawer?

I picked at the picture with the knife. The back was blank.

I put the photograph back and the locket in the box. Papers were strewn everywhere, around the chair and on the carpet, the desk a disaster. Every cubbyhole or drawer had been rummaged through and I hadn't found a clue. No passport, no documents. Not even a key to a safe deposit box.

I glanced around. Books, books, books, a globe, a tennis trophy on the mantel over the fireplace. Nothing which looked a likely place to keep old documents. Unless something was stuck in a book. But there were hundreds of books. It would take all day to look through each one of them, and I didn't have all day.

Maybe I should try his bedroom.

It smelled dusty but was bright with sunlight that entered in shafts through the mullioned panes of a bay window. It felt as though I were trespassing--a cat burglar creeping into someone's boudoir as I looked for a place to

31

begin. My gaze rested on the four-poster bed Papa and my mother had shared.

I tiptoed to the dresser and looked at photographs. Most were of me in various stages from birth through college. My mother held me in two, as a newborn and at about nine months. I quickly shifted my gaze to a photograph of Papa as a young man.

I slipped it out of the frame. I couldn't put my finger on why. Perhaps if I met someone my father had known 50 years ago, it would jar that person's memory.

I turned and fixed my eyes on an old steamer trunk on a stand at the foot of the bed. Inside were blankets, winter pajamas, cards, old magazines. And letters. Letters tied with a faded blue silk ribbon. The stamps were French, and the postmark on the top one read, *Calvi, Corse, 16-7-1933.*

Corse?

"Corsica" in English, the Mediterranean island my mother was from. The numbers were the date since the French put the day of the month first.

July 16, 1933.

That sickish, nostalgic feeling took hold. These letters had been written after Maman had abandoned me and Papa. I turned the stack in my hands. Should I read them? Could anything in them shed light on the current situation?

Perhaps.

But what else might I find? Just seeing them and her handwriting brought back the ache. As a child I had sensed that all was not as it should have been. My mother often seemed in a dark mood, the tension between Maman and Papa sometimes palpable.

One day, my father picked me up from school. I wondered why. He had never done so before and didn't say a word on the way home. When we arrived he asked me to sit with him in the living room, where he told me that he was to blame. It was his fault she was unhappy; his fault she had left. I didn't figure out until much later why, exactly. Actually, I didn't know for sure until a few weeks after I found those letters. Maman had left because she didn't feel loved by Papa. She had known he loved another, had loved another since before they were married. But I'm getting ahead of myself.

I sat down in Papa's stuffed bedroom chair and exhaled. Of course I didn't want to relive the pain, but I'd grit my teeth and do it. These letters might contain the clue I was searching for. Whatever Maman had said, whatever she had written couldn't hurt me now. My opinion of her couldn't sink lower.

On the other hand, this was snooping. If Papa had wanted me to see these, he'd have shown them to me long ago.

How would I like it if he read my mail?

Of course I wouldn't. But he lay in a coma and these letters might contain information that could save his life.

I untied the ribbon and opened the first one. It was written in French.

Calvi, Corsica
16 July, 1933

My dearest Paul,

> *I know you must feel that my actions toward you and little Claire are without justification. It may help you to know that I have not slept more than a few hours each night for the past several months because of the guilt that I feel. I do not expect you to forgive me for what I have done. Nevertheless, I feel I must explain what led me to take the drastic action of leaving the two of you.*
> *It is as though I were living--no, living is not the word--<u>existing</u> at the bottom of a dark pit--a cold, damp pit with no way to climb out. The feeling of helplessness was overwhelming.*

33

*It took away all my strength. Oh how I longed
for the sunny sky of Corsica, for the sweet smell
of the maquis and the scent of salt from the
Mediterranean. How I longed for the comforting
presence of my mother and father, brothers and
sisters, and uncles and aunts. How I detested
the brutally hot summers in Virginia, and the
cold, damp winters. It is true as well that I felt
her between us always, although I know you did
the best you could to push her ghost away. I
emerged from my pit only for brief periods in
springtime, and even then, not for more than
a few hours at a time. How lost I felt, how
completely alone, even with you beside me,
darling. Even with little Claire. The blackness
of it blinded me, until one day I realized what
my condition was doing to you and to little
Claire. Listless, angry, petty in the perpetuity
of my despair, I realized that you two would
be better off without me my darling, and that
I would be better off here as well.*

*Surely at times you must long for the
Windward Isle of your youth. Do you not?
Can you not understand? I know that it is
impossible for you ever to return, but as for me--
it was <u>not</u> impossible and my only hope for
salvation.*

*Perhaps I was wrong, but now it is
done. I know it is impossible for you to forgive
me and that Claire will grow up despising her
mother. This is my cross.*

*Please, darling, love her for me.
Embrace her. Kiss her for me everyday.*

> *Yours forever in heart,*
> *Camille*

She certainly seemed to have been unhappy, but
that didn't give her the right to run out.

Who was this ghost between them?

I reread the letter. The reference to the "Windward Isle" of my father's youth might be a clue. Windward Isle? What was a Windward Isle? Why was it impossible for him to return?

Over the next half hour I read all nine letters and they took their toll. They had been written in intervals ranging from six months to four years. They were filled with questions about me, reactions to photographs, references to the milestones of my life. The last of the bunch was dated six years prior, right after my graduation from college.

By the time I was done, tears streamed down my cheeks. I'd concluded it would be impossible to hold on to anger toward her any longer. I had missed her deeply and suffered terribly, but so had she. What an awful situation to find oneself in. What a horrible choice to have to make: your sanity or your child.

It took awhile, but once I had a grip on myself I went back to the first letter. "Windward Isle" was the only clue I'd found.

Why was he unable to return to the island of his youth?

Back in Papa's den I found a single-volume encyclopedia on the bookshelf and flipped to W.

> WINDWARD ISLANDS--group
> of islands in the Lesser Antilles,
> WEST INDIES, stretching toward
> Venezuela. They include St. Lucia,
> St. Vincent, the Grenadines, Grenada,
> and Martinique. The area is about
> 950 square miles and the people
> mainly Negro, producing bananas,
> cacao, limes, sugar, nutmeg and cotton.

I looked up each of the islands and all turned out to be English speaking except for the last one. As I read what the encyclopedia said, my heart began to pound.

MARTINIQUE--island in the Windward
group in the E. Caribbean, an overseas
department of France since 1946.
Discovered by Columbus c1493, it was
colonized by France as a sugar-growing
center after 1635; slave labor was used
until 1848, and much of the present
population is of African descent. The
economy still rests on sugar, and also
rum and fruit. The island is volcanic,
and so is rugged and mountainous but
very fertile. Its main town is Fort-de-France.

This was it, the only Windward Isle that was
French. It had to be the one.

Why hadn't Papa told me? What difference could
it possibly make? Why had he allowed me to believe he
grew up somewhere else?

I needed to find out more. This little encyclopedia
was okay for a quick reference, but it did not contain much
detail. I wanted facts, history. Was voodoo practiced on
the island? That might explain my father's reference to
magic. Unfortunately, there weren't any other books on
these shelves that looked as though they might be of help.

I checked my watch and realized I'd better get back
to the paper before O'Malley went looking for me.

But when I stepped into the shade of the big
magnolia and opened the door of the Ford, it occurred to
me that the main branch of the library was on my way--
only a few blocks from the paper.

Okay, so I was impulsive. Too bad if O'Malley
missed me. This was important.

Ten minutes later I pushed through the revolving
door of the main branch of the Richmond Public Library
and headed straight for the card catalog, the clicking of my
heels against the marble floor echoing throughout the
building.

I pulled out the drawer marked MAR-MUN and found only two entries for Martinique. Both were travel memoirs, one written in 1887 and the other in 1926.

At least they were a place to start.

The stacks were a bookworm's paradise, musty and moldy like a pile of old newspapers. Aisle after aisle of cloth-bound tomes were piled on shelves at least 12 feet high, but I soon found the row I was looking for and spotted *A Midsummer Trip to the Tropics*, the memoir written in 1887.

What could it possibly tell me about Martinique in 1902?

Well, it could contain a clue. My experience at the newspaper had taught me to look under every pebble.

I turned to the index and found a reference to Martinique on page twenty-six:

> We are ashore in St. Pierre, the
> quaintest, queerest, and the prettiest withal,
> among West Indian cities: all stone-built and
> stone-flagged, with very narrow streets, wooden
> or zinc awnings, and peaked roofs of red tile,
> pierced by gabled dormers. Most of the
> buildings are painted in a clear yellow tone,
> which contrasts nicely with the burning blue
> ribbon of tropical sky above; and no street is
> absolutely level; nearly all of them climb hills,
> descend into hollows,curve, twist, describe
> sudden angles. There is everywhere a loud
> murmur of running water, pouring through
> the deep gutters contrived between the paved
> thoroughfare and the absurd little sidewalks,
> varying in width from one to three feet. The
> architecture is quite old: it is seventeenth century,
> probably; and it reminds one a great deal of that
> characterizing the antiquated French quarter of
> New Orleans. All the tints, the forms, the vistas,
> would seem to have been especially selected or
> designed for aquarelle studies, just to please the

whim of some extravagant artist. The windows
are frameless openings without glass; some have
iron bars; all have heavy wooden shutters with
movable slats, through which light and air can
enter as through Venetian blinds. These are
usually painted green or bright bluish-gray.

So steep are the streets descending to
the harbor--by flights of old mossy stone steps--
that looking down them to the azure water you
have the sensation of gazing from a cliff. From
certain openings in the main street--the Rue Victor
Hugo--you can get something like a bird's-eye
view of the harbor with its shipping. The roofs
of the street below are under your feet, and other
streets are rising behind you to meet the mountain
roads. They climb at a very steep angle, occasionally breaking into stairs of lava rock,
all grass-tufted and moss-lined.

I flipped ahead--more of the same. Martinique
seemed like a splendid place, but the author's description
was of no use beyond providing a snapshot of the island
where my father had spent his youth. I returned *A
Midsummer Trip to the Tropics* to its spot on the shelf and a
few books away found the 1926 title, *Love and the
Caribbean*. According to the index there was a reference to
Martinique on page 36.

Once we went to St. Pierre.

From Fond Lahaye it is a three hour's sail
by canoe, along a coast indented with green valleys
that climb through fields of sugar cane. At the
foot of most of these valleys, between the stems of
the coconut palms, you see the outline of wooden
cabins. So concealed are these cabins behind that
façade of greenery that were it not for the fishing
nets hung out along the beach on poles to dry you
would scarcely suspect that a village was there.
Nor, as you approach St. Pierre, would you

suspect that in that semicircle of hills under the
cloud-hung shadow of Mont Pelé are hidden the
ruins of a city for which history can find no
parallel.

Ruins? What was this?

At first sight it is nothing but a third-rate,
decrepit shipping port, not unlike Manzanillo or
La Libertad. It has its pier, its warehouses, its
market; its single cobbled street contains the
usual dockside features. A café or two, a
restaurant, a small wooden shanty labeled
"Cercle," a somewhat larger shanty labeled
"Select Tango." A hairdresser, a general store.
At first sight it is one of many thousand places.
It is not until you step out of that main street into
the tangled jungle at the back of it that you realize
that St. Pierre is as it has always been, unique.
Even then you do not at first realize it. At first
you see nothing but greenery, wild shrubbery, the
great tagged leaves of the banana plant, with here
and there the brown showing of a thatched roof.
It is not until you have wandered a little through
those twisted paths that you see that it is in the
angles of old walls that those thatched cottages
are built, that it is over broken masonry, over old
stairways and porticoes, that those trailing
creepers are festooned; that empty windows
are shadowed by those ragged leaves. At odd
corners you will come upon signs of that old life:
a marble slab that was once the doorstep of a
colonial bungalow; a fountain that splashed
coolly through siestaed summers; a shrine with
the bronze body broken at its foot. Everywhere
you will come upon signs of that old life; *"Le pays
de Revenants"* they called it. With what grim irony
has chance played on the word. But it is not till
you have left the town and have climbed to look

down into the basin of the amphitheatre that contained St. Pierre and, looking down, that you realize the extent and nature of the disaster. No place that I have ever seen has moved me in quite that way.

What disaster?

And *Revenants?* The word meant ghosts. Why was it ironic St. Pierre was known as the land of ghosts?

I put my finger on the page and moved it rapidly along, skimming.

Here was something:

> At eight o'clock a gay and gallant people was preparing on a sunlit morning busily for its *jour de fete.* Forty-five seconds later, of all that gaiety and courage there was nothing left. Not anything. Certain legends linger. They say that four days later, when the process of excavation was begun, there was found in the vault of the prison a criminal, the sole survivor.

Earthquake? Volcano? This was incredible. What could have happened to destroy an entire town?

I searched ahead through the text, but the author apparently assumed his audience already knew. He did not so much as provide a date, nor did he say whether a volcanic eruption or an earthquake had caused the disaster.

I returned the book to the shelf and went to the reference section to look at an encyclopedia, one that would tell me more than the single volume at home.

Under the listing for Martinique I found the usual information about the economy, agriculture, government, and social conditions. And beneath a heading about the land itself, I came upon this:

> The island is largely mountains.
> The average elevation is 3000

feet. The highest point is Mt.
Pelée, 4583 feet, an active volcano.
Its catastrophic eruption in 1902
destroyed the city of St. Pierre,
killing an estimated 30,000 people.

The date, 1902, could it be a coincidence?
What had he said?
Fifty years ago, all the others dead, May the eighth.
May 8, 1902.

It was exasperating this didn't give the month and day, but they would be easy enough to find.

I hurried from the library to my car, moving as fast as possible in heels and a straight dress. Those darn spikes made it impossible to keep my hips from swaying. Men's heads turned, men on the sidewalk, men climbing the steps of old brownstones, men in cars all casting their eyes at me and straining rubber necks. I climbed in and slammed shut the door, wondering whether the man who held my future in his hands, O'Malley, had already missed me. But as I pulled into the parking lot next to the paper I decided to risk it. It would take only a few minutes longer, and nothing could be more important than saving my father.

People streamed in and out, past the glass doors of the newspaper building. A man held one for me and I headed straight for the elevator. But I didn't go up to the newsroom. I took the elevator down instead, hurried along a hallway into a dimly-lit room where bare bulbs in white porcelain sockets gave off an amber glow: the crypt-like cavern which held the archives of the *Richmond Times-Dispatch*.

I breathed in the scent of mold as I passed row after row of file cabinets full of microfilm, knelt by one and studied the labels. Fifty years ago the *Times* and the *Dispatch* must have been competitors, I realized, then pulled open the bottom drawer and rummaged through the contents until I found a small cardboard box which contained the spool of film that would give me answers. I

41

threaded it onto a projector mounted overhead in a cubicle, switched on a light that shone down on a white counter top and turned the crank. Page after page of the *Richmond Dispatch* rolled by.

There was nothing in the May eighth edition, but then there wouldn't be if it happened on that day.

How long did it take for news to travel back then?

On May ninth, buried on page six, was the report of a volcanic eruption in Martinique by a ship's captain who arrived in St. Lucia badly burned, his ship almost completely destroyed.

I cranked more pages by. Then my heart began to pound. A huge black headline was splashed across the front page of the May tenth *Dispatch*:

40,000 PERISH
ST. PIERRE, MARTINIQUE
DISASTER IS FULLY CONFIRMED

The entire front page was devoted to it.

"At seven a.m. on May eight," I read, " a stream of mud and fire from Mt. Pelée enveloped the city destroying every house in the community."

St. Pierre, described as a miniature Paris and "the jewel of the Caribbean," had been snuffed out in an instant. This report differed from the Britannica in the number of people killed and from *Love and the Caribbean* in the timing--seven o'clock instead of eight, three minutes verses 45 seconds. But there was no discrepancy about the intensity of the blast. The force of it was so strong that a tidal wave sent all 18 ships in the harbor to the bottom. Only one some miles away in open sea escaped, yet even this one was badly burned and all on board but its captain were killed.

It was like an atom bomb--Hiroshima.

This was what Papa had been talking about: *All the others--dead*, he'd said.

42

As I read the text I had difficulty holding back the tears. How horrible it must have been to lose everyone--everyone you knew, everyone you had grown up with, all of them snuffed out in one cataclysmic instant.

Why hadn't he shared this with me?

How had he survived?

Had he even been there?

All the others dead.

Was he somewhere beyond that four-mile radius?

Was he the man in jail?

I scanned for some reference to the survivor who had been mentioned in the travel memoir, but there was nothing about him.

Then it dawned on me. Of course not. The author of *Love and the Caribbean* had said the man in the jail was not discovered until four days later.

Someone behind me cleared his throat and I spun around to see the ruddy, cherubic face of Alexander O'Malley--smiling sarcastically. "Ah, Miss DuMond. Excuse me, I mean--ah, DuMond. So nice of you to join us here at the newspaper today."

"Well, you see, I didn't mean to . . . actually, the problem is my father is terribly ill . . . "

"No need to explain." O'Malley showed me the palm of his hand. "You're here, and I've found you. You see, I need someone to cover the school board meeting this afternoon. There's something of a brouhaha brewing--if you'll pardon the alliteration. I thought of you because it'll give you a chance to try your hand at something besides strictly Woman's Page stuff. I'm giving you the chance you wanted, DuMond."

Time to think fast.

"Mr. O'Malley--you, me, the *Times-Dispatch*, we're all in luck. I'm on to something that's going to win a Pulitzer. Did you know one of the worst disasters in history took place almost exactly 50 years ago? The exact date is next week, May eighth."

"Really, DuMond. And what disaster might that be?"

43

"A volcano erupted and wiped out an entire city in Martinique. Killed 40,000 people in three minutes--18 ships anchored there went straight to the bottom--makes Pearl Harbor look like a Fourth of July picnic. Here, look." I pointed to the front page of the *Dispatch.*

"My, my." O'Malley stepped closer. "Humm. I'd forgotten about that. Of course, I was only a wee lad at the time, you understand."

Why not go for it? Take a swing at the big one I told myself. "This has to be one of the most tremendous stories to come along in this century, Mr. O'Malley, and hardly anyone remembers it. My idea is to make sure they do. What I've got in mind is a front page feature for the Sunday Perspective Section. Let's see, won't be this Sunday--that'd be next Sunday. Yes. The eleventh of May." I fanned my hands. "Picture this: 'St. Pierre, Martinique: Then and Now.' I tell you I can see it, Mr. O'Malley. It's going to be good, don't you think?"

"I like it." O'Malley rubbed his chin. "But, how are we going to get the 'now' part? We can't send a fair young maiden like yourself to a place like Martinique."

"Really, Mr. O'Malley, you surprise me. I thought of it--I should get to do it. All I need is a travel advance, my bags are practically packed."

O'Malley stared at me for several seconds, then shook his head. "You've got to be kidding, DuMond. There's no way I'm going to send a cub reporter a couple of thousand miles away to a place where they probably still cut off people's hands for stealing a loaf of bread. Especially a *woman* cub reporter. Even if I wanted to, the publisher would have my head."

"It's not primitive. It's a department of France."

"Forget it, DuMond. The school board meeting is the best I can do."

O'Malley turned, but I put my hand on his shoulder. "Wait a minute, Mr. O'Malley, please. You've no idea how important this is to me. It has to do with my father and his illness. It's, it's very difficult to explain."

"For the last time, DuMond, even if I wanted to I

44

couldn't."

"What if I paid for it myself? What if I went on my *own?*"

His brow furrowed. "You mean like on a vacation? I certainly can't tell you where to take your vacation . . . DuMond."

"How about this, Mr. O'Malley. Suppose I take a few days unpaid leave and do the story on my own? If you decide to use it, you'll pay my expenses. Otherwise, it's on my nickel."

O'Malley frowned.

"Please, Mr. O'Malley. What have you got to lose? Nothing, right? It'll be one heckuva story, I guarantee it. And if it's not, well, you're under no obligation whatsoever. Really."

He held up a hand. "Okay, okay. I'll find someone else to cover the school board. But I'm telling you, you may have missed your big chance."

Minutes later, I was back at my desk and on the telephone to Eastern Airlines, my heart pumping. The men were back at their desks, too, puffing on cigarettes and cigars, smoke curling into the air. This was my shot. I'd save Papa and prove my worth to O'Malley at the same time.

"That's right," I said into the telephone. "Martinique. I need to get there as quickly as possible."

There was a pause at the other end of the line. Then, "That would be Fort de France."

"Nothing to St. Pierre?"

"The only airport I see is in Fort de France."

"Okay, then," I said. "How fast can I get there?"

"One moment, please."

While I waited I noticed others nearby staring at me with puzzled expressions, particularly Beatrice Blanton, the lady who wrote the society column, a rather hefty woman in her late fifties with a body shaped like an inverted pear and three chins that dangled above a single strand of pearls.

45

The Eastern Airlines ticket agent came back on the line. "Can you make a five o'clock plane to Atlanta?"

"Yes," I said. "Book it."

The agent explained the routing and I said I'd pick up my ticket and pay for it at the airport. Then I hung up.

"Did I hear you say Martinique? Why on earth, my dear?" Beatrice Blanton said.

I stuffed items from my desk in my purse and explained I was doing a story on the fiftieth anniversary of the Mt. Pelée eruption.

"I suspected it before, but this is confirmation," Beatrice said. "Alexander O'Malley has lost his ever-loving mind."

"If you must know, Beatrice, I'm doing this on my own," I said. "But, I disagree with you. O'Malley and the other men who run this world lost their minds a long, long time ago. It's high time a woman got a decent assignment at this paper."

"Well, I never--"

"And anyway, Martinique is not some backward place. It's a department of France for heaven's sake," I said.

Frank Lowry, a wiry little guy who worked the police beat looked up. "Did you say France?"

"That's right," I said. "France is certainly in the twentieth century. Right?"

"Well, I wouldn't be so sure," Frank said. "I was in France during the war, and my advice is . . . " He smiled and winked. "Take toilet paper." He pushed his hat back and pounded out a sentence or two on his Underwood.

I needed to go home and pack, but first withdrew money from the bank and stopped at the hospital. I glanced at J. E. B. Stuart as I hurried up the front steps of the curved brick building and through the doors to the reception desk. A little lady in white with a starched white hat looked up.

"I'm here to see Mr. Paul DuMond," I said. "He's a patient of Dr. Martin's."

The woman consulted a box of three by five cards.

"By the way," I said. "Is Dr. Martin in the hospital?"

"Yes, I believe he's making rounds. And Mr. DuMond is in room 313."

"Would you page Dr. Martin for me, please? Ask him please to meet Miss DuMond in her father's room."

"Certainly," the woman said.

I took the elevator to the third floor and followed signs to Papa's room. The door was ajar so I pushed it gently and crept inside. Sun shone between the slats, projecting a washboard pattern of light on his bed.

His hair looked so much thinner than I remembered, his face was gaunt and he seemed helpless and lost--flat on his back with a sheet over him, arms resting at his sides, a tube in one leading to a bottle which hung from a pole. He still stared at nothing, his eyes as empty and hollow as the ache I felt inside.

I kneeled next him. "Papa, Papa it's me, Claire."

Not a twitch.

"Papa, why didn't you tell me about Martinique? About the eruption of Mt. Pelée?"

Nothing.

I felt someone else's presence and stood.

"Sorry if I startled you, Claire," Dr. Martin said softly. He glanced at Papa. "Paul has been like this ever since he arrived. Hasn't moved a muscle."

"Have you found out what's wrong?"

Dr. Martin shook his head. "I don't understand it, Claire. I've seen cases in mental hospitals where people were catatonic like this. Move them into any position and they'll stay exactly the way you put them. But those people are schizophrenic, and schizophrenia almost always shows up when a person is still young. Under the age of 30, anyway. Paul's mind was razor sharp the last time I saw him. We played golf last week at the Club."

"Do you suppose his condition could be caused by an event that took place 50 years ago, Doctor?"

"I don't follow, Claire. What do you mean?"

47

I explained Jeff's theory and my discovery of the volcanic eruption on the date my father had mentioned.

Dr. Martin pursed his lips. "Claire, I've never heard of anything like it. And for a man of science to speculate on something like that, well, it wouldn't be a responsible thing to do." He rubbed his chin. "Now, I have read about witch doctors and the Evil Eye causing one of their tribe to drop dead. But 50 years later? Anyway, I'm sure your father doesn't believe in witch doctors. He always seemed like such a well-educated man to me."

"But do you think it's possible?"

"Well, I don't know." He shrugged. "Anything is possible, I suppose. I've been around long enough to see some pretty strange things." He glanced at Papa, then back at me. "I feel I should warn you, though, I wouldn't go around talking about this theory of yours to anyone else. It's the kind of talk that might land *you* in the mental ward."

"Thanks, Doctor, I'll remember that. Anyway, I'm going to Martinique to see what I can find out."

"All the way to Martinique?"

"I've got to do something, Dr. Martin." I looked at Papa. "If I don't find out what's behind this, I'm afraid he might die so I'm taking time off and flying down there."

"Where is Martinique, exactly?"

"In the Caribbean."

"Oh yes, I see now," Dr. Martin said. "Voodoo. Those Caribbean islands are full of voodoo, but I just don't see how a voodoo spell could last for 50 years."

I drove home on the road that wound past the park known as Dogwood Dell with its carillon and reflecting pool. But I hardly noticed the tower or its reflection, or the pink dogwoods all in bloom. I had a plane to catch and I was in a daze, convinced my father's life depended on me and me alone.

I was upstairs packing when the doorbell rang.

I scurried down and opened the thick plank door.

"Jeff, what a surprise."

He stepped inside.

"I called your office, Claire, and they told me you'd be gone for a week. What is going on?"

It was none of his business, but I didn't have time to argue.

"It came up suddenly. I was going to call you from the airport if I had time before takeoff."

I started up the stairs.

"Where are you going, Claire?"

"I'm sorry, Jeff, I don't want to be rude but I've got to finishing packing if I'm going to make the plane."

Jeff's eyes narrowed. "Go ahead and pack, but if you don't mind I'll tag along. Maybe you can tell me what's going on."

I climbed the stairs, past hand-colored engravings of plants and herbs that hung against flowered wallpaper, filling Jeff in as quickly as I could on the way to my room.

"You can't be serious," he said. "A beautiful woman like you going alone to an uncivilized island in the tropics?"

I searched through my dresser and closets, tossed garments into an open suitcase on the bed.

"It's not uncivilized," I said. "It's a department of France. Let's see, guess I won't need any sweaters."

"France! My case rests. Claire, you are a woman whether you realize it or not, and there are certain things women don't do."

"Take a good look at the calendar, Jeff." I threw a brassiere onto the pile. "We're now in the second half of the twentieth century. There is nothing women can't do or haven't done."

"Sure," said Jeff. "Women can fly planes and work in factories, but that's not what we're talking about here. We're talking about going unescorted to a place populated by dope smugglers, modern day pirates, good old fashioned thieves. You could be bopped on the head and sold into white slavery."

"Give me a break, will you, Jeff? I can take care of

myself."

"I don't want the woman I'm going to marry to be Shanghaied to Morocco, put up on a block and sold to an Arab sheik along with some camels."

"Let's not talk about marriage, okay? At least not until I get back."

"Let me come with you," he said.

Why was he so thick-headed? Reporting was my job and sometimes that required subjecting oneself to danger--at least it would if I ever got myself off the Woman's Page. This trip might turn out to be the way for me to do just that. But most important of all, my father's life was at stake. I didn't have any choice. I had to go.

Still, the poor guy did look worried and forlorn, and I had to admit as I glanced at him out of the corners of my eyes, he was cute when he was forlorn. Yeah, he was cute and he was hurt. Suddenly I felt sorry for him.

I snapped shut my suitcase.

"I know you're worried, but this is something I have to do. It's hard for me to explain--a very strong feeling--I think my father's life is in danger, and I believe the place I can find out why is Martinique--so I'm going there. It's not the end of the earth, I'll be back in less than a week."

I pulled my suitcase off the bed and started for the door.

Jeff cut me off, put his hands on my shoulders. "I love you, Claire, and I'm worried about you--don't you see?"

"Jeff. I've got a plane to catch."

"Damn it, Claire, at least let me give you a proper send off."

He pulled me to him and I dropped the suitcase. His arms closed around me and his face moved forward-- his eyes closed, his mouth puckered. I felt the softness of his lips, the warmth of his flesh and the firmness of his body against me. A tingly sensation began deep inside, rushed rapidly upward. I knew full well it would engulf me in a matter of seconds if I let it, so I exerted all my willpower and pulled away.

I leaned back into him, pressed my forehead to his chin and gave him a little poke in the chest. "I said I could take care of myself, didn't I? But who would have thought I'd have to begin so soon?"

3

I stumbled down the aisle and collapsed into my seat, my pulse doing 90 miles an hour. It'd been close, but I'd made it on board just as the stewardess had pulled shut the door. For a good three minutes all I could do was focus on my breathing, on the air coming in through my nostrils and out of my lungs, until my system was back to normal.

But now I was on my way.

Thank goodness the adjacent seat was empty, an unexpected bonus. The last time I'd flown I'd had to put up with a lecherous traveling salesman. I relaxed and let my body shift with the motion of the plane as it gained altitude and banked southward toward Raleigh and Atlanta. Now there would be time to think.

Should I be worried for my safety? I wondered. Jeff certainly seemed to think so. The idea I might be kidnapped and sold into white slavery seemed far-fetched, but it wasn't beyond possibility. That sort of thing still happened in France, especially in port cities such as Marseille, and Fort de France was a port city. A blonde with a build could bring an astounding price from an oil-rich Arab sheik. Well, I told myself, a person didn't get anywhere if she didn't take risks, and this was one I was willing to take. I was going into this with my eyes open; I'd just have to keep them that way.

I spent a lot of the time on that series of plane rides thinking about my childhood and trying to remember details which might provide clues to Papa's beliefs about magic and the supernatural. As far back as I could remember he'd been a faithful churchgoer. As for myself, I'd gone along with his wishes and attended Sunday school, church and Bible classes. But frankly I always believed the whole thing was a bunch of wishful thinking. When you were dead you were just that: dead.

And the concept of original sin was particularly hard to swallow. If one went along with it, one had to believe that even babies had sinful natures--although I had to confess that as an adult who had lived though World War II and read a newspaper everyday, the idea man was evil at the core wasn't hard to swallow. Nevertheless, as soon as I was old enough to make my own decisions, one of the first I made was to sleep in on Sundays.

To his credit Papa never insisted I go to church after I returned home from college. What struck me now, though, was his choice of churches. He was a full-blooded Frenchman, and everyone who knew anything about France knew France was 98 percent Roman Catholic. Yet Papa was a Southern Baptist. I seriously doubted a person would run into many of those in Martinique, so it must have been a denomination he'd decided on later in life.

I drifted off to sleep with that thought on my mind.

Midway through the night, high in the air somewhere between Atlanta and Miami, a dream jolted me awake. It was a replay of a conversation we'd had when I was 12. I'd asked him if we could switch to the Episcopal church since it was closer to our house--although the real reason was all my friends went there.

"If you want to change churches when you are older and on your own, that's up to you. Choosing a church is like buying a pair of shoes. Each individual should pick what fits him best. I've chosen to be a Baptist because of the ritual of baptism. The submersion in water is a symbolic death to sin; emerging from it a resurrection. A rebirth in Christ. The sanctification of bathing in holy water. A few drops on the forehead aren't enough for me."

There I was in an airplane at three in the morning with my eyes wide open, the drone of engines the only sound, thinking that those weren't the words of a man who took religion lightly. I wondered what had happened for it to become so important?

And was what had happened connected to his current condition?

The plane arrived just after midnight the following day. I'd never been so exhausted or wished so that a journey would end. Willpower and an intense desire to see what I'd find in Martinique carried me down a stairway which had been rolled against the plane. An Eastern Airlines employee bade me and the other passengers farewell and I started across the black tarmac toward a one-story terminal building and an open doorway with a bare light bulb shining above it. It must have just rained. Puddles had formed on the uneven surface and the air felt heavy. I put one foot in front of the other and reflected on the offhand comment by the ticket agent in Richmond about my embarking on longer than the average trip. The reality had been grueling, a change of planes in Atlanta, layovers and changes of aircraft in Miami, San Juan, and Phillipsburg in Dutch St. Maarten. I'd been traveling for a day and a half.

Inside, a drowsy customs agent in a round brimmed hat gave my passport a perfunctory glance and slapped a rubber stamp on a page in the visa section. The lights were out behind the airline ticket counters. The waiting area was deserted except for a man with a Panama hat tilted over his eyes, asleep on a bench with a dead chicken under his arm.

This wasn't Richmond, I thought as I stood in a daze at the area designated as the baggage claim. After a while what looked like garage doors swung open and a truck that might have doubled as a hay wagon backed to within five feet. An ebony-skinned man in a flowered shirt tied at the waist hopped out and hauled down suitcases, plopping them on the dusty concrete floor. I spotted mine immediately, lugged it outside into the warm night air and realized I was lucky to have found it before my fellow passengers because a single cab was all that waited. It sat under a palm tree--a black four-door Citroen with an upright grill and a little white sign on the roof. The driver looked up, the whites of his eyes accentuated by dark skin and jet black pupils.

"Where to, mademoiselle?" he said in French.

"La Residence de la Port," I said.

He nodded, and I was surprised when he turned the key to start the engine. I'd expected him to jump out to open the door and to take my bag. I shrugged, opened it myself and shoved the bag in.

At the end of the dirt road that led away from the airport, the taxi turned onto a two-lane blacktop highway. The road ahead was dark and wet, and I made a mental note to include in my newspaper story a reference to the surreal feeling of riding in the back of a taxi alone in a foreign country in the middle of the night. We bounced along in silence past dark vegetation. I noticed a couple of houses in French colonial style set far back from the road, and later, clumps of rundown shanties, some not much more than lean-tos, with corrugated metal roofs and no glass in the window openings. They were not like the shanty towns I'd seen in Virginia, and at first I couldn't put my finger on why. In the moonlight I could see the usual hens scratching in the dirt and goats and other animals housed in chicken wire pens, but this was different. Perhaps it was the silhouettes of palms against a tropical night sky.

"You are not from around here, are you mademoiselle?"

55

The driver's voice had a singsong quality and his French was heavily accented--a brand of Creole patois, I supposed.

"No, this is my first time in Martinique. I'm from Virginia," I replied. "I'm here to write a story about the fiftieth anniversary of the Mt. Pelée eruption."

"Virginia?"

The driver's eyes darted at me in the rearview mirror. An uneasy feeling settled over me.

"In the United States."

"You speak good French, mademoiselle. Very good."

"Thank you," I said. "My father is French. I think he was from Martinique in fact."

"Oh yes? What is his name?"

"Paul DuMond."

The driver appeared to reflect. "I am afraid I do not know him."

"No, I suppose not. He left a long, long time ago." Perhaps now was as good a time as any to begin my investigation. "What do you know about the Mt. Pelée eruption--if you don't mind me asking you?"

He glanced at me again. "Many, many people were killed. They say more than 30,000. It was the fault of the governor, who ignored Pelée's warnings. The volcano had been spewing ash for weeks and there had even been a few small eruptions, one that wiped out an entire town on the slope of the mountain and 600 souls with it."

"Why was it the fault of the governor?"

"He should have ordered an evacuation--the prudent thing under the circumstances. Of course, all things are clear to those who have the advantage of looking back."

"You say no one left St. Pierre? Why did they need the governor to tell them to leave if the volcano was so obviously active?"

"Perhaps some left, but if they did it was against the governor's instructions. To the contrary, he ordered people who lived in the surrounding environs to abandon their homes and come into St. Pierre, which as you might imagine had the unfortunate result that more deaths took place than would otherwise have occurred. At one point he even had a roadblock established, which was manned by soldiers under his command, to prevent the citizens of St. Pierre from fleeing to Fort de France."

The taxi had entered a city. Palms sprouted from tree wells along the curb between wrought iron street lamps. The style of the buildings with their double-decker piazzas reminded me of pictures I'd seen of the French Quarter in New Orleans. But no jazz was being played at that time of night, the streets quiet and deserted.

"It sounds completely crazy that the governor wouldn't allow the people to leave," I said. "What possible reason could there have been?"

"He did not want a flood of refugees to descend upon Fort de France. And in his defense, although he is difficult to defend given the outcome of his reasoning, a huge mud slide caused by the volcano 50 years prior went in the direction away from St. Pierre, sparing the city completely. He and others were no doubt convinced that if a major eruption did occur, it would follow the same course."

The driver slowed the car and pulled to a stop in front of a hotel portico.

"There was no damage then to Fort de France?"

"No, no, none at all. Fort de France is 17 miles from St. Pierre, which, by the way, is the total of your bill-- 17 francs."

I searched in my pocketbook for my purse. "Will you take American dollars? I haven't any French money yet."

"It will be my pleasure, mademoiselle. Three dollars should be adequate."

I gave him four. When my bag and I were on the sidewalk I said, "One more thing, driver. The man in jail, the sole survivor of the eruption, what do you know of him?"

He stared up at me from behind the wheel, his lips

pursed. I thought I saw a wrinkle appear in the dark skin of his brow. He put the car in gear and started off.

"Another time, mademoiselle. Let's save the answer for another time."

The next morning breakfast was delivered to my room as I'd requested, at eight o'clock sharp. I was up, bathed, still in my bathrobe and groggy from my trip--but eager nonetheless to get on with my quest.

As I ate, the taxi driver's face flickered in my mind. I recalled the whites of his eyes and his wry smile as he pulled away.

Why had he responded so rudely? If the legend of a sole survivor were true, surely it would be easy enough to find out.

I stuffed in the last morsel of croissant, washed it down with Earl Grey tea. It was time to begin. My clothes were laid out. I was in the tropics and would dress accordingly--khaki safari pants, a white, sleeveless linen blouse, and a Panama hat with a flowing white sash. I had come back to life after almost eight hours sleep and was beginning to feel excited. Because of my father's condition I supposed I shouldn't allow myself to think of this as an adventure, but rather as a deadly serious mission. But it was one of the first times no one was along to tell me what I had to do or how I had to act or who I was supposed to be. It was a chance for me to find myself, a journey I had longed to take ever since I could remember. I had no way of knowing then how much I would discover.

Minutes later, I descended red carpeted steps to the lobby, which I had not noticed the night before in my grogginess. I was surprised to see the hotel bustling with activity, and that the lobby area was larger than I'd realized, perhaps 40 by 40 feet. And it was higher, too. The ceiling, which was held aloft by Corinthian columns, stood at least 20 feet above a white marble floor.

I strolled past bellboys and elegantly dressed hotel

guests, I assumed most were French, and out a wide door to a busy city street that was different from any I'd seen-- like something out of another century in an exotic foreign land. As I walked along I sidestepped the droppings of horses and donkeys, which appeared to be the favored mode of transportation. Everywhere I looked the beasts plodded along loaded down with bags of rice, green bananas and raw sugar cane. Some pulled wagons full of fruit. The street was narrow and the sun still low so that the pavement was shaded by buildings on each side--for the most part French colonial structures with covered balconies where red hibiscus grew. Ornate ironwork between floors provided runs for purple bougainvillea to climb; the sky was bright blue above burnt red terra cotta tile roofs, punctuated with small white clouds.

I stopped to take photographs and look in shop windows. All the signs and prices were in French--much of the merchandise no doubt imported from the motherland. Except for people of European descent, the women wore flowered prints wrapped loosely around their bodies. Earthenware jugs balanced on the heads of some. Others wore turbans made of brightly-colored cloth.

As I moved along, the street opened into a wide area teeming with humanity. I plunged forward and arrived in an open-air market, the spectacle around me out of a travelogue--the sounds, smells, colors--the people in native dress haggling over the price of a skinned rabbit or a string of beads. It was a shame, I thought, Jeff was not there to enjoy it with me.

Row after row of stalls were filled with local produce--mangoes, olives, dates, coconuts, bananas, exotic fruit I'd never seen before. Chickens hung by scrawny legs, their naked bodies stripped of feathers, feet and heads still attached.

My stomach felt queasy and I tasted salty saliva. The sight of a butcher's bloody apron and the severed pig's foot he held up for a customer did not help. Then, thankfully, the smell of freshly baked bread and pastries reached me. I quickly moved in that direction.

My thoughts returned to Jeff. Perhaps I should have been more receptive to his attempt at affection, but darn it, why did he have to be so condescending? I was capable of defending myself--strong as a lot of men and smarter than most, at least if smarts were defined as something more than what one got out of a book. Take Jeff. He was *knowledgeable*--about archaeology. He should have been, he was a college professor. He'd run on for hours if I let him, expounding on some theory of the Incas, the Mayans, or the rise of civilization in Mesopotamia. It was his understanding of real live twentieth-century people, their thoughts, feelings, likes and dislikes, that was lacking. I supposed it wasn't entirely his fault. I knew him well enough to realize he didn't mean to be the way he appeared. Jeff was one of those scientific types with his head in the clouds.

I shouldn't have been so hard on him. He was one of those brainy people around whom others felt transparent. He didn't try to make them feel that way, and I was certain he cared for me. The truth was, most women probably would have fallen all over themselves to maneuver him down the aisle. Maybe something was wrong with me. Maybe my past--my mother leaving. Billy Hanover. God, I hadn't thought of *him* in a long, long while.

Enough. Time to think of something else, of the job I'd come to do. I needed answers and I needed them quickly.

Why did Papa think he was going to die?

That certainly seemed to be the case. Only five days to unravel the mystery--

Five? More like three. The return trip would take a day and a half.

Three days! Thoughts of Jeff had to go.

A black man looked at me and turned away. I pulled a pad and pencil from my camera case and tapped him on the shoulder.

"Excuse me, Sir," I said in French. "I'm doing a story on the fiftieth anniversary of the Mt. Pelée eruption--

an incredible catastrophe as I am sure you know. What can you tell me about it?"

The man's eyes grew round. He ran.

Had I been too abrupt?

I squared off and took a picture of a lady of African descent with a jug on her head, advanced the film, then took another of a scruffy white man with a two-day beard.

"Pardon me, Sir," I said to him. "You know about the Mt. Pelée eruption, I'm sure."

"Yes . . . from school . . . and of course the old people don't hardly talk of nothing else if you let them. I heard stories to make your nose hairs curl."

"Interesting figure of speech," I said.

His smile revealed rotten teeth.

"The survivor they found in the jail," I said. "What have you heard of him?"

He held hands before his face as though I were a vampire. In an instant he had disappeared into the crowd.

What was with these people?

A greengrocer took my arm and directed my attention to his large, ripe cucumbers.

"Magnificent," I said. "But I wonder if you would mind helping me with something. You see, I'm doing a story." I pointed to my pad with my pencil. "And there's something I need to know. This fellow they found in jail after the Mt. Pelée eruption--the lone survivor. It was a long time ago, of course, but surely stories of him abound. What can you tell me about him?"

His nose wrinkled. "I can tell you to mind your own business and move on," he said waving me away.

I started forward into the crowd. Was there some unwritten code against answering a reporter's questions in a market? Were the people here just too busy, or was there something in particular about my approach?

I spotted a street that led away from the pandemonium and headed for it.

My escape route emptied into an expanse of

manicured lawn, which turned into a park encircled by tall coconut palms. The walkways were bordered by Mediterranean laurel covered with pink blossoms. I detected the scent of rosemary. I strolled along gazing at the bright blue sky. The sun was higher now, the air still and warm. I took a handkerchief from my camera bag and wiped my brow--not a lady-like thing to do but I didn't realize someone was watching.

A white marble statue came into view of a demur young woman on a pedestal, dressed in a flowing gown. On the base in raised block letters was spelled out, "Josephine."

Napoleon's Josephine? Must be.

A man's voice startled me. "She was very beautiful. Like my Marie-Charlotte."

I spun around to see an old French gentleman with white hair and a bushy white mustache. He sat on a bench in the shade of a banana palm with a Panama hat in his lap, dressed in a tan tropical suit, white pinpoint cotton shirt and black knit tie.

"I'll bet you come here often," I said.

"Almost every day."

I sat at the other end of the bench. He looked old enough to have firsthand knowledge of the eruption.

After a moment I said, "Have you lived here all your life?"

"Most of it." He sighed. "I was born and raised in St. Pierre. Now St. Pierre is gone, at least the St. Pierre I knew."

Eureka, I thought. "I see," I said. "The Mt. Pelée eruption."

"Alas."

"Must have been awful. But you--how did you survive?"

"I left St. Pierre on the seventh. I was to be married on the tenth, that Saturday, but I had to go to Fort de France to make last-minute arrangements." He toyed with the brim of his Panama. "You see, the family lawyer was here, and I thought I needed a will. So I left my Marie-

Charlotte, thinking we would be reunited at the altar."

"How horrible," I said.

"I was 24. She was three years younger. It was the only time either of us had been in love." He shifted uneasily, but seemed compelled to speak.

"That day, the morning of the eighth of May, I awoke thinking it was the next to the last day I would ever spend alone." He looked into the sky. "It was a lovely morning--after one of the worst nights, ever. A night of thunder, lightning, unceasing rain. The sun broke through early and the sky became clear--bright blue. I took it to be a good omen."

His eyes returned to his hat. "Never have I known, never shall I know anything like the happiness and joy with which I dressed and bathed and shaved."

He sat in silence.

"What happened? Did you hear the eruption?"

"As I finished my coffee, there came two enormous explosions. The entire island shook. But I wasn't frightened. Why should I be? A road being cut through a mountain pass, perhaps. I continued, as did everyone in Forte de France, with what I had to do. I went to breakfast, tried to get my mind on something else."

"How did you find out what happened? When did you know?"

"I began to notice a worried look on people's faces. And the sky--which had been such a divine, royal blue-- became dark in a matter of minutes. A thin dust with pebbles mingled in was falling over the town. A man came running into the dining room of the hotel--no news was coming through from St. Pierre. The telephone line had been cut suddenly in the middle of a message, at the instant of the two explosions. Since that moment there had been . . . silence." He looked at me, sadness in his eyes. He shook his head.

"Were you frightened? Did you know at that moment? Or did it take more time to realize . . . "

"I tried not to worry. I told myself it was absurd to be frightened. But panic caught hold of the people in the

63

restaurant and panic is contagious. I left. I sought the company of friends and relatives."

"How long was it before you knew?"

"By 11 o'clock our nerves were gone. Three hours had passed and still no news. By then I was at my uncle's club, where we sat in silence staring at our rum punches, one thought only on our minds."

He let out a long, deep sigh.

"I shall never forget the suspense, the terror, the uncertainty. *Midday* and still no message had come through. The boat which was sent out to make inquiries had not returned. We worried, we waited. It was not until one o'clock that we knew."

His face showed pain. After a moment, he slapped his knee as if to shake off the memory.

"It is now 50 years ago. A lifetime. One can forget most things in so long a time. One thinks one's heart is broken, but it mends. One thinks one's life is over, but it isn't. One must pick up the pieces--make the best of it-- and that is what I did, eventually. I married, had children. Grandchildren, now."

A faraway look came over him. "Only . . . I don't know--it's difficult to put it into words. Since that day, I've felt nothing really matters in particular."

"A sad, sad story," I said.

"The ramblings of an old man."

"Did you know someone, a man perhaps a few years younger than you were at the time, whose name was Paul DuMond?"

"Paul DuMond? No, and I would rather not think about it any longer. It is much too painful. No more questions, please."

He stood and straightened his jacket.

I jumped up. "So sorry, but there is one more thing I am very curious about. The survivor, a man who was in the jail. What became of him?"

A strange look appeared in the old man's eye. He tipped his hat. "Good day, mademoiselle. I hope you will enjoy your stay in Martinique."

64

In an instant he was gone.

That evening, back in my hotel room, I sat by the window staring down at the street. A whole day was shot--wasted. Except for the old man, it seemed as though no one on this entire island had any firsthand knowledge of the eruption, and no one I had questioned knew anything at all about the man in jail. And as for my father, well, he might as well have grown up in Kalamazoo.

Two days left! I could feel myself beginning to hyperventilate.

Count to ten slowly, I told myself. It wouldn't do to have an emotional breakdown now, although I felt as though I were on the verge of one. I needed to remain calm and persevere. If I didn't get hold of myself and keep pushing, Papa would die from his mysterious affliction. His fate was in my hands.

Fate. Was everything predetermined, all decided, anyway? I couldn't believe that. A person had to take charge of her fate, make it happen. That's what I was doing--fighting to shape the outcome of Papa's fate. That was why I'd walked into O'Malley's office and asked for a decent assignment, to shape my own fate--for all the good it had done me.

But who knew? Maybe this trip to Martinique was part of the plan the Fates had for me, as well as for Papa. If I could write a terrific story it could be my ticket out of the woman's corner. But I'd have to get more information tomorrow than I had gotten today.

At least the old man's story would make good copy. Poor old fellow. It was impossible to grasp the magnitude of the catastrophe until it was put in terms of what it meant to a single individual. Then I could multiply by 30,000.

I leaned back in the chair and rested my head. What had Papa experienced that day? What had happened to him, and--what was her name? Angelique. Yes. Had she been killed? How had Papa escaped? Had he gone to Fort de France as the old man had?

65

Possibly, or maybe he and his sweetheart had a lover's spat, and he left the island entirely--before the eruption.

Not being with her during those final minutes could have been at the root of the problem, maybe the source of an enormous sense of guilt, especially if the two of them parted on bad terms with the future of their relationship unresolved.

The terms Jeff and I had parted on were not so good, either, were they? Suppose something happened to one of us before we saw each other again?

I looked at my watch. Seven o'clock.

I picked up the telephone. "Operator? This is room 26, Miss Claire DuMond. I'd like to make a person-to-person call to Mr. Jeff McDannon in Richmond, Virginia. The United States. Belmont three, one, five, three, six."

"Very good, mademoiselle. I shall ring back when I have him on the line."

Maybe that was it. Perhaps Papa never cleared the air.

Dear Jeff. Sweet Jeff. I shook my head. I'd been covering a symposium at Richmond College when I met him. He'd been the featured speaker. How eloquent he'd been as he explained the results of a dig in Egypt, but how he stammered, was at a loss for words with me. I'd known right away. It were as though I could read his mind.

What had it been? The way he diverted his eyes? Or how he seemed to have difficulty looking straight at me? He actually blushed, and then I knew--though I hadn't admitted it to myself for a long, long time. He was smitten. My smitten puppy dog. Oh, every now and then he kicked and screamed and protested, but underneath that's what he was: my puppy dog.

Come along, Jeff. Sit. Good. Now, roll over.

That had been two years ago. Two years.

It had been months before I let Jeff know who I really was, let him have a glimpse of the real me. It was a talent of mine that I could be whatever a man wanted, and

I was able to do it without relinquishing my own identity. I had a chameleon quality which enabled me to transform myself, part of my process of becoming. In his eyes, I became what he wanted to see: his dream girl. What he didn't know was that his dream girl existed in the eyes of the beholder. I'd had it happen before. So when I had grown close to him I shared my goals and ambitions, my desire to become someone who was *not* what he wanted, which of course was a doting wife who spent her time keeping the silver polished, barefoot and pregnant. No. If he wanted me, the real me, he'd have to accept something else--a person with goals. Lofty goals for a woman of that time.

The funny thing was, he said he didn't mind, that he loved me all the more. He wanted to set a date, wanted to become engaged right away, but I found reasons to put him off. Excuses, really. I liked my options open--the way they were.

Maybe something was wrong with me. Nothing was wrong with Jeff. Oh, his mind tended to get stuck every now and then in the rut of thinking men were superior. What else was new? Mid-twentieth century culture was to blame. One had to go back a long way to the earliest civilizations--civilizations where the earth goddess reigned--before one found a society which valued women more. To his credit Jeff had pointed that out. He'd said that in some ancient civilizations women were thought of as an extension of the divine because they shared the role of creator with the Godhead. Women gave birth. Men had the easy part.

Jeff did try to see my point of view. Even so I often had to remind him when he was behaving like an ass.

I stood, moved to the balcony, pushed the French doors open and walked outside. The air was warm and it seemed to hover close to my skin. There was almost no breeze, but the pleasant odor of hibiscus reached me nonetheless, and lingered--spicy sweet. Street lights flickered below.

It was curious . . . the man by the street lamp had

been standing there for an hour, I was sure of it.

Why'd he look away and bury his head in a newspaper?

People didn't stand under street lamps and read newspapers.

Did he think he was some sort of private eye out of a Hollywood production? His black shirt and white tie certainly fit the part of Bogart in *The Big Sleep*.

The telephone rang and I went back inside.

"Mademoiselle DuMond? I am so sorry, but your party is not home. Do you wish to try again, later?"

"Yes, operator--later."

I looked at my watch. Almost eight o'clock. Where on earth could he be? Out with the boys? Another woman?

Naw, not Jeff. He better not be.

I went to the French doors and stood to the side.

He was there, looking up at my window, craning his neck.

I moved into full view and the paper shot in front of his face.

How juvenile!

There was a rumble in my stomach. Small wonder. I hadn't eaten since breakfast.

What was the name of that restaurant? *La Belle Epoque?* Yes. Only a short distance from the hotel according to the desk clerk. It would be amusing to see what this fellow did when I walked past.

A few minutes later, I strolled through the lobby, which was illuminated in a delightful way that emphasized the high ceiling and supporting columns, and went out the front doors into the night. I passed within two feet of the man in the black shirt, who kept his back turned and the newspaper inches from his nose, rounded the corner and stepped into a doorway.

Footsteps came my way, then stopped.

I stepped back onto the sidewalk and to my surprise the street was empty.

I felt a flutter. Where had Black Shirt gone?

Why worry? I'd dealt with creeps before. I could handle this one.

The street was dark and the absence of other pedestrians made me uneasy, but I arrived without incident. My mood shifted, perhaps because I found the restaurant to be charming. The chairs and floor were dark stained wood. Candles in glass goblets on cloth-covered tables gave off a warm, golden glow. Large plants and oriental screen dividers created an intimate atmosphere.

I followed the head waiter to a booth along a wall near French doors pushed open. A gentle breeze caressed my face and shoulders. The waiter held my chair and I took the menu, but didn't look at it right away. The temperature was delightful. I could smell the sea. What a marvelous evening. Jeff would have enjoyed this place; the balmy tropical air.

A tall Frenchman with a cigarette dangling from his lips walked by my table. He stopped by a large fern, and stood, staring at me.

Why was it Frenchmen always thought of themselves as lady-killers?

I looked again a moment later and his eyes were still on me, a kind of hungry-wolf look in them. My neck hairs bristled.

I recalled the time I was 14 and walked past a construction site during the noon hour. All the workers had lunch boxes open, eating.

"Hey, baby!" one of them had shouted. "Whatcha doing tonight?"

Another let out a wolf whistle and they all chimed in with catcalls, whistles, and shouts of "Momma-momma-mía, getta load a those meat balls!"

Now I chalked up their behavior to the fact they were mostly males in their early twenties with IQs in the 65-to-70 range, but at the time I was totally befuddled and realized everyone up and down the block was looking at me--people coming out of stores, passing by in cars, crossing the street. It brought me to the brink of tears and I couldn't understand the hullabaloo from these grown men when the boys at school always seemed to shy away.

Men.

The waiter returned with a bucket of ice and a bottle of champagne. I glanced toward the fern--the wolf was gone.

"What's this? I didn't order wine."

He uncorked it. "An admirer has commanded me to bring this to you with his compliments."

He poured a small amount in my glass.

"Commanded you? What gentleman?"

I tasted it, nodded approval.

"I am sorry, mademoiselle, but he wishes to remain anonymous. He said to let you know only that he understands you have been inquiring after him today."

The waiter filled my glass.

"Me? Asking about him you say?"

He pushed the bottle into the ice bucket.

"That is what he said, mademoiselle. No more."

He bowed slightly and backed away.

The wine sparkled in the candlelight and tiny bubbles rushed to the surface in thin lines. I sipped--and wondered.

The man with wolf eyes?

No, the champagne arrived only seconds after he had left the fern.

Asking about him? Asking about *him*.

The man in jail?

It must be--certainly. He was the only man I'd asked about besides Papa.

I leaned out of the booth--the restaurant was full. Dozens of men here were old enough, and there was no way to have a look around without causing a scene.

Why didn't he identify himself?

Understand you've been asking about me. Well, here I am.

Unless he had something to hide . . . from a reporter.

That he once had been in jail?

70

That he *belonged* in jail?

Of course. That explained the man--Black Shirt-- watching from the street. Black Shirt wasn't old enough to be the one, but he must be connected--must work for him.

I looked at the bottle. *Chateau-Troyes,* 1932.

1932?

A 20-year-old bottle meant he must be a very successful former jail bird, and no doubt a very powerful one as well . . . with men working for him, keeping an eye on a reporter who was asking about him. Yes, *very* powerful.

I stood and headed for the door.

The head waiter's eyes grew round. "Mademoiselle, what is it? Are you sick?"

"Not sick. I am so sorry, I have forgotten an engagement." I hurried from the restaurant in the direction of my hotel, telling myself to calm down, it wasn't far.

I rounded the corner, scurried past the doorway I'd ducked into earlier. An automobile engine roared behind me and I looked back. Headlights approached fast.

I broke into a run--my heart pounding.

The engine grew louder, wound up in second gear, was practically upon me.

The car jumped the curb, bounced, swayed, two wheels left the ground.

I stepped into an opening, backed against the building, the car scraped the spot where I'd stood a half second before.

It skidded to a stop.

Get going. Move!

The engine roared again, tires squealed, wound up in first.

Oh, no--Where?

A drop in pitch to second gear.

Turn the corner, turn it now!

I stretched--made it. The car sped past--inches away.

The hotel--fifty yards! Run!

Tires screeched--then moaned as the car circled

71

back.

I ran flat out, top speed, the hotel clearly in sight--almost within reach--the whine of the engine growing louder, louder. I looked over my shoulder. It was nearly upon me. I leaped for a doorway.

The car hit a lamp post--sprayed glass--glanced off, skidded across the sidewalk, bounced off another lamp post, landed back in the street, spun halfway around, straightened out and sped away.

I lay face down on the pavement, trembling--my heart pounding, my mind racing.

A hand on my shoulder--*Oh God!*

"Goodness, gracious, Claire. Are you all right?"

What? Who? No, it couldn't be.

"The desk clerk said you'd gone to dinner. I came to find you and saw the whole thing. It looked as though that car was *trying* to run you down."

I rolled over. "Jeff?! It is you, but . . . I don't believe it. What are you doing here?"

"I was sick with worry about you, Claire. I couldn't think of anything else. I was useless to everyone, including myself, so I said to hell with it and caught the first plane south."

I sat up. "Ouch!"

"Are you hurt?"

He peeled away a torn flap of safari pants. "Your knee is skinned." He felt above, below. "Nothing's broken, though."

"Help me up, please."

He pulled me to my feet. I took a step, limped.

"Here, lean on me," he said.

I waved him off. "I'll be all right."

He took my arm. "Let's get inside the hotel and wash the grit off that scrape."

We walked through the door into the lobby. The heels of Jeff's boots clicked on the marble floor.

"The bar," I said.

The room was lit by candlelight. Only a few customers were at the bar. I sat at a table. Jeff went to the bar.

"Two brandies--cognac," I heard him say in French. "And a hot towel. This lady's skinned her knee."

His French was not bad, I thought, but his American accent was a little thick.

Moments later he placed a brandy in front of me, adjusted his glasses, and dabbed my knee with a warm, moist cloth.

I sipped the cognac, swallowed, felt the burning sensation of alcohol accompanied by a warm, comforting rush. I watched Jeff at work. He hadn't made that trip to the barber. His flat-top had grown another quarter of an inch.

"Tell me what happened, Claire."

I gave him the nutshell version, ending with the champagne and my flight in panic from the restaurant. Then I turned the brandy glass bottom up.

"Another round, bartender," Jeff said. Then to me, "This is actually worse than I could have imagined. People trying to run over you--for goodness sake."

Two more glasses of cognac appeared on our table.

Jeff stopped the man. "Tell me something, bartender. This fellow who survived the Mt. Pelée eruption because he was in jail. What's his game? Is he some kind of crook?" Jeff pulled a 50 franc note from his wallet and held it up.

"Drugs. Heroin. They say he supplies Chicago *and* New York."

Jeff handed him the bill.

"Tell me something else. If you wanted to find people old enough to remember the Mt. Pelée eruption, where would you go?"

"Cockfights, I guess. There's always a bunch of old guys there. The fights will be going on all day tomorrow because it's Sunday."

The bartender snapped his fingers. "Wait a minute. Sunday. It made me think of something. The old priest--Father Gaulois. The eruption is all he talks about-- the subject of half his sermons. Claims he left St. Pierre

73

only minutes before Pelée blew its top. You'll find him at the Church of the Sacred Heart."

"Good man." Jeff slipped him another bill.

I watched him walk away. A slow burn came over me.

"Have I ever told you, Jeff, that you're a certified creep?"

"Excuse me?"

"I mean, it's like you want me to hate you."

"What are you saying, Claire? I just helped you off the pavement, and cleaned your wound."

"You've horned your way into something that's my affair--not yours. If I were a man you never would have come."

"You're right. It's no secret I've fallen for you."

"If you really loved me, you wouldn't muck around in my business."

"Wait a minute. I'm here precisely because I do love you."

"You think I'm a frail, stupid, inferior being who needs a man to protect and think for her. You want to keep me in my place."

"Not true. I think you're smart--not think, *know*. And you're, you're strong, too. You play a helluva game of tennis."

"Oh my God, Jeff. You're so, so--patronizing."

I took a sip of brandy, swallowed--took another. Perhaps counting to ten would help . . . one, two, three . . .

Okay, so Jeff was a louse. Nothing new there. At this moment, though, he looked like a little boy--pouting.

Nine, ten . . . yes, that was better.

He took a sip of brandy and sniffed. He did look hurt. I hated to see him hurt.

"Give me a break, will you, Claire?" He shrugged. "I'm sorry if I offended you in some way, but frankly, I don't know what you're talking about."

"I'm sorry I blew up at you," I said. "But suppose I explain it to you one more time. Playing traditional roles over and over like a broken record keeps women in their place. You get to be the knight in shining armor, I'm always the damsel in distress."

"What do you want--I should be the damsel?"

"What a minute, let me finish. So--you come dashing on stage to rescue me from harm's way."

"What's wrong with that?"

"It's my turf. I'm on assignment--at least in a way I am. I mean, the newspaper isn't paying me exactly, but if I can bring back a story O'Malley likes, it will get me off the Woman's Page. You know how important that is to me, and it's important I do it on my own. Besides, I don't follow you on your archaeological digs so I don't see why you should follow me here, see? I don't need or want your assistance, don't you understand?"

"All I've done so far is help you up, and mop up a little blood."

"No, that isn't all you've done. You found out something in two minutes I've been busting my you know what all day to find out."

Jeff blinked and an impish smile appeared.

"Now I get it. You've been one-upped. Doggone." He shook his head. "Guess this means you're not going to sleep with me tonight."

4

The next morning I sat in front of the mirror in my hotel room plucking my eyebrows and wondering what I'd gotten myself into. A drug smuggler, or more likely one of his henchmen, had tried to run me down in the street. Had that little episode been the end of it? It did not seem likely.

Although my hair was sandy blond, my brows were dark and thick, the kind that needed constant attention. One thing was certain, I was not going to all this trouble for Jeff. No, sir. It was Sunday and I was going to visit a priest. That called for extra effort.

I stood and held a sun dress to me made of a Liberty of London flowered print in autumn tones. The length was below my knee, so the bandage over my scrape would be hidden. It was low cut, too, so there would be an inch or more of cleavage. The thin straps would reveal a good deal of bare skin around my neck and shoulders. Jeff would think it was too daring. Nevertheless, the colors looked great next to my cream complexion.

Jeff would survive. The dress would do nicely--

76

especially topped off with the straw hat I'd wear to protect myself from the sun. So what if a few heads turned? It was too hot to wear something tight. This was the tropics.

No, Jeff wasn't a reason to make myself look fetching. A glimpse of partially exposed breast would only encourage him to make some smarty-pants comment which I'd simply have to give right back to him. I put on the broad-brimmed hat, looked in the mirror, turned from side to side. I searched my cosmetic bag for hair pins.

Why did Jeff have such a knack for pushing my buttons? His attempt at a joke about me not sleeping with him, for example. Maybe I wouldn't have reacted so violently if I'd thought it really were a joke. Fact was, I'd gone to bed with him twice--once when we celebrated my landing a job at the newspaper. That time the champagne was to blame. The other was the night he returned from a three-month dig in Egypt. My joy at seeing him caused me to forget myself.

Both encounters ended up as disappointments. Sex might be okay for some women--but not for me.

Yep. Jeff expected this romantic tropical setting to cause me to forget myself again. He was wrong.

Eat your heart out, Jeffrey.

On the way downstairs I wondered how I should act toward him this morning. Slightly miffed? A bit aloof? Cool as a watermelon on ice? Heck, why bother to figure it out. Play it by ear.

I strolled between the columns. He stood and waved as I entered the dining room, a big smile on his face which accentuated the crow's-feet around his eyes and the laugh-lines that came from years of archaeological digs in the sun. He actually was handsome in a gangly sort of way. The dimple on his cheek was enough to make a girl's nose hairs curl, to borrow a phrase from that scruffy man in the marketplace. If only he'd do something about the haircut. He looked dapper otherwise--in a blue and white striped seersucker suit, starched white Oxford shirt and yellow paisley tie--an ensemble that fit with the white linen tablecloths, bone china and silver napkin rings.

He held a chair, slipped it under me deftly as I sat.

"Two days left, Jeff. We'd better make this a quick breakfast."

"Coffee, croissant, and fruit are on the way." He put his napkin in his lap with a flourish. "Not still smarting from last night, I hope?"

"We agreed not to talk about it."

"Aye, aye, captain."

"And no more Mr. Smart Alec."

"Hold on," Jeff said. "You go too far. You're asking me to go against my nature."

Breakfast arrived. The waiter served us coffee.

When he'd left I said, "If you won't promise to cut out the wise-guy routine, at least promise no more Sir Lancelot dashing about opening doors and blocking the way while you wait for me to get off the elevator." I took a sip. The coffee was strong. I wished for tea, poured in cream.

"Gentlemanly behavior is ingrained in me," Jeff said. "You know I've tried to change, but I find it's quite impossible. Blame it on my parents."

I studied his face. He was actually enjoying this, probably seeing how far he could push before my temper flared--the scientist in him experimenting.

Carefully, I applied jam to a croissant.

"I believe it is possible to overcome an unfortunate upbringing," I said. "Of course, one has to recognize one's deficiencies, work on them and *want* to change."

Jeff removed his glasses and pinched the bridge of his nose. "What if a man likes treating a lady like a lady?"

"What if the *woman* would rather be treated like an equal?"

His lips puckered. "If a man treats a *lady* like an equal, that's not treating her as well as she deserves. I mean, you don't run around and open the car door for one of your male friends."

"Precisely," I said. "By opening the car door, you're telling a *woman* in a subtle way she's inferior, she's not capable of doing it herself. But we've been over this ground, so let's just move on, shall we? I'll try to assist you in your retraining by calling attention to your little *faux pas* when you make them, like the one a minute ago when you held my chair."

"Are you determined to deprive me of the pleasure of holding your chair, Claire? Just now, for example, it gave me a really good shot down that low-cut dress of yours."

I gave him the icy-watermelon glare.

The waiter placed the check in front of Jeff. I grabbed it, scribbled my room number and initials.

Jeff dabbed his napkin at he corners of his mouth.

"To the Church of the Sacred Heart," he said and stood.

Walking out of the front door, I experienced a déjá vu sensation. A black Citroen was waiting at the curb, a little white sign on the roof. The driver looked up at me, large whites encircling the jet black pupils of his eyes.

I opened the back door and Jeff climbed in after me.

"The Church of the Sacred Heart," he said.

The driver pulled down the lever and began edging through heavy pedestrian traffic, past horses and donkeys pulling wagons.

I was still seething and felt the driver deserved a little of my wrath. "I've been wondering, driver, why wouldn't you tell me about the man in jail?"

He glanced in the mirror. "Who?"

"You know perfectly well who I'm talking about, driver. The Mt. Pelée eruption? Apparently, the man is still alive, a drug smuggler who goes around terrifying innocent people."

He smiled and nodded. "You got it right that time, mademoiselle, which is exactly why I did not say anything about him to you. You never know who might be friend of whom, you understand? I'd rather keep mouth shut, give

79

tongue a rest. Can save neck much discomfort. Comprehend?"

Ten minutes later, the Citroen struggled in second gear as it climbed the steep grade of the hill overlooking Fort de France and its horseshoe-shaped harbor. Water glistened far below, its deep blue set off from lush green vegetation by a thin band of white sand. I glanced at my watch. Almost ten o'clock.

Jeff made a move for his wallet, and I put my hand on his arm.

"Wait here, please, driver." I handed him a bill. "We're going to see Father Gaulois, then we'll need a ride back."

"You won't be able to see him now, mademoiselle. It is almost time for mass."

I looked at the front door of the church and saw people filing in.

"Isn't mass at eleven?" Jeff asked.

"Ten o'clock," the driver said.

"Oh, no," I said. "We've just blown half the day."

"Not blown. This is just a detour," Jeff said. "Driver, is there a place around here where cockfights are held on Sunday morning?"

"This is Martinique, monsieur. There are cockfights *everywhere* on Sunday. It's a wonder the Church does any business."

"Take us to one, will you?"

The driver put the Citroen in first, gunned the engine and let out the clutch. "I know a nice place in *Trinité*," he said. "They have a building, the Gallodrome, with five different galleries. One has a piano and a bar."

"Perfect," Jeff said.

I gazed out the open window, felt the warm breeze on my face as we rolled by deep green foliage, wide leaves, thin leaves, tall curved palms and short squatty ones.

"How far is it to *Trinité*, driver?" I said.

"Two kilometers beyond the next pass."

"By the way, now that we're practically old

80

friends, what's your name, driver?"

"They call me Toussaint."

"Toussaint--All Saints. Your birthday is the first of November?"

"Yes, mademoiselle."

I chuckled. I knew it was a custom in French countries to name children for the saint on whose day they were born, but this was the first time I'd met anyone named for All Saints Day.

As we rode along, I struck up a conversation with Toussaint. My mood grew lighter. I enjoyed the patter of his Creole dialect. It was more fun--and easier--to ask him questions about his family and his life in Martinique than to deal with the tension between Jeff and me. I managed to stretch it out until we rolled to a stop beside the Gallodrome.

Jeff did not attempt to pay. I handed Toussaint a bill. "Wait here, please."

We walked toward the rickety wooden structure and a cheer went up. It actually seemed to wobble.

"Think it's safe?" I said.

"I seriously doubt they go by the same safety codes we have in the States, if that's what you mean."

"You don't have to come, you know."

"Wouldn't miss this for anything."

A man at the gate collected five francs from each of us, which got us through the gate. We followed a line of people into an opening, a kind of tunnel which led to one of the galleries.

Inside was a round pit, about 20 feet across, surrounded by a throng of on-lookers who sat on wooden bleachers or stood in back. Jeff and I took ringside seats vacated by two unhappy-looking men who stormed past pounding their hats against their thighs and complaining about the stupidity of chickens.

I settled in, looked around, took the camera out of my bag as well as the light meter, which I used to get a reading. A lot of old men were there, but a lot of young men, too.

I attached a telephoto lens and scanned the crowd. The only women I saw looked like fugitives from the red-light district. No doubt Jeff thought it would be unsafe for me to be there alone, but I was certain the reason no women were present was that women in general were more civilized than men. It was difficult to imagine a more barbaric form of recreation than watching two birds peck and claw each other to death.

Two men, each holding a rooster, came through gates on opposite sides of the pit and approached a circle drawn in the dirt. They held up the cocks. The crowd buzzed. Shouts and wolf whistles filled the air.

I snapped a picture.

The man next to Jeff said, "Ten francs says Green wins."

"You're on," Jeff said. "Keep your fingers crossed, Claire. We've got the one with the red tag."

The two men knelt on opposite sides of the circle, set the cocks on the ground and held them for a moment before they let go.

The birds flew at each other, the crowd jumped to its feet with a roar. There was a such a whirlwind of a fight, feathers flying, I had trouble determining which cock was which. Everyone around me bounced up and down in a frenzy shrieking encouragement to whichever one they'd bet on.

After a few minutes, though, the fight seemed to have gone out of both birds, and the noise of the crowd settled to a buzz. The cocks eyed each other, gasping. One moved cautiously in an encircling maneuver, its head low, jutting back and forth. Then it took a couple of strutting steps, but it stayed well clear as the other cocked its head and gave his opponent a look as if to say, "Ready for some more, big guy? Try one step closer and see what happens."

By some signal I missed the owners took the birds simultaneously by the wings and placed them at the edge of the circle, five feet apart.

Jeff shook his head. "I think Old Red's a goner."

Both birds flapped their wings, which lifted them in the air. The crowd roared, Red lunged forward with a vicious peck to the back of Green's neck, and Green--clearly defeated--showed Red his backside.

"Hard to believe," Jeff said.

Jeff's neighbor shrugged and handed him a ten-franc note.

"Hope you won't find it patronizing if I use some of my winnings to buy you a drink tonight," Jeff said. "By the way, have you noticed the man over there in the black shirt and white tie? Hasn't taken his eyes off you since we sat down."

"Black shirt? Where?"

"Be discreet, will you? Straight across, third row up."

I scanned the crowd and the man I'd come to think of as Black Shirt looked directly into my eyes, jumped to his feet and headed for the exit.

"It's him," I said. "The man who was watching my window."

"Uh-oh!" Jeff looked right, then left. "Better make a dash for it--he could corner us in nothing flat."

I got to my feet. "If we haven't been already."

I tore up the aisle, then down the corridor toward the outside, leading the way. A few feet from the opening Black Shirt stepped into my path and held up his hands. I pulled up, swung my camera around my head as though I were winding up for the Olympic hammer throw and let it fly. The telephoto lens hit him in the forehead so hard his feet left the ground. He let out a scream as he landed on his back. I grabbed the camera, sprinted, didn't look around until the taxi was in reach, but when I did, Jeff was close behind.

"Church of the Sacred Heart," I said, gasping as I climbed into the car. "And step on it."

"I'll say you'd better step on it," Jeff said, pulling the door shut. "They're not going to take that lying down."

Toussaint rammed the car in reverse, backed, then

pulled the shift lever into first and shot across the bumpy dirt surface of the parking lot. I hung on as we skidded onto the blacktop highway. As he ran through the gears, I examined my camera and saw that the lip of the lens was bent.

"Took a pretty good lick," I said.

"You got his attention," Jeff said.

"Didn't seem the proper time to stop and chat."

"Probably not," Jeff said. "Guess we'll never know if all he wanted was a match."

I shrugged and shoved the camera back into its case. "Shoot first, ask questions later, right? I was only following whoever-said-that's advice."

We rode in silence for a few minutes until I noticed Toussaint spending a good deal of time looking in the rearview mirror. I turned and glanced out the back. A hundred yards behind a black Peugeot disappeared from view as we went into a curve.

I saw it again when we were on a straight stretch. It had gained 20 yards or more.

"We've got a problem back there," I said softly.

Jeff turned to look. "Oh, Lord."

I leaned over the front seat. "Don't let that car behind us catch up, Toussaint," I said. "Whoever it is is connected with that dope smuggler we were talking about, remember? The one who survived the Mt. Pelée eruption? We had a little go with him in the stadium."

"You mean Bébé Dominique? The gangster? My God." Toussaint stomped the gas.

The car accelerated as the motor wound up tight and we fishtailed around a curve, throwing me into Jeff. I grabbed for a strap that hung from the post between the front and rear seats and missed it as the car swayed the other way. Finally I got my fingers around the darn thing, inched them through until the strap was in my palm. Once I had a grip on it I held on tight.

Jeff looked out the back. "He's gaining on us."

We fishtailed around another curve and tires squealed. I was thrown toward the open window this time. My stomach lurched when I looked down a cliff to rocks hundreds of feet below.

The Peugeot pulled within 25 yards, so close I could see two men in the front seat. I couldn't make out if it was Black Shirt behind the wheel, but I stopped worrying about who it was when I saw a gun emerge from the passenger's side, followed by a puff of smoke and the crack of a pistol.

I screamed and pulled Jeff down with me to the seat, his big brown eyes inches away.

"What's that line about a kettle of fish, Ollie?" he said.

We slammed into another curve, tires squealing.

"Okay, smarty pants, what would *you* have done?"

"Diplomacy, perhaps. Bit late, now."

The car leveled out. Toussaint shifted into a higher gear. The pistol cracked again and again. There was a loud smack. Jeff and I were showered with tiny shards of glass.

Something happened, a sense of calm came over me, an inner peace that seemed to say not to fight it, to accept my fate. It was clear we could not escape, but somehow it didn't matter that we were going to end up smashed against a tree, over a cliff, or stopped and facing a bullet between the eyes. Whatever happened, everything would be all right. I can only describe the feeling as an odd sense of resignation. With it came the realization that it was time to tell Jeff I really did care for him, that I was glad he was here no matter what I'd said. On top of it I wanted him to know how terribly sorry I was we were going to die. It was my fault.

"Jeff, I've something important to tell you--"

Suddenly I was thrown forward into the back of the front seat. The brakes moaned; the car skidded. It yawed and I was thrown backward as the motor roared, then forward as we screeched to a stop.

For a few seconds that seemed longer I heard nothing, except birds chirping. Then Toussaint said, "For

85

this ride I expect a large gratuity in addition to the fare and the cost of the rear windshield."

Jeff and I slowly raised our heads above the seat.

"What happened?" Jeff asked.

"The Army has arrived," Toussaint said. "Not on horseback as in your American movies. In this instance, I had to take us to them." He shook his head. "They appear to be rather unhappy. No doubt it has something to do with the fact that I crashed through their precious gate."

I followed his eyes and saw two men in olive green uniforms, pistols drawn, running toward us. The taxi had come to a stop in a courtyard surrounded by drab looking buildings in the middle of which was a flag pole flying the French Tricolor.

"Well, I'll be. An army base," Jeff said.

"French foreign legion," Toussaint said.

When soldiers surrounded the car I thought we'd gone from facing death at gunpoint by angry mobsters to death by military firing squad. But tempers cooled a few degrees when Toussaint explained the situation and apologized profusely for not stopping for the sentry.

One of the soldiers opened the door and I stepped out unsteadily. My knees felt weak and my legs wobbled as though I'd been on a ship for days and had not yet regained my affinity for land. The soldiers waited impatiently, and Jeff stood by watching with a blank expression on his face as I settled the bill with Toussaint. Then the men in olive green led Toussaint toward one of the featureless cement buildings, through an opening between palms which stood on each side of a narrow walkway. I wondered what they were going to do with him and wished I could help, but no one seemed willing to listen to my protests. The poor guy should have been treated as a hero rather than of as a fugitive from justice.

I rode to Fort de France on Jeff's lap in the backseat of a jeep, squeezed between two buck privates, each of whom I estimated to be approximately 19. I did my best to keep my eyes focused on anything but them--the foliage of the rain forest, the shanties with corrugated roofs, the occasional colonial style sugar plantation house with large porch and columns--because I could sense that their post-pubescent hormones were running wild. Every time we went around a curve I was thrown into one or the other of them, who would glance at his buddy and say, "Ooh, la la," with a silly grin.

"Ooh la la, we are sitting very close, all of us." Then he would roll his eyes.

"*N'cest pas?*" And the other would roll his. "Very close. Yes, very close--indeed."

How times had changed. When I was 16 sending bucks like this into fits of horniness would have been a dream come true rather than a mild embarrassment. I had, after all, been virtually ignored by boys my own age in middle and high school. How many times had I played the wallflower role? And how painful it had been. Although I never did find the wart on the end of my nose, I was convinced something was wrong with me.

Then boys' attitudes toward me shifted--although it was a while before I realized it. Papa said I was a late-bloomer.

I looked at one of the fuzzy-faced privates beside me. His eyes grew wide. He looked about to float off on a cloud of ecstasy. I didn't want to know what was going on inside his head. He reminded me of Billy Hanover, a boy I'd dated when I was 19.

"Got my greetings from Uncle Sam today," he'd said one day. "First boot camp, then England. They say there's going to be an invasion force assembled there the likes of which this planet's never seen."

"Oh, Billy, no," was all that I could manage. Every male I knew under the age of 30 had been drafted, but still, the news came as a shock.

"I wanna marry you, Claire. I know it sounds corny, but you're the woman of my dreams."

After all that rejection by boys in school, I was far from used to having anyone feel that way about me, and so flattered and touched I almost violated my intuition and accepted his proposal. But in the end a feeling deep inside won the struggle and I told him I wanted to wait until he came back before making a commitment.

The jeep hit a bump, jostling me, and I heard another, "Ooh la la."

A dozen of my friends had married their beaus, had become war brides. I wondered now why I had been different, why I had turned Billy Hanover down. I liked to keep my options open, it was true. But I could also be impulsive. This trip to Martinique was proof of that. No. There was something more than my basic nature at work. The loss of my mother perhaps. I'd known I couldn't handle losing someone else.

"Thank God we're here," Jeff said.

"Here?"

"At the church, remember? Let's go."

"Oh, right." I stood and struggled past the private who reminded me of Billy. I couldn't help but rub against him, and he let out another, "Ooh, la, la."

The soldiers hooted and waved as they drove away, and Jeff and I waved back as we climbed the steps to the church.

I looked at my watch. Ten minutes after two.

"It's hard to keep from hyperventilating," I said. "The ticking of the clock is starting to get to me."

"We've got more than 24 hours," Jeff said. "We just need things to start breaking our way, that's all."

Inside, the church was spartan--a peaked beam ceiling above a bare stone floor and walls, no glass in the windows, wooden benches, a painted plaster crucifix behind candles in wooden holders--but it felt cool inside and somehow welcoming.

No one was in the sanctuary, so we went out through a side door, where we found a confessional and a door to an office.

I knocked.

"Come in."

An old priest sat behind a wooden desk piled high with books and papers. The office was simply furnished-- a stone floor, no rug. There was a framed black-and-white sketch of Jesus on one wall with a crucifix hanging from a nail below it, a modest bookshelf on another.

The priest stood and motioned for us to take seats in two straight back wooden chairs in front of his desk.

"Welcome," he said in French.

He wore a beige burlap robe and had a kind face which seemed pale for a tropical resident. His ears stood out at 90 degree angles from his head. His skin was sprinkled with liver spots. I judged him to be in his late sixties or early seventies.

"Are you Father Gaulois?" I asked.

He nodded.

"Then I'll come right to the point," I said. "We're in Martinique looking for information about my father. He's about your age, and his name is Paul DuMond."

The priest peered at me over wire-rimmed half-moons and I sensed his pulse gaining speed. He stared at me for a second longer, then shook his head. "I knew a Paul DuMond in St. Pierre, but he could not be your father. He joined the saints in 1902, as did so many others."

"He must have left before the eruption," I said.

"Impossible. Paul DuMond was my friend--my very close friend. I would have known."

"Wait," I said. "I've an old snapshot of him."

I searched in my camera bag and produced the photograph, which I'd wrapped carefully in cellophane.

The priest stared at it.

"Yes, this is the Paul DuMond I knew. . . . But--"

"There's another thing, I believe he had a sweetheart whose name was Angelique," I said.

The old priest's eyes grew wide. "It must be. But how can it?"

"There's only one way," I said. "He left before the eruption."

"And never looked back," Jeff said. "He never talked to anyone about what happened, at least as far as

89

we know."

"He's in a coma, Father," I said. "Has been for a week and he's spoken only once, a delirious kind of rambling that made no sense. From what I could make out, I believe he thinks he's going to die on Thursday morning."

The priest's brow wrinkled, then relaxed. "Fifty years to the day," he said. "Even the day of the week--a Thursday I shall never forget."

"What can you tell us about those final days?" I said.

Father Gaulois rubbed a temple. "Looking back, it is clear Pelée gave ample warning. She blew smoke and scattered cinders for weeks and weeks. And there were mud slides as well. On the fourth of May, one town-- Ajoupa Bouillon--was completely destroyed, its residents sucked into steaming crevices that opened in the side of the mountain."

"Why didn't the people leave?" I asked.

He shrugged. "The governor said we would be safe. I, for one, believed God would protect us. Besides, St. Pierre was a comely city. It is difficult for one who was not there to understand the grasp it had on those who were part of her. All its narrow streets were bright with color, alive with activity. The culture of Versailles, the Carib, the mysteries of darkest Africa all were there.

"Even so, some urged evacuation, but the governor said the problems with Pelée would pass. The editorial pages of the newspaper supported his contention based on the informed opinions of esteemed scientists from the Lycée of St. Pierre. But now, with the clarity that comes from the vantage point of time, I have no doubt that politics came into play. The eighth of May was election day, and native voodoo priests pointed to Pelée's behavior as evidence the gods were angry with the established party--that it was time for change. The governor wanted status quo. If he had recognized the danger of the volcano, it would have been the same as admitting there might be something to the charges." A faraway look came into his eyes. "The eighth of May was also the *grande fete* of the

Ascension for that year, and I believed our Father in heaven would protect us." He shook his head. "But I have learned that it can be dangerous folly for man to attempt to predict God's will. Instead, our Savior chose that day to call to paradise the inhabitants of St. Pierre and they ascended into heaven with Him, where they shall remain until the day of judgment."

Father Gaulois crossed himself.

"But you escaped," I said.

"It was God's will, and by his grace." He crossed himself again. "It had been a terrible night of rain and storm, but when I awoke the clouds parted and the sun broke through. Then, it happened while I stood on my balcony, gazing up.

"Some people go through their entire lives without such a revelation. Indeed, deep insights rarely come. I am fortunate to have had glimpses of the Eternal from time to time, but this was so much more, as though the Savior Himself whispered in my ear. I knew that day would be the last for the city of St. Pierre but the first of a new life for me. I would leave the city and become a priest. No longer would I be Jean-Luc Gaulois. I would be Father Gaulois of the Holy Roman Catholic Church."

"Jean-Luc? My father said the name, Jean-Luc, when he spoke."

The priest nodded. "I am not surprised. We were close friends--best friends. After my revelation, I ran to find your father--to beg him to leave the city with me. But he was not in his apartment."

I leaned forward. "Father Gaulois, is there anything that might give us a clue? Why would he believe he's going to die? It is as though he were in the grip of a magic spell--a curse. You mentioned voodoo priests. Is such a thing as a curse possible?"

"Most certainly. There was a woman in St. Pierre, a *séancier*, and her son, a *quimboiseur*, who lived in the mountains behind Pelée, above the town of Basse Pointe-- some kilometers north of St. Pierre. Your father had a fascination with these people and their beliefs, although I for one did not approve."

"Pardon me, Father, what is a *quimboiseur?*"

"A sorcerer. They are common in Martinique. It is the influence of primitive cultures--of Africa and native Carib."

"Could this sorcerer have cast a spell?"

"As I told your father and many others since-- magic is evil, the Scriptures are clear on this. It is the devil's work and should be left alone."

"Could this *quimboiseur* still be there?"

The priest's gaze drifted to the ceiling. "Was the *quimboiseur* a young man then? Yes, I suppose he was. And superstition says they live many centuries. Some think they are immortal. But I am not superstitious."

I turned. Jeff was sitting silently, taking it in.

"We've got to find him," I said.

"You're right, Claire. I think this is our break."

5

Although Toussaint had been quick witted enough to pull into that French Foreign Legion base and gain us a temporary reprieve, the thug who'd been after us certainly would be scouring the island. I'd have been on the next plane if it weren't for Papa. Black Shirt surely was the sort who wasn't going to rest until he had revenge, but at least now we knew where we needed to go and whom we needed to find. Armed with this knowledge and the buoyant feeling it gave, Jeff and I convinced each other the gangsters would be unlikely to look for us 15 or 20 miles away at the other end of the island. That's where we needed to go to find the *quimboiseur.* Our only problem was, we didn't have transportation. So we went to the hotel and changed, then crept around the streets glancing over our shoulders. We soon learned that almost everything was closed on Sunday.

Finally, Jeff got onto something.

"It's the best we can do," he said. "A taxi is too obvious. We don't want to be noticed by our friend Black Shirt, and there are no cars for sale or rent today."

He stood astride a small motorcycle, gunning the engine, blue smoke curling into the air. He reminded me of a proud twelve-year-old with a brand new bike.

"This baby will get us where we need to go." He pointed to the engine which looked only slightly larger than one might find on a model airplane. "125 cubic centimeters of raw power," he said. "Hop on. It'll be dark before long."

The contraption hardly looked powerful enough to carry both of us at once, but I threw my leg over it, wrapped my arms around Jeff and we were off with a sputter. It was a good thing I'd put on a fresh pair of safari pants because a dress would have been hiked up around my waist in a matter of seconds.

Minutes later, I'd settled in and was looking over Jeff's shoulder as the motor whirred and he guided the bike toward the highway called *La Route de la Trace.* It would take us through the tropical rain forest to the village of Morne Rouge and then to Basse Pointe.

Morne Rouge, Basse Pointe . . . strange sounding names. *Strange sounding names* were words of a song that was popular during the war, and in my mind I could hear a woman sing it, her smooth, melodious voice coming over the tinny speaker of Billy Hanover's car radio: "Those far away places with strange sounding names, far away over the sea--"

Billy Hanover kissed me and for a moment I thought his tongue would gag me. A question flashed: *What doesn't a girl have to endure?* But I was busy being an enchantress, the vamp Billy wanted me to be--pale of skin, full-breasted, intellectual, sexy, aloof. So I kept my thoughts to myself.

"Oh Gosh, Claire, I'm gonna miss you," he said as he unbuttoned my blouse. Then he unhooked my bra and his hands went darting to places they weren't supposed to go. In two seconds they were up my dress, tugging at my panties.

Time to draw the line.

"For the love of Pete, Billy, stop it. Stop it, now."

"But Claire, darling, you can't deny a man who's headed into battle. This may be our only chance for love, don't you see?"

I was young and stupid and I liked the guy, felt for him, felt his unspoken fear of dying, his desire for me--the ache in his loins--his deep, fervent and thoroughly calculated hope of making a score. It would carry him forward--sustain him--provide a memory more valuable than anything I could give. Before I had a chance to think about what it would mean to me, I felt the pain. But I didn't struggle, bit my lip, decided the best course was to grit my teeth. It scared me though, especially because of the way he breathed and panted like a wild animal out of control, and I felt excruciating, grating agony, as though I were going to split open.

Then he let out a sigh, rolled over, and lit a cigarette. The smoke from it curled into the air and the song continued on the radio. The top was down and I looked up at stars encircling a quarter moon. I was thoroughly, totally, completely revolted, but didn't let on because it was our last night together. I was disgusted with myself--disgusted for allowing Billy to take my virginity in the back seat of a car, disgusted with men because they were such beasts, and disgusted with sex because it was so, so, well . . . so disgusting.

But that was long ago, nine years to be exact. It was better not to think about it, so I pushed away the memory, straightened my back, squared my shoulders, felt the wind in my hair and told myself I should be in a good mood. Things were looking up. I was still under pressure-- the clock ticking relentlessly. I'd have to find answers fast and return to Fort de France by tomorrow afternoon to catch the last plane out. But now I knew what we were looking for, the sorcerer who lived in the hills above Basse Pointe.

Imagine. A sorcerer. How very, very odd.

Could magic really exist?

Did this sorcerer still exist? He might have died a

long, long time ago.

Take things one step at a time, I told myself. Think positive, enjoy the warm air against your face and in your hair, the lush green scenery, the palms silhouetted against a sky now growing a deeper shade of blue, your arms around Jeff's waist, the sputter of the motorcycle engine.

The bike's little motor settled into a low, murmuring hum, almost gurgling like water falling serenely from a fountain into a reflecting pool. We passed giant bamboo, chestnut and mahogany trees, a valley filled with enormous ferns. Mountains called *Pitons de Carbet* came into view.

"Look," Jeff said. He pointed to a huge poinsettia covered with vivid red blooms.

"Amazing," I said. "Must be 12 feet tall."

"They're native to the tropics," he said over the hum. "Actually, what look like flowers are leaves that have turned red. They do that when the days are only ten hours long and the nights fourteen. That combination triggers something."

"That's why we have them at Christmas then. The days are short."

"True, but they're really hard to grow in a greenhouse. Florists make them bloom by using lights that go on and off at precise times. It's called good old Yankee ingenuity."

"Damn Yankees," I said.

Steep mountains loomed ahead, and we started up the road that knifed between them.

"It's hard to believe that sorcerers operate in this day and age," I said. "Do you really think there's a chance we'll find him?"

"Sure. It's possible, anyway. I'm not surprised they still exist in this part of the world."

"What do you know about them?" I asked.

"Not much. I know natives practice voodoo in Haiti, and I assume it's similar to what's here in Martinique."

"Seems so strange. Double bubble toil and

trouble."

"I won't pretend to be an expert," Jeff said. "But from what I know, voodoo is a mixture of Catholicism and African beliefs brought from Africa. The supreme being is called *Bon Dieu* in Haiti, but lesser deities also exist. Some of them have the names of Christian saints, some of African gods. Others are the spirits of ancestors."

"And what about these--what did Father Gaulois call them? *Quimboiseurs?* Where do they fit in?"

"I imagine they're some sort of priests," Jeff said. "If I'm not mistaken, voodooists think demons are lurking just about everywhere you turn. Of course, you can't see them. These demons as well as the spirits of the dead inhabit an invisible realm. But a lot of them would like to be back in the flesh, in the physical world. If a person isn't careful, he can become possessed--his body taken over by one of them. I suppose these *quimboiseurs* help people guard against that sort of thing by leading ceremonies that pay homage where it's due which keeps the nasty ones at bay."

We were on our way up a mountain now, the motorcycle struggling. After a bit I said, "What do you mean, an invisible realm?"

"You've heard of the happy hunting ground? The idea of a spirit world is fairly pervasive in pagan cultures. Some tribes believe that witch doctors can put themselves in a trance and cross over to the other side to get advice from their ancestors."

This other side sounded a lot like the idea of heaven to me. I was about to ask Jeff just where it was supposed to be when we passed over the summit and saw a valley of thick, lush vegetation bathed in the amber light of late afternoon. The sky was purple and streaked with orange. The undersides of clouds reflected yellow light and were rimmed in pink. They seemed close enough to touch. For an instant I had the sensation I was part of that scene rather than an observer of it. I was *one* with it--an extension of all I saw, and all I saw was an extension of me.

97

The motorcycle picked up speed going downhill. The feeling faded. Yet I remembered Father Gaulois' words about glimpsing the Eternal. I was about to tell Jeff about it when I noticed he was studying the rearview mirror.

"Hey, keep your eyes on the road," I said.

"I think we've got a problem. A black Peugeot's back there. He's gaining on us."

"Oh, no. Way out here? How could he know?"

"Maybe they never let us out of their sight. This is the first really long stretch of straight road we've had."

Jeff rotated the throttle and the engine wound up to a high pitch. "Duck down out of the wind." He leaned forward, his head inches above the handle bars.

The wind blew my hair wildly as I rested my head on his back. We whizzed by the ramshackle houses of Morne Rouge. I caught a glimpse of slender palms arched over the road, rising up from both sides like swords in a military wedding. Suddenly, I felt a thud and the air was filled with white feathers and the screaming cackle of chickens.

"I always thought they were able to get out of the way in time," Jeff shouted as he hit the brakes, sat upright, pushing me back. The bike skidded, he put his foot down and we slid to a stop in the middle of an intersection.

"Glad no cop was there to see me run that stop sign," Jeff said.

"Or run over that chicken."

The motor had died. Jeff kicked it back to life, gunned the engine, let out the clutch.

"Look back." Jeff took the turn to the right. "See if you can spot them. I want to know if they see us head in this direction."

I kept my eyes on the road behind as long as I could. It disappeared behind palm trees and tropical foliage.

"Didn't see them."

"Good. There's only a 50-50 chance they'll come this way. Can't know we're headed to Basse Pointe."

"Unless they talked to the priest."

"Right," Jeff said.

The road that led toward Basse Pointe turned out to be a series of hairpin turns which climbed a range of steep interior mountains. It was narrow and the going slow with no guard rail. In some places the sides dropped hundreds of feet.

"Look," Jeff said.

Miles away to the east, across a valley, a huge mountain loomed against the darkening sky. Its peak was shrouded in pink and purple clouds.

"The infamous Mt. Pelée," I said.

Jeff nodded.

"It'll be night soon," he said, his eyes back on the road. "Still, I don't think we should use the headlight."

We came to an overhang where the foliage dropped away. In the dim light of dusk I saw a black Peugeot three turns below, moving fast. I tapped Jeff's shoulder and pointed as it sped around a curve.

"Rats," he said. "At least we're almost to the top."

The road ahead disappeared over a crest. When we reached it Jeff shouted, "Hold on, Claire, here we go!"

The bike picked up speed as we barreled downhill like an airplane in a power dive, except we did not go in a straight line. The road was curved and winding. We swerved in one direction, then the other. I hugged Jeff and clenched my teeth as we leaned low. The ground rushed by underneath in a blur--around and back and around and back--perilously close to the edge. Our momentum pushed us closer and closer on each turn. First we had a foot leeway, then an inch. If we went over the side, we'd experience a free fall of a thousand feet into the murky jungle below.

At last we came to a straight stretch. The road disappeared into darkness. I felt the way a dive bomber pilot must have, locked in a harness, hanging forward against the straps as he headed straight for a Japanese ship, his finger on the button ready to push, but wanting to score a direct hit, waiting to get closer and closer and closer, the guns of the ship spewing puffs of black smoke, puff after puff after puff, every gun on the ship throwing them out. On and on he'd go not caring any longer if he were hit. Not only not caring but expecting it, wanting to put his bomb down the stack of that ship. But I cared and I wanted to scream in Jeff's ear to ease up. I watched in disbelief as he rotated the throttle wide open. Suddenly we were on top of another curve, the rear wheel skidded and we--the bike, Jeff and I--hit the foliage broadside.

I was thrown--twisted into the air through 360 degrees--tumbled forward, my arms outstretched into darkness. I bounced hard on my stomach--the air rushed out of me--and came to an abrupt stop. Only my wrists were visible in the shadows, my hands submerged in mud.

I lay there for 30 or 40 seconds which seemed forever, trying desperately to inhale.

"Claire! Are you all right?"

It was Jeff. He knelt beside me, put his hands on my shoulders.

I pushed myself up, gasping.

He felt my arms and legs.

"Nothing broken," he said.

"Yeah, but I probably scraped my scrape."

He stood and reached out his hand.

"Let's go. We don't have much time."

I pulled up. "Where's the bike?"

"Kaput--frame's bent. Our friends are going to see where we left the road. We need to hide."

I followed him through the underbrush until he stopped and put a finger to his lips.

"Listen."

There was a screech of car tires. Doors slammed.

"There're two of them at least," Jeff said. "Thank God it's almost dark."

An electric torch flashed on and scanned in our direction. I crouched, pulling Jeff with me.

I could hear the men's voices speaking French. I flinched at the word they used for me--*putain*--whore.

One said, "This way. They can't be far."

Jeff motioned for me to follow and moved forward on all fours. As I crawled up an embankment through the foliage my hand slipped around a rock that fit my palm nicely--yet it protruded an inch or two out the bottom. If those men caught up with us I was going to need this to defend myself.

The ground leveled out. Through the darkness I saw Jeff turn and motion to me. He pointed to an opening in the ground, moved into it and disappeared. I heard him yelp.

I pushed my way in after him, felt myself fall. The next thing I knew I came to a teeth-rattling halt on top of him.

"Are you all right?" I said.

His hand clutched his forehead. "Just a bump."

I dropped the stone and pulled his hand away. I could barely see it was so dark.

"You're bleeding," I said.

"Don't worry--I'll live."

He looked up, past me. "Uh-oh."

I followed his eyes and saw the moon through an opening ten feet above. It was pitch black all around.

"Let's move away from the entrance," Jeff said softly. "They'll never find us in here."

I followed him into darkness, settled myself against a boulder next to him, and a shiver ran through me. It was the first time I'd felt cold since I arrived in Martinique.

Jeff put his arm around me.

"Jeff?"

"Yes, Claire."

I could barely see him in the dim light.

"How are we going to get out of here?"

"You would think of details at a time like this."

"That hole is straight up--out of reach."

Jeff was silent.

"You'll stand on my shoulders and climb out," he said at last. "Then you'll throw me a vine or something."

Jeff lifted his arm. The luminous dial of his watch appeared. "We'll wait an hour and a half. Those thugs

101

will have given up by then."

I closed my eyes, breathed in deeply and exhaled a long, slow sigh. How incredibly tired I felt.

Images whirled through my mind: The statue of Josephine, the old man holding his Panama hat. Rotten teeth turning and running away, chicken feathers flying. Then I saw Black Shirt's startled face as the camera hurled toward him, the priest behind his desk. Someone chased me and I ran as fast as I could, frantic but able to move only in slow motion.

Jeff called from far away.

"Wake up, Claire. Time's up."

"Already?"

"You've been asleep."

I reached out. He pulled me to my feet.

We moved under the opening. Jeff studied it.

"It's high, all right."

He knelt. "Climb aboard."

I put my knees on his shoulders, my hands on his head. He stood and I almost lost my balance, but steadied myself.

I looked up. "I'm nowhere near it."

"You'll have to stand."

"Easy for you to say."

I pulled one foot up to his shoulder, almost lost my balance, grabbed his hair--pulled hard.

"Ouch!"

"Steady, boy."

I brought the other foot in place. Jeff took hold of my legs. Slowly I rose from a deep knee-bend position, holding onto his hair for balance. Once my legs were almost extended, I let go and began to straighten up. I wobbled. Jeff took a few steps which brought me back into balance.

The moon was directly overhead--I stretched out my arms.

"I can't reach it, Jeff. We're short."

I knelt, grabbed his head, slid to the ground.

"How short?"

"Four, maybe six inches. But that's just to touch it."

Jeff looked around. I followed his gaze. The cave disappeared into darkness.

"There must be something to stand on," he said.

"It'll have to be two feet thick, maybe more if I'm going to get a firm enough grip to pull myself out."

"Let's circle out from the moonlight and see what we can find."

I walked behind for about ten minutes, my hand on his back, taking small steps.

"Watch your head," he said. "Ouch--darn it. Wish we had a flashlight. This looks like as far as it goes."

We moved back toward the light and sat against the rock where I'd slept. My heart palpitated and I began to hyperventilate.

"We're trapped, Jeff. We're gonna die here."

"Whoa, Claire--take it easy. We'll be able to see better in the morning when the sun shines through that hole."

"It's my fault. Why'd I have to hit that guy?"

He put his arm around me.

"They tried to kill you with that car. You had a reason."

"Think so?"

"Shoot first. Ask questions later."

I snuggled close.

"Jeff?"

"Claire."

"I'm glad you followed me to Martinique."

He gave me a squeeze. "And I'm sorry I don't treat you as an equal, but I promise I'll try harder from now on. I just haven't been able to stop thinking of you as so much more than equal."

His face was inches from mine. Shadows from the faint glow of moonlight had formed in the laugh-lines.

"I think you're pretty special, too," I said.

His lips touched mine, and I melted against him. That tingly feeling started somewhere in my lower half and rushed upward, spread out, threatened to engulf me, but I realized this might be the end anyway. What the hell, I'd let it take me where it would. For an instant I thought of Billy Hanover headed into battle and supposed there was nothing like knowing you were going to die to make you feel like having sex. At that moment, facing death, I was more alive than I had ever been. I kissed Jeff's ears, his neck, breathed in the musky scent of his sweat, blood, lingering aftershave. I found the buttons of his shirt, undid them, and parted the shirt, pushed it off his shoulders and let it fall away. The tips of my fingers touched, caressed, felt the muscles of his chest and arms.

He fumbled with my blouse and I had to help him. Finally I undid the buttons myself and let the blouse slide off.

I smoothed the hair on his chest. He pulled me to him and I felt his strength, the firmness of his body, the power of his muscles as they flexed. He drew me into him, close to him, making me part of him. A kind of magnetism melded us--a tingling spread throughout me, a fluttering like a gentle breeze, a heavenly breeze, a puffy white cloud that carried me away. And yet there was a frenzy to it, a wild unpredictable frenzy, a yearning, aching, gnawing, a wild desire that had to be fulfilled. I was diving now into a pool of warm welcoming water, deeper, deeper, losing myself in that strange, wonderful pool, his lips instruments of pleasure that made music that danced and spun around me, all over me, through me . . . tingling, flickering, spinning around and around in a whirlpool, deeper into incredible bliss, into fantasy and unimaginable ecstasy. For once I was completely in myself, not split, not standing to one side and watching. I was in unity and harmony, at one with myself and at one with Jeff and at one with the universe. I knew for the second time that day that all things were one and I was part of all things, united with the cosmos. I was soaring, dipping, turning, flying higher and higher--up, up, up--then swooping down, down, down. Then up again, down again, up, up, higher and higher each time, each time more and more intense.

Nothing could stop me, nothing would stop me. This was ecstasy, this was what really feeling was about. This is what I'd been missing, and it was better than anything I'd ever imagined possible. If only it would last and last, and last, but it couldn't last, nothing that wonderful could last. But I would try to make it, try to draw it out, until . . . I couldn't, but I must, it must.

Then came an incredible surge that started in my toes and moved up, all the way up, until it engulfed my entire body as it rushed from inside out in thrilling, joyful upheaval. It began to fade slowly . . . slowly. Finally, I collapsed on Jeff's chest, gasping and out of breath. I lay for a long time without speaking.

At last, when my breathing had returned to normal and so had his, I caressed his cheek and pressed a finger to his lips. He kissed it and let out a sigh.

"If I smoked," he said, "I'd definitely have a cigarette, right now."

Doggone it. Why did he have to remind me?

6

I blinked and lifted my hand to shade my eyes. A shaft of light poured through the opening and formed a bright white circle on the gray stone floor of the cave. I'd half expected to wake up to find the events of the night before were a dream brought on by spicy Creole cooking--a nightmare of being pursued by thugs, a fantasy of sexual passion. But it had happened.

The memory of sex sent a quiver through me. I'd had no idea love-making could be like that. The race down the mountain and through the woods into the cave had been an aphrodisiac, a kind of foreplay that broke me out of my frigid shell. I'd have to arrange to be chased by criminals more often, although now maybe that wouldn't be necessary.

Jeff was still asleep, a forearm covering his eyes, an underarm exposed. Should I wake him with kisses? Return him to the state of arousal of the night before? Be the sexy little kitten he no doubt wanted me to be, the sexy kitten I would no doubt be in reality the very next chance I got?

There would be time enough for that if we were indeed stuck here. How long did it take to die from hunger, or thirst?

Not a pleasant thought. I pushed it back, told myself I didn't come this far to die.

I found my clothes and put them on. With the cave lit as brightly as it probably ever would be, now was a good time to explore.

I turned slowly in a circle, searching.

The cave was an oval that became dark and narrow at each end. Perhaps it was an underground riverbed at some point in its geological history. Maybe it still was when heavy rain came. I reasoned that if water passed through, an opening was required for the water to empty out.

I crept in the direction that seemed to be downhill. As I moved along the ceiling and floor came closer together. I was forced to crouch, then crawl. Finally, I found myself in a space no more than two feet in diameter, total darkness ahead of me.

Should I go back and wake up Jeff?

Naw, let him sleep, I thought. Press on. I could handle this. Besides, I wouldn't venture out of earshot.

I elbowed forward into the darkness, the moldy odor of stale air in my nostrils. Underneath was rock, smooth against my hands, which seemed to confirm my theory of it being a water pathway. I scooted forward several feet, rested, then scooted several more.

After awhile the going seemed easier. I was moving without difficulty. Suddenly I realized I was headed straight down. I slid, picking up speed, carried by my own weight. I put my hands on the sides and pushed hard. This slowed my descent but my weight kept pushing me forward and I continued slipping. I dug in the toes of my shoes and spread my legs--finally came to a stop.

I was hanging. If I relaxed even a little I would surely fall who knew how far--ten feet, 50 feet, a hundred? I was inside a mountain--a tall mountain, holding on for dear life, surrounded by total darkness.

107

"Jeff! Jeff! Can you hear me!"

How far away was he?

"Jeff! Jeff!"

Please God, let him come.

"J-e-e-e-ff!"

After an eternity, I heard him.

"Claire! Claire! Where--are--you?!"

"Jeff! At the lower end--there's a passageway, a tunnel!"

"I'm coming Claire!" His voice was closer now, but my wrists were beginning to ache I was pushing so hard.

"Careful, Jeff. This tunnel turns a corner and heads straight down. I'm hanging on to keep from falling." *God, am I hanging on.*

I felt his hand on my foot. "Thank heaven you're here."

At last I could relax my wrists--somewhat anyway.

"Why didn't you tell me, Claire? . . . "

"Just checking the lay of the land . . . you were asleep, and, and--you looked so peaceful, that's all."

I felt his hand close around the other foot. "Okay, let's pull you out."

I pushed and he pulled, but I slipped farther down.

"Let's think about this," Jeff said. "Water must flow through here when it rains."

"Check."

"Water's gotta come out somewhere."

"Check."

"It's easier to go forward than back up."

"I see where you're headed, but what if this shaft drops a hundred feet?"

"Can you hold on while I back out and turn around? I think I can brake us both if I'm headed feet first."

"Think?"

"Not much choice."

I spread my legs and dug in my toes. My wrists were throbbing, but in less than a minute I felt him take hold of each foot again.

"Spread your hands flat against the sides and push," he said. "We'll get to the bottom of this."

"Cute, Jeff. I wish I'd thought of that."

"So you could have kept it to yourself?"

"Check."

We inched downward for what seemed an hour. My arms ached. I felt as though the palms of my hands had turned into giant blisters. My wrists were numb. I didn't have much strength left in them. Gradually, the sides of the passageway were growing wider and wider apart. I had difficulty applying enough pressure to make a difference.

"Got a problem, Claire." Jeff puffed and wheezed. "I'm having trouble holding on to you. You've got to help."

"I'm doing my best. The walls are too far apart."

"You're slipping."

"It's just too wide."

"Oh, no!"

I fell. I put my hands out and hit a glancing blow, turned a flip, landed with a chilling splash.

"*Claire?*"

I shot to the surface. "I'm okay, I'm okay. Thank God, the shaft empties into a pool of water."

"I heard. Can't go down any farther myself. Out of the way, I've got to jump."

A splash--spray landed on me.

Jeff came along side. "This eliminates one problem."

"Which?"

"We're not going to die of thirst."

"That's comforting."

"Notice something else?" he said.

"What?"

"We can see each other."

He was right. There was enough light to make out his face. I could see him replace his glasses from wherever he'd held them, the dimple in his cheek and his flat-top, now flattened by the water.

"The light is coming from that direction. Come on,"

109

Jeff said.

I swam behind him for 30 yards to the water's edge. He climbed out and offered me a hand.

"Always the gentleman," I said as I pulled up.

"Please, don't start that again."

"Just kidding." I wrapped my arms around him, gave him a wet kiss, pressed against him.

"Ummm. . . . I like the way you kid."

My arm around him, his around me, we moved toward the light. A large, underground chamber opened up. Shadows danced on the rocks between orange streaks of light.

"What would cause that glow up there?" I asked.

A singsong patois came from the darkness. "Welcome to cave of ancestors of children of Martinique."

Jeff moved in front, hands out. "Who are you? What do you want?"

"It is I who should ask such questions, if I had not the sight of a *quimboiseur*. This my home."

He spoke French. Well, not really French, more a rustic patois--thick Creole with an English word mixed in every now and then, and every now and then one I didn't understand at all. But I got the gist of what he said. I could see him in the shadows. He wore no shirt. His trousers were cut off and ragged above his knobby knees. His chest was covered by a necklace--strands of white beads, sea shells and the bones and skulls of small animals.

"You're the *quimboiseur* who lives in the hills above Basse Pointe," I said in French.

"And you are daughter of Paul DuMond." He smiled--his teeth white next to his dark skin--a twinkle in his eye.

"How could you know that?"

He hopped from the boulder, landed in front of us. "*Quimboiseur* know, see--all." He touched a finger to his temple and smiled, then shrugged. "Beside, you look like. There is family resemblance. Come. I expected you."

I took Jeff's arm and we walked behind him into the

middle of a shadowy circle of boulders and hanging rocks which reminded me of pictures I'd seen of Stonehenge, except this Stonehenge was in the center of an enormous underground chamber formed by a dome-like roof of stone that rose to perhaps 50 or 60 feet.

The *quimboiseur* sat cross-legged in the shadows in front of a fire and motioned for us to join him. The orange light danced in his eyes and on the beads and bones of his necklace.

"How did you know we were coming?" I said.

"You ask questions, your father ask questions. You both need learn: Bird's job to sing. Fish to swim. Sun to shine. Cloud's job to rain. *Quimboiseur's* job to know."

"Then you know we're here to find out why my father is ill--why he thinks he's going to die on the anniversary of the Mt. Pelée eruption."

"You just like father. Ask question, then answer."

"I don't understand."

"You say, 'Why my father ill?' Then you say why: 'He think he going to die.'" He opened his hands as if releasing the answer. "People do what think. Story older than mountains and sea. Reason chicken cross road. First think, then do."

"Cause and effect," Jeff said.

"Okay, okay," I said. "Why does he *think* he's going to die?"

"Now you ask correct question." He stared into the fire and the light danced in his eyes.

After a minute or so I said, "You do know, don't you?"

"Am thinking how to tell."

"Is it really all that difficult?"

"One thing to know with head. Not same as with heart."

"Sorry to butt in," Jeff said, "but we'd better get some information fast, and get back to Fort de France. We've got a plane to catch."

The *quimboiseur* held up a finger, cocked his head. "Best way for you is look. See for self."

"See for myself?" I said.

"I help you enter place where all things before and after present moment dwell. Then you see for self what happened."

"Sorry, but I'm afraid I don't understand."

"I think he wants to take you to the invisible realm. The spirit world we were talking about," Jeff said.

"You *must* be kidding."

"It way for you to *see*," the *quimboiseur* said.

This guy is nuts, I thought. "Suppose I get stuck there and can't get back?"

"Look, you don't think such a place really exists?" Jeff said in English so the *quimboiseur* wouldn't understand. "Well, neither do I. Just go along and see what happens. It's a way to get some answers."

"Easy for you to say."

"Probably, he's going to hypnotize you. Then describe events so they become vivid in your mind."

"Now I get it. You want me to go a long with this, don't you, Jeff? So you can write a paper. Jeff McDannon the scientist. Well, I'm not so sure I want to be hypnotized."

"Just pretend, Claire. Close your eyes and pretend, that's all. Even if you do drift off, I'll be right here. I'll stay on the alert. Trust me. I won't let things get out of hand."

The *quimboiseur* threaded his fingers, turned the backs of his hands toward himself and pushed out. His knuckles cracked. He picked up a tambourine.

"You want see what happened, or not?" he said.

I looked at Jeff. "I guess we *do* need to find out."

"That's why we came."

"You're right, we're wasting time. Let's get on with this."

He began tapping the tambourine rhythmically. "First, preparation. You have much tension. Must release."

"You better believe I'm tense. You'd be tense, too, if someone was trying to catch you and kill you, and suddenly you found yourself trapped in a cave." *And sitting with a certifiable lunatic who's about to lead you off to Never Land.*

"You are safe and must relax. Now let go. Look in fire and relax." He pointed at the fire. "Let problems go. Look in fire and relax."

There was nothing to lose, right? I focused on the fire and tried to calm myself.

He tapped the tambourine. "Look in fire and relax . . . look in fire and relax . . . " His voice settled softly into a chant. "Look in fire and relax . . . look in fire and relax."

I watched the flames. They pulsated and curled, glowed--started nowhere, ended nowhere--vibrant, alive. The *quimboiseur's* voice and the tapping came from far away, melodious and soothing. I tried not to let them get to me but was having difficulty holding on. Jeff had said he'd watch out, that he wouldn't let anything happen, so I told myself I didn't need to worry. I was as safe as if I were at home in my own bed.

The tapping and his voice continued melodiously. They kept on and on until they were part of me and I was part of them, at one, at peace, alive.

"Now come to place above and behind eyes . . . now come to place above and behind eyes . . . "

The spot where I'd focused hopped on an elevator and swooped up inside my head. The fire was a blur. I was inside my head now and the fire was an orange glow somewhere far off. I was relaxed, incredibly relaxed . . .

"All tension pour out now and leave . . . all tension pour out now and leave . . . "

There was a rush of letting go, a release, the ecstasy and comfort of slipping into a bed after a long day--of closing my eyes and feeling sleep descend. I was safe. Nothing could harm me while wrapped in the arms of sleep--sweet, gentle sleep.

Far, far away, barely audible, was the chant, "You come to place now . . . to hole in hollow tree . . . you come to place now . . . to hole in hollow tree . . . "

I was no longer asleep but I still felt at peace. It

seemed as though I had awakened to find myself in another place, a place unlike any I had ever seen. I stood in mist up to my ankles, before an enormous redwood. A dreamlike quality, a fuzzy glow, radiated from everything around me, from the tree, from the leaves, from the gnarled old limbs. I could not see the ground under my feet because it was covered with the mist. In the distance everything receded into mist. The tree had an opening in the trunk large enough to walk into. The voice and the tapping of the tambourine were very distant now--as if inside my head, in my imagination.

"Spirit guide meet you now and go . . . spirit guide meet you now and go . . . "

A huge gull, bigger than I, came out of the mist, swooped down and landed in front of me. His head came toward me and he cocked it to one side and he looked me over with one eye. Apparently satisfied, he turned and offered me his back.

What was I to do? The bird was no doubt a metaphor of some sort I had created in my mind. I was thinking it should have been a dove, not a sea gull. But what difference did it make? I might as well go along. Jeff was back there watching out for me, and I wasn't really going anywhere. This was a dream, a realistic dream. Jeff had assured me that's all it would be, and surely Jeff knew about these things. So I climbed on and straddled the gull like a horse. He turned to the redwood, took a few quick steps, lifted free of the ground. My stomach lurched as though a high-speed elevator had started off.

I soared on the gull's back into the tree opening and suddenly he was gone. I was in a long dark tunnel with a light far at the end, inky blackness all around. I was floating and had the sensation others were near me, but these others were trapped. Some seemed frightened and tormented, not knowing which way to go, but it was obvious to me, and I headed to the light. I tried to say something like, "Come on, follow me," but they remained where they were, confused, or perhaps haunted by demons. I realized they couldn't *see* the light. I was moving toward it now, past those who apparently did not know which way to turn. I tried to speak to them, to call out to them, to urge them to follow--but no sound came from my lips.

As I drew nearer to the light I saw someone at the end of the tunnel waiting in the glare, a silhouette surrounded by brilliant white. As I approached I realized it was not a person, not a physical person, not flesh and blood and bones, but an ethereal entity, almost transparent, a three-dimensional being of light, a woman with the kindest face I'd ever seen. She seemed familiar, although I could not recall how I knew her. She embraced me, told me she was here to help, but she did so without speaking, did so with some sort of mental telepathy. She pointed and I looked down and saw the circle of stones in the cave. She and I were hovering high up above it near the stone ceiling. Jeff was there and so was the *quimboiseur*, who was still chanting and gazing into the fire. Most startling of all was my own body lying between them, as if asleep.

Perhaps sensing my concern, the being pointed to something I hadn't noticed before. A long umbilical cord connected me--my ethereal body--to my physical one below. The cord was translucent like the rest of me and I understood the presence of it to mean I wasn't dead--not disconnected from my body entirely. I was only temporarily outside my physical self. Nevertheless, I must admit, I felt a quivering uneasiness.

How could this be a dream and how could all this be happening inside my head if I could see myself, my body, lying on the floor of the cave? I supposed I'd always sensed my physical self wasn't really me because of the strange tendency I had to stand outside myself at times as an observer. Even so, I needed my body didn't I? I mean, I existed now, in this strange disembodied state, but *where* did I exist? I tried to call out to Jeff, to make him see me, but no sound came from my mouth. I had no vocal cords, no throat, no larynx. I was obviously invisible except to myself and to this other ethereal being who was able to communicate with me as I with her--mind to mind without spoken words.

The being seemed to sense my distress and took my hands and looked into my eyes. Her face was kind and sweet and loving, so delicate and full of light words do not do it justice. All I can say is that she radiated love and it helped sooth my uneasiness--for the moment at least. She seemed to communicate that this current state, this disembodied journey I was on was part of my larger journey, something which had been planned since before I first emerged from this realm as a newborn. It was something I absolutely needed to do. I must trust and come with her.

I do not remember every detail of this part of my journey or what followed but am almost certain she quoted Scripture: "In my Father's house there are many rooms." At any rate, I understood there were a number of levels or zones or areas--rooms seems too limiting a word--in this nonphysical realm where I was, and that these were the provinces of different souls. In order to view what I had come to view I needed to bypass many of them and enter a dimension comprised solely of thought where even ethereal bodies such as ours did not exist. She communicated that in this place I would inhabit the thoughts of others, as though I were inside their minds. It was the way I would come to know what had happened to my father.

She reached out her hands and I took them and the next thing I knew a great canopy of blue sky was above me, the most incredible pure blue with white swirls of cotton candy clouds floating by. The sun was warm on my neck. Below was the island of Martinique jutting out of a deep blue sea like the top of a mountain range.

I glided down, down, as a harbor filled with ships docked by stone quays came into view. White masts gleamed in the sun. The flags flew from their sterns--the blue, white, red of the French Tricolor, and the red, white and blue of the Stars and Stripes--the Swedish yellow cross on a light blue field. Streets and people were so close I felt I could reach out and touch them--as well as houses, quaint, queer flagstone houses painted in a clear yellow tone that contrasted delightfully with the burning blue ribbon of tropical sky.

I skimmed over red tile roofs pierced by gabled dormers, and looked down at narrow streets, nearly all of which climbed hills, or descended into hollows, curved and twisted at sudden, unexpected angles. It was a delightful city, uplifting, except that gray volcanic ash was on everything, the roofs, on ships in the harbor, the streets, in places pushed into piles several feet high. Everywhere too was the murmur of falling water. It sprung in silver columns from fountains scattered here and there, poured through deep gutters carved between cobblestone streets and absurd little sidewalks, some no more than a foot wide.

From sun it appeared to be early morning.

I pulled up and stopped, hovering there on the roof peak, invisible even to myself. Through a window a few yards away, I saw two men arguing. One was middle-aged and looked like a refugee from the Paris underworld--a French apache--thin mustache, strap t-shirt with a tuft of chest hair protruding out the top. The hair on his head was oiled and slicked back. A hand-rolled cigarette dangled from his lips. He grasped the cigarette between an index and middle finger, sucked in, then threw the butt on the floor and ground it out, exhaling purplish-gray smoke.

The other man was much younger, a light-skinned mulatto with short, kinky hair, a flat nose and a brow that protruded over small, angry eyes. His biceps bulged and veins stood out on his thick neck as he clenched his fists, shook a finger at the man in the t-shirt and shouted an obscenity.

A young woman, perhaps 16 or 17, cowered behind the older man. She had shiny, jet black hair that fell straight to the middle of her back, smooth, tan skin and crisp features--a beauty by any definition. She looked familiar. I remembered where I'd seen her. She was the girl in the picture in the gold locket.

The older man took her by the arm, whipped her

117

around in front of him and threw her into the grasp of the mulatto. The mulatto's mouth curved upward. He threw back his head and laughed.

I remember thinking someone should recruit this guy for that spooky radio show, *Inner Sanctum.* Then I blacked out, went into a spin, twirled, fell through time and space, spinning, heading somewhere. But where? Into a whirlpool? It seemed so, but this wasn't water this was space--infinite, like the space in a dream, and I was flying out of control.

Could it be I was headed into another dimension?

A series of images flashed before me that seemed to be memories--a large French colonial mansion with pillars, sugar cane swaying in a tropical breeze, an apothecary shop. They were not my memories. I'd never before seen sugar cane. How did I know?

As the images sorted themselves out, it became as though my mind had merged, had fused somehow with someone else's. I now viewed my surroundings from inside that person's head. I had no control over what was happening and could only watch and listen and feel. It were as though I was sitting in a movie theater while a three-dimensional film played all around me which not only communicated the external action but the thoughts and feelings of the protagonist. It was unnerving. I thought of my body lying back in the cave, looking asleep, but really an empty shell on automatic pilot. No matter what Jeff said or thought or theorized about hypnotism, no matter what double talk he might use to explain what was happening, no way was this going on inside my head. This was as real as anything I'd ever experienced, sensed or felt while wide awake using the brain enclosed in the skull and covered with flesh and hair far, far away in 1952.

A thought came to me. Perhaps I only supposed my body was back there on automatic pilot. I could no longer see it so there was no way to be sure.

I hoped to heaven the pilot--me--got back to the controls.

Out of Body, Into Mind

May, 1902

7

As I think back it is like a dream, blurred as a photograph or a movie when shot through a lens coated with gelatin. For what seemed several minutes I experienced an uneasy darkness. Then whomever I inhabited awoke suddenly, pulse racing, and I could sense that he--I was certain it was a male--was wet and clammy, covered with perspiration. A fist clutched at his intestine.

What he felt was fear. Welcome to the club, I thought. Whomever it was swung his feet over the side of the bed, sat up and struggled to remember a nightmare. What had he been dreaming? About Angelique? Yes, Angelique.

I realized I must be inside Papa's mind.

His memory of the nightmare flashed before me. Someone was pulling her away and she was screaming, "No, no, no!" but his feet were stuck in soggy wet volcanic ash. He could not pull them free and his grasp did not extend far enough to reach and pull her back. He watched, horrified and helpless, as her arms flailed and her face--contorted in agony--receded into darkness.

No longer was there any doubt of the identity of the girl in the gold locket. She was Angelique.

My father crossed the room to the washstand as he shook off the memory, poured water into the basin and splashed it on him. He had a feeling, a kind of knowing in his stomach. He didn't think it was a result of the nightmare. He was certain something must be terribly wrong.

When he looked in the mirror I was shocked, for it was not the face I expected, not Papa with wrinkles, gray hair and a hint of jowls from skin which had begun to sag. I saw instead a young Frenchman, blue eyes, dark eyebrows, and a few boyish whiskers.

He toweled off, emptied the contents of the wash basin into the chamber pot, dressed and hurried out the door and along a cobbled street.

What struck me next was the stench of sulfur, like rotten eggs. It hung in the air and rose from the cinders scattered everywhere. I noticed the cinders were not only on the ground, they were falling from the sky. Mt. Pelée was erupting. The volcano would certainly destroy St. Pierre at any second and the question was, would we make it to safety? Why wasn't he running?

I concentrated as hard as I could in an effort to project my thoughts into Papa's mind and make him see what was going on. After several minutes I knew it was useless. He was oblivious to my presence, oblivious to what I was thinking; totally focused on finding his beloved Angelique and not in the least concerned about the ash.

He descended steep stone steps to the *Rue Victor Hugo,* hardly noticing a view of the harbor through falling ash that I found incredibly bizarre. Gulls soared above tall masts bathed in a kind of hazy light. The sea was gray, no horizon. The scene simply faded into the strange rain of falling cinders.

He hurried past a fountain that showered a silver spray over bronze Tritons, the only objects anywhere to be seen that weren't covered with stinky gray powder. He turned a corner, hopped a gutter, passed by a boulangerie and climbed the steps to Angelique's apartment.

He wanted to pound on the door but thought better of it, lightly tapped the louvered shutter instead.

There was no answer.

He tapped harder. Still no answer.

Then he gave in to his first impulse and pounded on the door.

"Angelique! Angelique! Are you there?"

What time was it? Seven o'clock? Angelique's father was probably curled up in an alley sleeping off a hard night of drinking, Papa thought, but where was she?

Papa. I cannot continue to call him that. I no longer thought of him as Papa, he was so obviously a young man--younger than I, although it seemed awfully strange. It occurred to me that in a very real sense he wasn't Papa, not yet. He wouldn't be for quite some time. All at once the idea came into focus which had nagged at me off and on all my adult life, but which I had never before put into words. A person never really is, not in a static sense of having arrived at a form that's static and unchanging. A person is a person because they are becoming, always moving toward being. Life is not life because one has accomplished a goal, but rather because one is moving toward a goal, continually unfolding.

So I began to think of Papa as someone else: as Paul, a 19 year old, alive and virile with blood pumping through his veins and lust in his heart and worlds to conquer. He went down the steps, circled to the front of the building, entered the shop where customers waited in line.

"Bon Jour, Paul," the proprietress said to him as she handed someone a baguette.

I could see only where Paul directed his sight, but he kept his eyes on this woman long enough for me to realize she was the angelic being who had met me at the end of the dark tunnel.

"Good morning, Madame DuPont," Paul said. "Have you seen Angelique? She's not upstairs."

"No. I've been in back baking bread."

"Her father?" Paul asked.

"Bahf! That man! The most terrible racket this morning--two men shouting so loud all the world could hear--such obscenities!"

"But he is not there either."

"No longer, perhaps. Thank heaven."

Paul wished the proprietress a good day and headed out the door. I saw that activity was picking up. Women swept cinders from stone stoops, men were leaving their homes--no doubt headed for work. A woman led a donkey loaded down with vegetables covered with gray volcanic ash.

Paul climbed steps to a second-floor balcony and weaved between pots of red hibiscus and purple bougainvillea, which he dusted lightly with a hand. He arrived at an old wooden door and knocked.

"Jean-Luc? Are you up?"

"Enter."

Jean-Luc sat at a table drinking coffee--small, pale, black hair and large ears. I recognized him instantly as the priest Jeff and I had spoken to even though now he was not much older than a boy. The look in his eyes had not changed and the expression on his peach-fuzz-covered face was that of someone wise beyond his current years.

"Angelique is missing," Paul said.

Jean-Luc peered at Paul over the lenses of wire-rimmed half-moons. "You should not be so upset." He waved Paul into a chair. "Providence actually may have blessed you, my good friend."

Paul helped himself to coffee. "What does Providence have to do with it?"

"Perhaps she ran off with a sailor."

"That would hardly be a blessing."

"Dear, dear Paul. Do you not know that women are responsible for the fall of man--our expulsion from the Garden? I for one say stay away from them. This one in particular. She is much too pretty. Find a homely one if you must abide their company."

That Garden business with Eve taking the rap was

123

just the sort of thing that had turned me away from religion. Paul echoed my sentiments. "The ravings of an old priest from the mouth of a young man," he said. "Amazing."

Jean-Luc smiled and sipped his coffee. "You are a passionate fellow, Paul, and that's good. You live life. Surely you will live it to the fullest as time goes by. The only trouble is, you let the lower half of your body do the thinking. What about balance? Perhaps you should think about that."

Paul was hardly listening. "Where could she be?" he said.

Jean-Luc shook his head. "For a pretty one, Angelique is nice enough. But I cannot help think she'll cause you grief. Her father's a drunk, her mother's a mulattress--and on top of it, a *séancier*. Imagine."

"I know. You didn't sneak into the smokehouse to save me, just to have me waste my life by marrying the wrong woman."

"Her brother is a *quimboiseur*--a witch doctor! Voodoo, Paul, voodoo. It is dangerous."

"Her *half* brother. And not a bad fellow--interesting, really."

"Remember, I warned you."

In his mind's eye Paul could see Angelique's face and her curvaceous body. "All I ask, Jean-Luc, is that you accept her," he said. "I plan for us to marry, want all of us to get along."

"Yes, yes, of course. You are my friend, my best friend. When the two of you are one, she will be my friend, also. I will accept her as a sister." Jean-Luc sighed, and took another sip of coffee. "You went to her apartment?"

"A terrible dream awoke me--a nightmare. She was being taken--pulled away against her will. I ran to her." Paul shivered. "I do not know how to describe the reaction. It were as though an empty place had formed inside me, as though she were gone--is gone."

"Perhaps she left because of Pelée. I have considered leaving myself to escape the stench of it."

"To me the smell of Pelée proves one can get used to almost anything. I hardly even notice it now." Paul waved the thought away. "The volcano has been wheezing and coughing for a month. Why would she choose now to leave? Anyway, she would tell me first."

"You tried her mother?"

Paul swallowed his coffee, stood and went to the sink. "They say when you meet the mother, you see the daughter in 20 years. I have been putting that off, but it appears that now the time has come." He rinsed the mug and turned it upside down. "I must go to work, but at lunchtime I will do it."

A few hours later, Paul descended a narrow street. Directly ahead was the harbor and the tall masts of ships. The fall of ash had subsided for the moment and gulls circled above--soaring, diving, screeching. A dark cloud from the volcano passed over the sun, and the breeze from the sea suddenly felt cool and brought with it the odor of salt water and fish mingled with the stench of sulfur.

He directed his attention to shingles that hung above the shop doors--an importer of linens, a sail-maker, an import-export broker. His eyes fixed on one that displayed a woman's hand holding an ornate bottle and the words, "Fragrances and Potions of the World."

A bell rang as he went though the door. No one was inside. A woman's voice called out, "One minute."

He looked at a glass display case that ran from front to back, inside of which were many different kinds of bottles. His stomach twitched. In a moment the door at the back of the shop swung open, and a woman dressed in vivid red appeared. She was not as Paul had imagined-- far from old. She appeared to be in her thirties and she was stunning, tall and straight with long delicate arms and fingers. She had the same exotic look Angelique possessed, but more pronounced, higher cheek bones, more angular--like an upside down triangle. She might have been Polynesian, but I guessed from what Jean-Luc had said that she was a mixture of Indian, African and

European.

"I, I am Paul DuMond. Angelique's Paul."

"I see." She studied him.

"I went to her apartment this morning--she is not there. By chance, is she here?"

"You show concern--care--for her. A novelty."

The precision of her speech and pronunciation startled me. I thought I detected an underlying nuance of Creole, but it was far from the rustic patois spoken by the man I now assumed was her son, the *quimboiseur*, the fellow I could thank for sending me on this journey.

Paul was puzzled by her comment. "Concern? I do not understand."

"Men of European descent rarely care at all for women of mixed heritage, except when they want to fornicate with them."

Blood rushed to Paul's face. The tingle lingered.

She chuckled and beckoned for him to follow her into the back room, waved him into a chair at a small round table covered in black.

"Tea?"

His throat had clamped shut and the words came with difficulty. "Thank . . . you."

A cup of dark, steaming liquid appeared before him.

"Cream? Sugar? Lemon?"

He couldn't speak, shook his head.

She sat. "You love my Angelique?"

The warm liquid cut a new passage. "More than I thought possible."

She leaned forward. "Give me your hand."

"Pardon?"

"Your hand."

He pushed his hand toward her, palm up. She studied it, massaged it with her thumb.

"You and your father. There is trouble between you."

"If you knew my father, you'd understand."

"Tell me."

126

"He is cruel, overbearing--unreasonable. He wants me to drive the workers with a whip. I cannot be as he wishes--as he is. My insides would rot."

"And your mother?"

"She defends him--fears him--obeys him. She has lost her soul. I tried--tried so hard to reason with him, and with her. It cannot be done. On my eighteenth birthday, I left."

She squeezed his hand. "Now you seek love, understanding, companionship."

"I have my friend, Jean-Luc. He grew up on the next plantation. Now he lives here with his aunt--attends the Lycée of St. Pierre."

"You are very close."

"I would die for him."

"And Angelique?"

"I would die for her as well. Never have I met someone such as her. Never have I felt this way about a woman. She is in my thoughts night and day."

She looked at his palm, and her brow wrinkled. "I see."

He pulled his hand away. "Where is she? Please tell me."

She shrugged. "I do not know, except, she is somewhere nearby. She is being held against her will. Her father is responsible. The man is despicable."

Paul wondered how this woman and Angelique's father could once have been lovers. She gave him a knowing look as though she had read this thought.

"How did I come to couple with such a man? He was handsome then, as you are now. We felt for each other as you and Angelique now feel for each other."

Lust, Paul thought, but what he felt for Angelique was more.

"I must find her," he said. "Save her."

"Do what you must. It will not change the outcome."

"What do you mean?"

"You will not remain together--not now. You are

destined to be separate." She nodded, as though she had turned up the last card and it had been the one she'd expected. "I have seen your palm," she said.

A few minutes later, Paul pushed through the swinging doors of the *Bistro du Port* in the *quartre vielle*, and moved past burly lunchtime diners on his way to the bar. The place looked like a saloon out of a cowboy movie: dusty plank flooring, wood tables and chairs, a long mirror behind the bar.

The bartender glanced up.

Paul said, "Henri Dubois--have you seen him?"

The bartender dried a glass with his apron and placed it upside down on the counter top. "Yes. He had his usual half liter of Pastis for lunch, capped it off with three shots of Calvados." The man shook his head, picked up another glass and began to wipe. "I think one of his boots is really a bucket."

"What happened after that?" Paul said. "Is he passed out behind the bar?"

"He was still conscious when I last saw him--staggering toward the *Bar Normandie*."

Paul weaved between derelict horse carts mired in wet volcanic ash and fended off black marketeers hawking their wares, most of which he assumed were stolen goods. In the past few days anarchy had come to the streets due in part to the large influx of refugees from rural areas at this end of the island, as well as to the disruption caused by falling ash and the panic generated by tremors which had not only shaken the city but in one instance caused a bridge to collapse killing 20 mourners in a funeral procession. Paul felt the situation growing worse hour by hour. The day before he'd witnessed a great wave which had damaged ships and installations along the harbor and he knew of disasters to villages in proximity to Pelée. Closer to home the pox had broken out in the mulatto quarter, reason by itself to get out of town. The constant drumming and chanting of voodoo priests in their efforts to ward off evil spirits made it hard to think.

By this time I'd figured out that it was May 6 and that in 40 hours Mt. Pelée would blow its top and snuff out the entire town. Paul wasn't going to die but the pain he might have to endure could be great, and I'd feel whatever he felt, experience whatever he experienced. A scream was building inside that no one would ever hear. I couldn't communicate with anyone. But there was one small hint of hope. A plan was forming in his mind. If he could find Angelique and if he could think of a place to go, he'd leave.

As he continued along the street he fleetingly considered returning to his boyhood home. The thought of his father and of his father's cruelty came crashing in: the time his Papa had locked him in the smokehouse, his Papa's drunkenness, the shouting, the cursing, the back of his Papa's hand. Paul pushed away the thoughts. He reflected instead on how ironic it was that Angelique's abuse at the hands of her father had brought them closer together, and had created a bond through the sharing of awful secrets.

He stopped before a red door, knocked, and thought how vile a man her father was to spend the siesta hour in a whorehouse.

He tapped his foot while he waited. The realization flashed in his mind that Angelique probably had not told him all the evil her father had done. No doubt her shame was much too great.

An eye appeared in the peephole, and the door swung open to reveal a woman with her hand on her hip, artificial red hair piled on her head, orange lips, and a tight, kelly-green bodice that pushed her breasts up and out, creating deep cleavage.

"My, my," she said. "We'll have to draw straws for you."

Paul walked inside and saw a curved staircase with half a dozen painted young women dressed in negligees. They leaned over the banister to look at him. Most wore practically nothing. One fleshy, one buxom, another thin. None looked shy.

He diverted his eyes to the madam. "I'm here to find Henri Dubois."

"A friend?" she said.

"Hardly. Were is he?" Paul moved toward the stairs.

She held up her hand. "He is occupied--you may not go in."

The rage inside Paul burst loose. He pushed past the woman. She grabbed him but he pulled away. The girls screamed as he took the steps two at a time.

The madam called out, "Charles, Charles, come quickly. We've got a trouble-maker."

Paul flung open the first door on the hallway but the room was empty. His heart pounded. Red flashed before his eyes. The second door was locked.

He kicked it open.

Henri Dubois sat on the edge of a bed wearing only a strap t-shirt, a tuft of hair protruding out the top. His mouth dropped open. A young woman knelt between his bare, hairy legs. She turned and looked at Paul with large doe's eyes, as though caught in the headlights of a speeding car.

"What have you done with Angelique?"

"Get the hell out of here," Dubois said.

Paul lunged and the girl scampered out of the way. He slapped Dubois hard, grabbed him around the throat and shook him. "Tell me where she is."

Henri Dubois' eyes bulged. He gasped for air as his fingers pried and clawed at Paul's hands. His face took on a purplish tinge. His eyes bulged as though they might pop out.

An arm encircled Paul's throat and pulled. A knee pushed into his back. "Let him go, or I'll break your spine," a man's voice said.

Dubois rubbed his throat and grasped. "You fuzzy-face, self-righteous little bastard. Angelique is--was mine to do with as I please. You had no claim on her."

Paul struggled, twisted. The bouncer pulled him

from the room.

"Where is she, Dubois?" he screamed.

"She brought a higher price than you could ever pay--paid a helluva gambling debt."

Paul shouted again, now in the hallway: "Where is she, Dubois? Tell me, or I swear by the eyes of the blessed Virgin, I will kill you."

"Bébé Dominique's your man. Try messing with him and see what happens."

The bouncer dragged Paul down the stairs amid the hoots and jeers of prostitutes, placed a foot on his back and shoved him into the street. He rolled over in ash that smelled like rotten eggs, sat up and glared at the door as it closed.

Now at least he knew who had taken Angelique: Bébé Dominique, a slimy and ruthless piece of scum. He even had an idea where he might find him, and he vowed that no matter how dangerous and evil the man might be, he would get Angelique back from him.

That evening, the incessant thumping of drums and the sound of voodoo chants and screams was coupled with pandemonium in the streets. Even so, Paul remained relatively calm as he moved along *Rue Victor Hugo*. He was a man who knew what must be done.

Earlier, an "Action Committee" appointed by the governor attempted to deal with the volcano by washing the volcanic ash from the streets. All they had succeeded in doing was to turn it into a sticky mire so difficult to navigate that wagon wheels became stuck in it, with the result that numerous carts and carriages sat abandoned.

Scores of people trudged along aimlessly, dazed, some with the hollow eyes of those stunned by having seen unthinkable horrors. Many were refugees from the countryside who had watched their loved ones swallowed up by cracks in the earth or scalded to death by molten lava. An entire sugar refinery near the slopes of Mt. Pelée had been covered by a slide and 200 or more workers buried alive. Reports such as this had created panic so palpable the air hummed with it. All the while voodoo drums continued accompanied by cries and shouts and chanting.

Paul stopped when he reached the top of one of the stone stairways to the harbor. It was almost dark now as he watched a torch flare in the mulatto quarter and heard the drumming rise in ferocity. A burst of shouting was followed by more torches being lit, one after the other. He could see a procession forming. The drumming continued getting louder and louder. Chanting whipped up the crowd. Arms flailed and white teeth flashed in the glow as the mulattos called out to each other and to whatever god they believed to be present. Then up the *Rue du Collage* they came toward the place where Paul stood, led by a dancer with paint streaked on his body like a savage Indian or a bushman from Africa. In the flickering light of torches the dancer shook and turned and spun in wild and frenetic delirium, a demon or a devil prancing toward us out of a fiery hell. I felt the strong impulse to run but Paul stood firm. I was trapped.

More of this bizarre and horrific parade came into view. Behind the dancer was a procession of men, chanting and swaying, holding small animals in their hands above their heads, chickens and ducks and geese. Two men carried a trussed goat, and one held a squealing, squirming piglet in his arms. I understood from Paul's thoughts that these were sacrificial animals, that the procession was on its way to the Cathedral of Saint Pierre where their throats would be slit and their blood thrown against the walls. Apparently, the voodoo priests were convinced the Christian god was causing the volcano to spew and spit and cough. They were determined to appease it with their offerings of warm blood and the spirits of these screaming, writhing, helpless creatures.

When I almost could not bear it any longer Paul turned away and hurried along a narrow alley. Up ahead a sign came into view, *Casino Royale*. I understood that he had been there before, but only once when he and Jean-Luc went out of boyish curiosity to see the St. Pierre underworld. It was populated with pimps and prostitutes, thugs, professional gamblers, smugglers and white slave merchants, as well as unwary sailors who were lured there with the promise of a good time, plied with rum and fleeced. Paul and Jean-Luc had experienced the latter firsthand and resolved never to return.

An enormous man with a bald head and baggy pants tied around the waist with a sash stood inside the front door--muscular arms folded across his chest. Paul walked past and stopped at the entrance to a room filled with cigar smoke and the chatter of people who milled around gaming tables--roulette, craps, blackjack.

He knew he must be careful how he approached the man he sought no matter how worried he might be about Angelique. It was said the man would slit a throat for the pleasure of watching blood spurt from the jugular.

Paul looked from one gambler to the next for a powerfully-built, light-skinned mulatto named Bébé Dominique, a well-known bookmaker, gambler and loan shark. Then Paul saw him slap the blackjack table, let out an expletive and point to the spot where he wanted the dealer to place a card. When it was turned he slapped his hands together as though he'd been sure what it would be.

The player in the next seat took a card, uttered words of disgust, turned his over and left the table.

Paul slipped into the vacated seat.

Bébé sized him up. "You're the anchor, you know that?"

"Excuse me?" Paul said.

"This is one of those new games from New Orleans, so you are obliged to learn the strategy. All of us," Bébé pointed to himself and the others at the table, "are playing against him." He pointed to the dealer. "You're the anchor."

He pointed to the space between Paul and the dealer. "See? No one's between you and the dealer--understand?"

"I must confess," Paul said, "I have never before played this game."

"Magnificent," Bébé said.

"Bets, please," the dealer said.

Paul took a handful of money from his purse, formed a stack of one-franc coins, and put one in the rectangle marked for bets.

"Look," Bébé said. "The anchor's an important spot, see. You need to know when to pass."

Paul said, "When the dealer gets to me, I will be grateful if you tell me what to do."

The dealer dealt each player two cards facedown, one face up and one facedown to himself. The dealer's up-card was a four.

Paul had a nine and a two. "What is the object of the game?"

"You need to beat the dealer. You need to have more than he does without going over 21. If he's got the same amount as you, you lose. Only thing is, the dealer's got to take a hit up to 16 and he's got to hold on 17. Understand what I said?"

Paul was about to say he did not understand, but the other players passed. The dealer asked him if he wanted a card.

Paul showed Bébé his hand--11 points. "I should take a card, correct?"

"You're the anchor," Bébé said. "You take a hit and the rest of us give you another mouth right there." He pointed to Paul's throat.

"Pass," Paul said.

The dealer turned up his cards--a ten and a four. He drew one, a jack. Everyone at the table chimed approval. Bébé gave Paul a slap on the back.

"You did all right, boy," he said. "See, if you had taken that card, you'd have had 21, which would have been okay for you, but this way he got it and busted, so we all won. Get it?"

Should Paul question this logic? Not unless he wanted an extra mouth.

They played blackjack for an hour and a half, with

Bébé coaching Paul on every hand. Judging from the growth of Paul's pile of money, they were doing very well.

"I've had enough of this," Bébé said.

"All right. Let me buy you a drink," Paul said. "I wouldn't have won without your help."

They stepped up to the bar. Paul asked for beer and Bébé ordered a shot of dark rum.

"Do you always win like that?" Paul said.

Bébé beamed. "Yeah. Nothin' to it."

The bartender put down their drinks.

Paul lifted his in the gesture of a toast, and they clicked glasses.

"I guess that means you don't have to work," Paul said.

Bébé downed his shot in one gulp and pointed to it for a refill. "Never worked a day in my life and don't intend to. Still, what you can get in this place is peanuts. There's a helluva lot more in St. Pierre for the taking than you'll find in here."

"How so?"

"I like to make book, see. Lately, I been making book that Pelée ain't going to blow. I'll give anybody 200 to one it's just not going to happen. You should see the suckers taking me up on it. What these dudes don't understand is--it's got to blow for them to collect--but if she blows, they ain't going to be around to collect." He threw back his head and laughed so hard he had to wipe tears from his eyes.

"That is amusing. Have you any others?" Paul said.

Bébé downed the rum and gestured for another shot. "Got a million, brother. Take that ship--the American steamer, Cape St. Cloud? They'll be off-loading cargo for the rest of this afternoon and all day tomorrow. About ten o'clock tomorrow night, I'll be off-loading their entire purse, payment in gold and silver for ten tons of cargo. Even if Pelée blows and everybody lives to collect, I'll be able to cover it."

This is incredible, Paul thought. "Really?" he said.

"That must take courage."

Bébé threw down another shot. "Brains is what it takes. And a strong stomach. At that time of night the crew's either asleep or ashore getting laid. So in a case like that what I do, see, is walk up to the guy who's on watch, put a gun to his head and tell him to take me to the guy who guards the safe. When we get there, I blow his brains out. Then I tell the guy who guards the safe it's his turn next if he don't open it." He shrugged. "Works every time."

Paul couldn't believe what he was hearing.

Bébé gestured to the bartender for another round. "Yeah. It's the brains that does it all right. The ones splattered all over the place." Bébé guffawed and slapped the bar. Paul wondered if it was possible to be more thoroughly disgusting.

"A guy like you must have a lot of women running after him," he said.

Bébé's brow furrowed and he threw down another shot of rum, slammed it on the bar and pointed to it to be filled again. "Yeah, they drops their pants for me wherever I go, but to tell you true, I ain't got much use for them." His eyes looked like slits. His lips moved one way and the words came out another. "Just this morning I had this dandy little virgin handed to me--the kind most guys'd give their left nut for. Not me. She's worth a lot more with her cherry intact. Sold her to the captain of that French ship headed for Libya, *Les Champs*. He'll sell her to a sheik, and she'll bring a pretty price, too, if she ain't all worn out 'tween now and then."

I would have blushed if I'd had a body and blood to blush with. I felt rage building inside Paul--could sense it was all he could do to maintain control.

Bébé raised the shot glass, cut his eyes toward Paul, took half of the rum in one sip, and returned the glass to the bar. Then he reached over and grabbed Paul on the rear. "Personally, I prefer tight little buns like yours," he said.

Paul flung Bébé's hand away with all his strength.

136

"Take your sleazy paw off me you filthy, degenerate scum."

"Why, you little--" Bébé lunged for him.

Paul stepped to the side and gave Bébé a shove as he passed, which increased his velocity. He rammed headfirst into the wall with a bone-crunching thud, then slid to the floor.

"Looks like you'll be out for the night. Too bad it isn't permanently," Paul said, and he reached into his pocket, threw down some money and turned toward the door.

After a few steps a burly arm encircled him and the flat edge of a knife was pressed against his throat. "You slimy pail of puke," Bébé hissed. "Let's show everyone here the color of your blood."

The bouncer grabbed Bébé's wrist. "Please, Bébé, not here. You know how the boss feels about messing up the place."

Paul struggled loose and scrambled for the door.

Bébé called after him, spewing venom. "Sleep well tonight, you sonofabitch. One day soon you're gonna wake up dead."

Two hours later, Paul wore a sailor's cap pulled down so it almost covered his eyes as he weaved and staggered up the gangplank of the French steamer, *Les Champs.*

"How many rounds of rum you have, swabby?" the man on watch said. "What's a matter, can't you hold it?"

Paul hiccupped, belched, and stopped halfway up to hang his head over the side. He made the sound of throwing up, then called out, "Must have been some bad ale, mate."

"Right, swabby, sure. Had everything to do with the quality and nothing to do with the quantity."

Paul reached the deck and staggered in the direction of the man. "Here, mate." He reached in his pocket. "Here's something I want to show you."

The man stood and took a step. Paul staggered until they were face to face, then clamped his hand over the man's mouth, spun him around and placed a knife firmly against his throat. "I do not wish to hurt you, but if you make a sound, I will send you on your way to God, understand?"

The watchman nodded--his eyes wide.

Paul took his hand from the man's mouth and stuffed a rag in it. "The girl they brought on board this morning. Take me to her." He put another across the first and tied it, then produced a rope and tied the watchman's wrists and arms in back of him.

"Let's go."

Paul held him with the point of the knife between two ribs, and the man led him down dark steps, moonlight from above casting eerie shadows.

"Do not take me to the wrong place," Paul said, "or your shipmates will be mopping your blood in the morning."

Before long we were down two decks--a rectangular light above, darkness below. We came to a door and the man grunted.

"You first." Paul shoved him, pushing the door open.

A kerosene lantern lit a narrow passageway. Paul tightened his grip on the watchman, and turned up the lantern's wick. Barrels were stacked from deck to rafters. Three barred doors stood in a row. He pulled the man along as he looked in each.

A frightened young woman peered at us from the darkness. Her expression transformed to joy, her dark eyes sparkled, her teeth flashed white. She flung herself against the bars.

"Paul, Paul--where--how? Oh, Paul."

Paul pressed a finger to his lips, then turned to the watchman. "Where's the key?"

The man shrugged, shook his head.

Angelique pointed. "Up there."

A rusty metal ring with a key on it hung from a

138

wooden peg above Paul's head.

A voice came from the stairwell, "Who's there?"

Oh no, Paul thought. He pushed the night watchman against the barrels.

The voice came again, "Who's there?"

Paul grabbed the key, inserted it into the lock and twisted. Angelique threw herself into his arms just as the stairwell door opened. "Get behind--stay close," Paul said, and a man with a lantern stepped into the passageway and held it up.

"Who are you--what are you doing here?"

Paul rushed at him and shoved with all his strength. The man tumbled backward. The lantern flew out of his hand and crashed on the deck. Flames followed spilling kerosene.

The man bellowed, "Mayday! Mayday!"

Paul grabbed Angelique's hand and pulled her with him through the door, took two and three steps at a time, glancing back when he reached the top to see that the well was filled with fire.

A bell clanged. Men shouted. Someone barked orders above the din. Paul kept hold of Angelique and they scurried across the ship to starboard, stopped at the edge and looked down. It was 20 feet to the water.

He looked at her--she looked at him. They shrugged and stepped off the side together. Paul sucked in air as his stomach lifted to his throat. Angelique's hand slipped away when he struck the water, his weight and momentum pushing him deep.

He rushed to the surface, popped out with a gasp and saw her three feet away--treading water in the moonlight--her jet black hair wet and flat against her, her lips slightly parted and streaks of soot on her cheeks and her forehead.

He pointed to the opposite pier. "That way," he said.

The bell clanged and the shouts and the cries of men from the *Les Champs* grew more and more frantic as Paul and Angelique swam away from the ship. But as we passed between the piles, the clamor became muted. By the time they were 200 yards away across the wide stretch of water and almost to the quay, the sounds blended into the background noise of drums and the shouts and cries of voodoo priests.

Paul lifted himself onto the concrete surface and stretched out his hand to Angelique. She emerged gracefully, slipped into his arms, pressing herself against him.

"Oh, Paul, Paul, dear Paul, I thought we would never be together again--that my life had ended in that cell, a slave."

She kissed him, and again I would have blushed if I'd had the equipment.

"Come." He took her hand. "Your mother's shop is not far."

They hurried up the steep hill that climbed away from the wharf.

"Let us make a plan," he said. "You will spend this night and tomorrow with your mother."

"But if they come for me?"

"Your mother must hide you, but neither of us can stay long in St. Pierre after what has happened. Even so, I have unfinished business to attend to."

The sign with the hand holding a bottle came into view.

"They will probably be watching my mother's shop. You will not be able to return," Angelique said.

"Stay hidden. Meet me on Thursday at noon at the cave of your half brother in the mountains."

Paul raised his hand to knock. Angelique blocked the forward motion of his arm.

"Maman will be upstairs, asleep. It is not necessary to wake her."

She knelt and tugged at a stone near the base of the doorway until it slid out. She removed a key.

Paul closed the door carefully so that the bell would not sound. They crept through the shop to the back room. Angelique lit a candle and turned to Paul. She was inches from him, haloed by the glow. She pushed back her hair, her eyes sparkling black onyx surrounded by olive skin streaked with soot.

"I've something for you," Paul said. He took a small box from his pocket and opened it to reveal heart-shaped gold lockets, one with his photograph, the other hers.

"It is the picture we had taken," she said.

"Cut apart now," he said, "but together always in spirit."

He took the locket with his photograph and fastened it around her neck.

"I will wear it until I die."

"As I will this." He put the one that contained her picture around his own neck and she reached behind to help him with the latch, which brought her face close to his. He wrapped his arms around her, pulled her close and kissed her. Arousal burst forth as she pulled him down on a day bed. She rolled on top of him, straddled him, her face above him in light from the candle's glow flickering on the curves of her cheeks, her nose and her brows. Her mouth turned up in a mischievous smile. She pulled her dress over her head.

He reached out, touched her, caressed her, tracing her exquisite shape. She placed her hands over the backs of his hands and pressed them to her.

She leaned forward, unbuttoned his shirt--pushed it away--kissed his neck, his shoulders, rubbed against him. Then she slid to one side and Paul raised up as she helped him pull off his trousers. Her eyes sparkled in the candlelight.

"I want you to do what no man has ever done," she said. "What no man other than you will ever do."

She straddled him, guided him until they moved together, her eyes closed, and they moved and they moved and they moved. And before long he was very near the edge, creeping closer and closer to it, as close as one could get without falling off on the other side into ecstasy, at one with heaven, on a voyage of rapture, a divine journey into the unknown, farther, farther, deeper, deeper. He and his love were one, united. He wanted this to go on and on and on. He wanted to hold onto this moment in time. But he could not hold on, because no one can stop a moment no matter how wonderful that moment may be . . . because one must continue unfolding. . . .

Control slipped away at the instant she cried out. Her body flushed and she seemed frozen above him in contorted rapture. At last she collapsed on his chest, gasping.

Paul lay with his arms around her, felt her body wet with perspiration as he stroked her, inhaled the sweet, musky scent of her. After a while, which seemed all too short a time, her breathing became more regular. She lifted her head, her dark eyes inches away, a corner of her mouth curved upward. She said, "No matter what happens, Paul, we will always share this night."

Uh-huh, I thought. If she only knew.

The question now on my mind was, would we get out of town in time?

8

It is no less than incredible to be inside someone else's head--know their thoughts and feelings and view what happens around them as they see it. What I experienced that night was all the more astonishing because I'd done it from the viewpoint of my father. No matter what happened from then on my life would never be the same. Imagine. I'd lived the previous 28 years thinking my father had come into the world full grown, prudent and dignified. That he'd been an irascible young man, more impetuous than I'd ever been, was a revelation which added a dimension that evoked new respect for the advice and counsel he'd given me over the years. He'd experienced firsthand the passions and the woes of growing up. He had made his own share of mistakes. Big ones.

I remained awake long after he fell asleep. In fact I didn't sleep at all because my body was sleeping elsewhere and the mind never slumbers. Rather, it journeys to other realms, such as the one of pure thought I now inhabited. Of course one usually remembers only snippets of these nocturnal sojourns as dreams.

It was dark, I could hear voodoo drums in the distance and the constant chanting. Occasionally the scream or squeal of an animal as its throat was cut. I wished to heaven I could return to Jeff and the cave and my body but I knew I must stay to learn why my father believed he was going to die 50 years hence--on the morning of May the eighth.

I wondered about Angelique. Would she be killed?

And Jean-Luc. How would he escape?

And Bébé? I'd not realized his identity at first but midway through the night it came to me. Toussaint had said the name of the dope smuggler, the man in jail, and it'd been Bébé Dominique. So my father's nemesis was the lone survivor, surrounded by stone walls three feet thick.

What I thought about most though was passing through the tunnel and hovering above the circle of rocks where Jeff sat with the *quimboiseur* and my body. I also thought of the being of light who had welcomed me, the lady from the bakery. I'd always believed the idea of an afterlife was wishful thinking. Where was heaven, for example, on the dark side of the moon? But now I realized dimensions exist other than the three known in the physical world. Because one can't see something doesn't mean it isn't real. People couldn't see germs before microscopes, but they've always existed.

I spent a good deal of time that night revising long-held ideas. Ever since I'd been old enough to think for myself, for example, I'd believed life was an accident. A bunch of atoms and molecules had come together by chance to form the building blocks, carbon and whatever, and were struck by lightening. This squirming mass of jelly had evolved into all the varied forms of life now on the planet. But that theory seemed out the window because life was more than it appeared.

Physical bodies were a medium, they were mere vehicles, as was the entire physical world. Something was underneath it, behind it--an intelligence with a purpose, although for the life of me I couldn't figure out what the purpose was. This intelligence and the light were the same. Everything whether alive or inert, grew out of it--was connected by it. This fit the sensation I'd had on the back of the motorcycle at dusk--that all is connected, everything is one. One life. Mountains, valleys, clouds, trees and people are no more separate than a person's head from her foot. I knew at that moment that the light guides the evolution of the universe and life, which explains how higher forms had evolved from single-cell creatures--how stomachs and livers and eyes and kidneys came about. They were not accidents.

I also thought of what the being of light had said, the verse she quoted from the Scriptures, "In my Father's house there are many rooms." The physical world I'd thought was all there was, was only one of many.

My reverie was interrupted by my father's stirring. He was waking up. I wished to goodness he'd take Angelique and get out of St. Pierre. But he had other ideas. Before long I knew what they were.

He spent most of the morning on the docks, where ships were unloading much needed supplies. By early afternoon he sat on the concrete surface of the quay with his back against a barrel of salt pork, watching the activity on board the American steamer, Cape St. Cloud. It was a good spot from which to observe the relationships of the officers and men to one another and to the ship. He was in the shade and the sun was hot that Wednesday afternoon in May. For the moment no cinders were falling on St. Pierre. The stacks would remain until the ship was completely unloaded and her hold empty. They provided cover. He'd be in trouble if the wrong person saw him. The wrong people included Bébé, of course, and the man from the French ship, *Les Champs*, who had discovered him in the area of the brig.

It was possible the man would not recognize him. The description which had been circulated was sketchy. It said only that Paul was a tall Caucasian in his early twenties and listed his hair color and eyes inaccurately as brown. The man with the lantern apparently did not have a good look at him in the darkness, and the night watchman--whom Paul bound and gagged--was killed in the fire.

Unfortunately, Angelique's description was as precise and accurate as it could be without actually providing a sketch. They were sure to learn about Angelique's mother and go to her shop. With luck Angelique's mother had foreseen this and hidden her somewhere else, or best of all, gotten her out of town completely.

Paul was wanted for breaking and entering, destruction of property and murder. She was wanted as his accomplice. Paul knew the two of them must leave Martinique for good. That would not be easy. It was 17 miles by foot across two sets of mountain ranges from Basse Pointe to Fort de France on a road that was not much more than a Carib Indian path.

Most people traveled from one place to another around the island by boat, but going by a boat in this instance was out of the question. St. Pierre was between Basse Pointe and Fort de France. A boat would stop at St. Pierre on the way. That was too great a risk. It would be better to make their way on foot to Grande-Riviére, a small landing about five miles from Basse Pointe, where they could catch a ferry to one of the neighboring islands, St. Lucia or Dominica.

It would not take long to connect Paul to Angelique. Paul knew that by now he had probably been identified as a prime suspect. The police no doubt were keeping an eye on Jean-Luc as a result. Paul was sad he would not be able to to bid him farewell face to face. To do so would put both of them in danger--Paul of being caught and Jean-Luc of being drawn into the affair as an accomplice.

The thought of Jean-Luc triggered the memory of being chained in the smokehouse. He was put there after the midday meal by his father, who was drunk and in a rage. According to his father he'd failed to drive the workers hard enough--not hard enough to finish harvesting

25 hectares of sugar cane on the plain of Riviére Salée by his father's deadline.

Word of his incarceration had spread to the neighboring plantation.

It was after dark, Paul was semi-conscious, delirious, his tongue and throat parched, the smokehouse an oven. He heard a sawing noise. The door slowly swung open with a creak.

Jean-Luc scolded the noisy hinge, "Quiet."

Once inside he said, "It is impossible to believe a Frenchman would do this to his son."

He sawed through the shackles on Paul's wrists. Paul collapsed on the dirt floor. Jean-Luc dragged him outside where the air was cooler.

"Here--drink," he said.

The water felt so cool and life-giving. When he was able to speak he said the words which still echoed in his mind, today, "How shall I repay you?"

Now that the police were after him, it appeared he would never have the opportunity.

Paul's mind suddenly became alert. He sat up. One of the men he'd targeted from the ship was walking down the gangplank. Actually, walking was not the right word. It was more like a waddle, his short arms swinging, his barrel chest and potbelly leading the way. He wore a striped knit shirt and brimless hat with "SS Cape St. Cloud" embroidered on the band.

He glanced at Paul but did not slow down. Paul jumped to his feet and followed, careful to stay far enough behind so he would not be noticed. They took *Rue de Marseille* and climbed the hill to *Boulevard Marché*. Paul felt a sudden gust of wind, looked up and noticed gulls diving, swooping, screeching more frantically than usual. Ahead, in the direction of Pelée a black cloud had formed and it was gathering momentum as it headed toward St. Pierre. More cinders on the way.

The man turned onto *Boulevard Marché*. Paul followed him into the bustling open air market. The crowd's demeanor appeared more tranquil than the night before, perhaps because of the respite from the shower of ash--a respite Paul estimated would last roughly five more minutes.

The man from the ship stopped at a stand that sold silver jewelry from Mexico. He pointed to a necklace of graduated silver beads. While the merchant and the man negotiated a price Paul wondered how he would approach this American. His English was less than perfect, even though he'd studied it in school and heard it spoken by visitors from the English-speaking islands of St. Lucia and Grenada.

He noticed the American had trouble communicating. He did not speak French. The merchant did not know English, or at least, pretended not to.

Paul used the English phrase he'd been practicing in his mind. "Pardon me, my good man, I would like to help." Then in French to the merchant, "What are you trying to do to my friend, rob him? He offered you the perfectly acceptable price of five French francs."

The merchant gestured, palms up. "The price, monsieur, is ten francs."

Paul put his hand on the American's arm, so he wouldn't walk away.

"Your asking price," Paul said to the merchant. "Both you and I know that's triple what you paid for it. Five francs will return a tidy profit."

The merchant threw up his hands. He handed the American the necklace and plucked the five franc note from between his fingers, a scowl upon his face.

"Say, that's all right." The man offered his hand. "Manny Oliver."

"Paul DuMond, Mr. Oliver. Pleased to meet you." Certain English phrases rolled right off his tongue.

"Call me Manny." He stuck the necklace in his pocket. "Something, ain't it? Know damn well every one a them frogs speaks English, only they pretends not to when it's to their advantage. Clip you blind, if you let them."

"Pardon?" Paul understood only half the words--

148

and none of it made sense--except that someone spoke English.

"Ain't important." Manny touched his hat. "Guess I'll be going my way." He started walking.

Paul fell in beside him and wondered how to broach the subject on his mind.

Manny turned. "Something I can do for you?"

"Yes, there is something." Paul searched for the words.

Manny put his hands on his hips and thrust his chin in Paul's direction. "No need to be bashful. Out with it, mate."

The words came with difficulty. "Someone is going to rob your ship, tonight."

Manny's brow furrowed. "Someone's gonna rob our ship?"

"Yes, the American steamer, Cape St. Cloud."

"What the--" Manny looked in both directions, back at Paul. "How do you know that?"

Paul lunged ahead in English, "This man say, is going to rob the American steamer, Cape St. Cloud. Is very, very, bad man."

"Sounds like it," Manny said. "Tell me more."

That night, the man on watch leaned back in a chair pretending to doze. Paul sat nearby on the deck of the Cape St. Cloud in the black shadow of a lifeboat opposite the gangplank, listening to the ever-present voodoo drums. He leaned against a banister rail and wondered where Angelique was at this moment.

I was thinking, *nine more hours till she blows, let's get out of here, Paul,* as he gazed at the sleeping city of St. Pierre and watched lights in windows flicker out one by one. Now all were dark. The only light came from the bluish glow of gas street lanterns that climbed away from the harbor.

Paul's eyes looked skyward. He saw the orange glow lining the clouds that mushroomed above the city and beyond the foothills surrounding Mt. Pelée.

Yes, Paul, it's an orange glow, all right, and it means it's time to get out of here.

Every 30 seconds or so lightning flashed. He counted until there was a clap of thunder, followed by a low rumble. A gust of wind touched his face. He could sense heavy moisture. A burnt scent was mingled with sulfur fumes. He calculated the storm would arrive in ten or 15 minutes.

The sound of footfalls on the quay drew Paul's attention. He leaned forward and spotted Bébé walking at a quick pace, swinging his arms. Bébé touched a bulge in his trousers, which Paul assumed was a revolver.

Bébé reached the Cape St. Cloud, climbed the gangplank at the same quick pace, stepped onto the deck a few feet away, drew the gun and pulled back the hammer. "If you want to live for a few minutes longer, take me to the safe and the man who has the combination."

Paul got up, covered the five feet between himself and Bébé without a sound, wrapped an arm around his throat and pressed the barrel of a gun to his temple. The night watchman ducked out of sight.

"Drop it, Bébé," Paul said. "This is payment for Angelique."

Suddenly half a dozen men with guns drawn surrounded Bébé, too.

Bébé dropped his. The men shackled his hands behind his back as he regarded Paul with contempt. "You double-crossin' sonofabitch. I'll get you for this if it takes the rest of my life."

He spat. Paul stepped aside.

Manny came between them and took Bébé's arm. "Let's go, fella. There's a nice, cool jail cell waiting for you. You're gonna have some time in there to think about revenge."

"You maggot." Bébé's eyes locked on Paul. His upper lip quivered. "You did this to me for that *putain*? I'll get her, too. I'll get both of you."

Paul stuck out his chin. "You can rot in hell."

Manny and two of his men led Bébé down the

gangplank. "I don't care if you're in China, I'm gonna get you and Angelique, and I'm gonna get your mother and your father and your sisters and your brothers and anyone else you're related to and I'm gonna fry their balls. Then I'm gonna make you eat them, you slimy bastard."

They reached the quay. Bébé looked up at Paul and spat.

Manny said, "Don't know much a what this frog is saying but I can tell he's a mean one. Guess you've done your good deed for the week, getting him off the street."

When they were about 25 yards away, Bébé finally took his eyes off Paul and turned to one of the men who'd shoved him, and spat at him--which solicited an even bigger shove.

Paul had expected to be elated to see Bébé carted away, but was left with a feeling of emptiness instead--like a hungry man who finishes the first course of a long-anticipated meal, only to find the rest is burned in the oven. He decided to figure out why later. The storm was coming. It was time to get moving.

Agitated air swirled and picked up momentum as he jogged up *Rue de Marseille*. By the time he reached the corner it had become a steady wind with so much force he could lean against it with all his weight and not fall forward. When he turned onto *Boulevard Marché* a bolt of lightning crackled down and struck so close it almost knocked him off his feet. The boom reverberated in his head and blue spots lingered before his eyes. It scared the proverbial you know what out of me, but he kept on running. Then rain came in a torrent, but he did not stop. He knew he must get out of town or risk being caught by the police, or worse, by one of Bébé's henchmen.

Lightning struck again a block and a half away. He turned and climbed a stone staircase two steps at a time to *Rue Victor Hugo*. Rain poured so hard he could barely see 20 yards ahead. At least it had washed away a good deal of the mire of volcanic ash, which made the going a little easier.

151

Minutes later, he spotted a horse-drawn wagon coming toward him, an old two-wheeler like the ones farmers used to truck produce to market from the hills. This one contained no vegetables--only a driver and two men in the back who took turns with a liter of rum.

"Hey sport!" one man in back called out. "Which way ya headed?"

"Basse Pointe."

"Climb aboard. Ain't fit out there for man or beast." He took off his hat and used it to motion for Paul to join them.

Paul caught up and jumped in. "Raining just as hard in here," he said with a wink.

"Yeah, but we got rum," the second man said. His grin showed two teeth missing in front.

He offered Paul the bottle.

"How far you headed?" He raised the rum to his lips.

"All the way past Morne Rouge. You'll only have a few miles more to walk," the man with the hat said. He wore a small mustache similar to Angelique's father.

"Helluva storm, ain't it?" the man with missing teeth said.

"Weather's been crazy ever since Pelée started acting up," Mustache said. A flash of lightning was followed a fraction of a second later by a clap of thunder.

"She's gonna blow. I know darn well, she's gonna blow," Missing Teeth said.

Mustache took the bottle of rum and mopped the mouth with his sleeve. He gestured to Missing Teeth with his thumb. "Thinks God's gonna rain fire on St. Pierre on account of it being like Sodom and Gomorrah." He shook his head and raised the bottle.

The rain continued to pour.

"You're darn right it is," Missing Teeth said. "Place's teeming with whores, cutthroats, thieves, traders in flesh and sin." He reached for the bottle. "Hey, take it easy with that."

"Not to worry," Mustache said. "There's more

152

where it came from." He stuck his hand under a pile of hay and produced another liter.

"You really think she's gonna blow?" Paul slicked back his hair and felt water run down his back.

"First the Riviére Blanche was swollen with boiling mud," Missing Teeth said. "Then the entire town of Ajoupa Bouillon was swallowed up and most of the people there along with it. Cinders have rained from the sky every day for a month. Don't you think she's trying to tell us something?"

"It wasn't so bad today," Mustache said. He passed the bottle.

Paul took a swig and handed it to Missing Teeth, who pointed the mouth back at him. "She's trying to tell us something--that's sure. She's trying to tell us to repent." He raised it to his lips. Large bubbles rushed upward as he swallowed. He wiped his mouth with the back of his hand. "She's quiet now, all right. She's quiet because she's building steam--building up for the really big blow." He tapped his chest above his heart. "As my sainted mother used to say, we'd all better repent--come to Christ--that's what she used to say."

Lightning flashed. Rain poured down.

In spite of the rain, they had to wake Paul when the wagon reached the spot on the trail past Morne Rouge where he'd asked them to let him off.

He hopped out and stood in the darkness waking up, watched the wagon roll away--a silly grin on Missing Teeth's face. Mustache waved at him from under his floppy hat. Paul bid them goodbye, and the wagon disappeared around a curve.

He held out his hand palm up. The rain had slowed to a fine mist. The lightning and thunder had stopped.

A faint hint of light glowed in the east. The clouds seemed higher and not as thick. It wasn't far now to the cave of the *quimboiseur*--a few miles perhaps--but it was all uphill. He guessed he'd arrive sometime after daybreak.

He walked along the trail and looked for the narrow path that led up the side of the mountain. Images of Angelique and him together in the back room of her mother's shop ran through his mind--the sparkle in her eyes, the curve of her mouth. He almost could not believe that such a magnificent woman and such ecstasy could be his. The thought filled him, sent waves of energy through him, swept him forward.

He found the spot where the path veered off and headed toward the cave in the mountains. It would be rough going, but he didn't care. He had wind under his wings: the beautiful, passionate Angelique and the anticipation of a long life with her stretched out to infinity. They could go wherever they wished, do whatever they wanted . . . well, perhaps that was not completely true. They could go almost everywhere. Some places they could not go--places where the French authorities would be looking for them. They should stay away from the French West Indies and mainland France. But there was Africa, America, Algeria, Argentina, Australia--and that was just the beginning of a long list of possibilities.

Time passed and it was lighter now, predawn gray. I wondered when it was going to happen: the eruption. It certainly couldn't be that far off, I thought as Paul moved easily up the mountain, climbed over boulders, ducked under leaves of giant ferns. Missing Teeth's words came to him--words about repentance. The face of the night watchman from *Les Champs* flashed in his mind--the wide, pleading eyes and the fear.

Missing Teeth said Pelée would rain fire on St. Pierre because it was a place of sin, a Sodom. If there were justice in the universe, if the law of cause and effect the *quimboiseur* had spoken of to Paul were true, if what a person gave out came back--then, Paul thought, he'd built up a huge debt. He'd burn in hell, or spend many unhappy lifetimes to repay it. But no matter what the price, no matter how many lifetimes he spent pushing a stone uphill only to have it roll back down--he told himself he'd do again what he had done on Friday. He would rescue Angelique. If all that he ever received in exchange was that one blissful night together, it was value well received. As Angelique had said, it was something they would always share.

Paul made good time. It would not be long now before he arrived--for breakfast, it seemed. Rays of sun shot over the horizon, and patches of blue appeared between the clouds. It was going to be a beautiful day, he thought.

But I knew otherwise.

9

I wondered whether people were held accountable for transgressions in the physical realm. I hadn't seen any Saint Peter with a long white beard when I'd arrived on the other side. I wished Paul would think about whatever it was the *quimboiseur* had told him. I was curious to know more, although I was also on edge, expecting Mt. Pelée to blow its top at any second. He didn't think about it, though, at least not then. I decided I'd talk about it with Jeff or maybe even the *quimboiseur* if I had the good fortune of making it back to my body--which I hoped to goodness was still in the cave where I'd left it.

About an hour after Paul split off from the men in the cart, he arrived at an overlook not far from the cave of the *quimboiseur.* He stepped onto a giant rock where the land dropped away to a valley well over a thousand feet below, walked to the edge and gazed at a view that took his breath away--mine, too, though in my case, figuratively speaking. Only after a storm was the air in Martinique this free of humidity, the colors--greens, blues--so vibrant. This was especially true on that particular day.

156

Everything had been covered with ash before the storm but the deluge had made the whole world sparkle. In the distance, beyond the valley, Mt. Pelée towered over everything, dwarfing the other mountains. Farther still, just to the left, was St. Pierre and the sea. The air was so clear I could make out the masts of ships in the harbor. The water glittered turquoise close in and gradually became dark blue farther out. It were as though we could see over the edge of the earth, the Caribbean descending out of view to form a razor-sharp horizon.

Something drew Paul's attention back to Mt. Pelée. A black cloud expanded rapidly out of the side which faced St. Pierre. It was odd to see a cloud grow from a mountain but of course I knew what it was. It appeared to be smoke, but judging from the rate of expansion Paul realized it might be an explosion--a very large explosion.

An eruption? Was Mt. Pelée erupting?

Darn right it was.

He was knocked back, literally lifted off his feet and at the same time stunned by a deafening clap, a crack so loud his head might as well have been positioned between crashing cymbals. I experienced this unfortunate experience along with him.

Before he was able to get up, another clap reached him. The ground beneath him shook, quivered and swayed like the deck of a ship in a storm.

Paul stayed on his back unable to think or move, felt the earth and the stone on which he lay tremble and quake for what seemed an eternity, until finally, thankfully, everything was still. He rolled to his side, pushed himself up and saw that the black cloud now completely engulfed St. Pierre, blotting out the sea and the expanse of sky in that direction. It continued to billow and grow--upward, outward, ever larger.

At first he could not make himself think--his mind was a void. Then a kind of reverence took hold. The scene which unfolded was totally sublime--an incredible explosion, miles high and wide--vivid and awesome evidence of the power of nature and the wrath of God.

157

Then fear presented itself. His mind began to work, first slowly, then rapidly as the implications of the catastrophe clamored for attention.

What about Angelique?

God, he thought, if there is a God, please don't let her be in St. Pierre in the midst of that holocaust.

He turned from the horrific scene and ran, ran as fast as he could toward the *quimboiseur's* cave.

To him it appeared as though nature herself held him back--leaves of giant ferns, banana palms, mahogany and chestnut trees brushed against him, slapped across his face. He pushed them out of the way and ran as fast as his aching legs would go. He must reach the cave. He must find her. The sickening dread was a lie. She would be there--she must--and he would run into her arms, lift her off the ground, swing her around and kiss her. She would laugh with joy and release of tension, for she would have been worried about him as well.

The opening of the cave came into view. Paul's heart sank. The *quimboiseur* stood alone, his bare back to Paul, a spear upright in one hand. He looked in the direction of St. Pierre where the enormous cloud climbed still higher in the sky.

"Quimbo! Quimbo! Where is Angelique?"

Quimbo turned. The solemn look on his face said much more than words.

Paul reached him. Between gasps he said, "Angelique, is she here?"

There was sadness in Quimbo's eyes. Paul looked past him to the expanding cloud, fell to his knees, brought his hands to his face and sobbed. "No, no, no. It cannot be."

The *quimboiseur* placed his hand on Paul's shoulder. "Is wheel of life."

Paul's vision was blurred. He wiped his eyes. A putrid mass surged in his stomach. "The wheel of life? Birth, death, birth? How can it be? Her life had just begun."

Quimbo shrugged. "Old destroyed so new can come."

A flush of blood burned Paul's neck and face. This wheel of life business wasn't an explanation he was willing to accept. Why should this be the fate of Angelique? She was as innocent as a lamb. For the love of God this could not be happening--it mustn't happen.

"You're a sorcerer, Quimbo, you can make magic. You must bring her back."

Quimbo lifted his staff and brought it to earth abruptly. "Quimbo not work black magic. Not interfere with fate."

"Look, Quimbo, what's happened isn't fair. Angelique doesn't deserve to die. You must agree on that. She's had an awful life. So have I. Together we were going to--"

"You not know mind of *Bon Dieu*." The *quimboiseur* raised a finger to his temple. "I not know mind of *Bon Dieu*. *Bon Dieu* have purpose, plan."

"Please, Quimbo. She is your half sister. You do not want her dead."

Quimbo shrugged. "Dead, alive. It not matter. She still exist, only not here with us."

Paul held out his hands, palms up. "That's just it, Quimbo, don't you see? Maybe she is on the other side, crossed-over, or whatever you call it when you're no longer in your body, but that's not where she wants to be. That's not where we want her, is it?"

The *quimboiseur* shook his head. "I not interfere with will of *Bon Dieu*. It dangerous."

"If you don't want to, why don't you help me do it? Put me in one of those trances. Send me to see this, this *Bon Dieu*. Let me talk to him. Maybe we can strike a deal."

A twitch shimmied in the corner of Quimbo's eye. "You not know danger you ask for. I not do for your own good."

Paul put his arm around the shoulder of the medicine man and walked with him to the entrance to the

159

cave. "Look, why not let me worry about the danger. Without Angelique I don't have a life."

As they went inside the cave, Quimbo looked up at him--his large eyes searching. "You not know what you risk. This moment, this now, it one small peck in time. What came before, what come after, that what important. You interfere, you change this moment, you risk disaster for yourself for all time--past and future."

.Darkness closed around as they entered the large chamber. Orange light danced and flickered on the stone. In a few moments they reached the circle of rocks and the fire. Paul motioned for the *quimboiseur* to sit.

"I'll worry about my past and future, Quimbo. Just help me enter the spirit world, old friend. You know how important it is to me."

The *quimboiseur* looked at him for several seconds without speaking and when he did speak, his words came slowly. "Mistake can take several lifetime to undo. Maybe never undo."

"Quimbo, I've built up plenty of debt already. It is going to take quite some time to pay it off. One lifetime more or less really doesn't seem to matter. Everything's riding on this one, so let us get on with it." He took the locket from around his neck, opened it and looked at her photograph. "I must save her, Quimbo. I am nothing without her, absolutely nothing."

The *quimboiseur* shook his head. "I not feel good about, but do." He picked up the tambourine and began tapping it rhythmically. "You have tension. Must release."

"Yes," Paul said. He rotated his shoulders in a circular pattern.

"Let go, Paul. Look in fire and relax." Quimbo pointed at it. "Let problems go. Look in fire and relax."

The *quimboiseur* continued tapping the tambourine, rhythmically. "Look in fire and relax . . . look in fire and relax . . . " His voice settled softly into a chant. "Look in fire and relax . . . look in fire and relax . . . "

Paul watched the flames, how they pulsated and

curled, how they glowed--started from nowhere, ended nowhere--vibrant, alive. Soon Quimbo's voice and the tapping seemed to come from somewhere far away, outside Paul.

"Now come to place above and behind eyes . . . now come to place above and behind eyes . . . "

The spot swooped up inside his head. The fire became a blur.

"All tension pour out now and leave . . . all tension pour out now and leave . . . "

Paul experienced the rush of letting go as he released the horror of the eruption, the evil of Bébé, the drunken wrath of his own father.

Far, far away, barely audible, Quimbo's chant continued. "You come to place now. . . to hole in hollow tree . . . you come to place now . . . to hole in hollow tree. "

Paul stood in mist up to his ankles, before an enormous chestnut tree. A dreamlike quality pervaded what he saw, a blurry glow radiated from everything above, below, around him. As he studied the tree, he saw an opening in the trunk.

A huge black bear bounded up to him, stopped and offered his back. Paul climbed on, straddled the bear below its shoulders like a horse. The bear bounded back through the hole, almost threw Paul off. He held tight to the animal's thick coat and pressed his knees into the animal's body with all his strength.

Then Paul was surrounded by darkness and he could feel the presence of others near him, those who had lost their way. Suddenly, ahead he saw a circle of light and realized he was in a tunnel. He headed toward the light. It became brighter and brighter until he reached it and passed to the other side.

He found himself in what seemed to be a current, a river of air, that pulled him along, surrounded by a hum he recognized to be the thoughts of others. Hundreds, perhaps thousands were swept up in this flow. All were moving at the same fast pace, gliding effortlessly, drawn by an invisible force. They stretched in front like cars on

161

an interstate at night, except the lights weren't red and the surroundings were not black, but a luminous, infinite gray. He now recognized these lights were other souls. A few were yellow. Now and then a sky blue one could be seen, but most resembled dirty white snowballs that glowed much brighter than their surroundings. Paul glanced down and saw that he, too, was white--a wispy white gossamer with tiny flecks of yellow.

Paul was drawn into a sea of souls that converged from all directions, a giant mixing bowl, where he and the others swirled in slow motion.

After a time he felt himself pulled into what seemed a tributary. It became quiet. He was moving along a translucent corridor, filmy and frosted, a fabric of energy that bulged in places, stretching into the distance where clusters of lights could be seen which resembled bunches of fireflies that did not blink. Paul understood these to be colonies of souls with similar vibrations, souls that knew each other well and banded together between incarnations.

Presently he felt a familiar pulling of minds reaching out to him and he had a strange sensation of being home. He was no longer surrounded by the infinite, luminous gray. Above him was an overcast sky. He now had feet, perceived himself to be back in his body, and was standing on land, land that was as flat as the ocean. Wet, cold marsh stretched as far as he could see. Yellow-green areas interspersed with tall grass arose between patches of gunmetal gray water. Cattails swayed gently in the cool, damp breeze.

Paul looked behind, half expecting to see the opening to the translucent gray corridor, but all he saw where more cattails and gunmetal gray water. Ahead, a footpath led in the direction of what appeared to be a mound of rocks, or perhaps a castle, far in the distance.

As he moved along, it became clear that ahead was neither a castle nor an outcropping of rocks, but a village built on a mound in the middle of this flat, featureless land. It resembled the Mont-Saint-Michel, a medieval town off the northern coast of France. As Paul approached, he experienced a strange, *déjá vu* sensation. He could not recall when, but it were as though he was returning at the end of a long journey, as if he were a knight who had gone to fight for the return of the Holy Land and had remained away for many years. At last he was coming home to his native land. He arrived at the base, walked through a portal in the stone wall, and turned uphill between houses and shops which lined a narrow, cobbled street.

He passed an old woman in a black dress with a scarf around her head who swept stone steps. She did not look up. He passed a man wearing a black beret who came out of a cross street leading a donkey loaded down with sacks of grain. Chickens scattered, then scratched and pecked at kernels of wheat which had fallen between the cobbles. Next he went by a blacksmith's shop where the smith stoked coals and worked the bellows. He removed a red-hot horseshoe from the fire, placed it on an anvil and pounded. Sparks sprayed with each ring of the hammer.

Should he stop and ask directions?

Directions where? Where was he headed? The fact was, he didn't know.

He looked up and saw the sign of the Rising Sun on a tavern.

He went inside. A log fire blazed in an open hearth. Candles glowed in hurricane lamps mounted on rough hewn wood pillars. Men sat at tables drinking and talking. Others leaned against the bar. A barmaid passed by balancing a tray loaded with frothy mugs of beer and cider.

He stepped to the bar, ordered a beer. A moment later the bartender placed a mug before him, foam spilling down the sides. "You're early, aren't you?" he said.

"Early?" Paul took the handle of the mug.

The man rested his elbows on the bar. "We didn't expect to see you back so soon."

"This trip was, I guess you might say, unexpected." Paul lifted the beer. "Where can I find the man in charge?"

Wrinkles appeared in the bartender's brow. "The one in charge? Now I see. That'll depend on what sort of business you have."

"It's a delicate matter," Paul said. "It has to do with saving somebody's life."

A corner of the man's mouth curled upward. I saw a twinkle in his eye.

"Yes," he said. "I didn't think it was your time. You came back early to change the outcome of an event."

"That's it, precisely," Paul said.

"You'll find your man at the abbey. Turn right when you go out the door and stay on this street to the top. Just ask for the abbot."

Paul downed the beer, took a few coins from his pocket and placed them on the bar.

Five minutes later, he stood at an iron gate and pulled a cord which rang a bell.

One eye peered at him through a peephole.

"I'm here to see the abbot," Paul said.

"Paul?"

"Yes."

The iron gate swung open and a short, thin monk with dark hair cut in a bowl motioned for him to enter, an enormous smile on his face. "Why it is you." The monk embraced him. "We did not expect to see you--not for quite some time. Come in, come in. The others will be so happy to see you." He paused. "But, what are you doing here?"

"The others?"

"The brothers, of course."

"I do not understand," Paul said.

The monk stepped back and regarded him. "I see. You do not remember. This is not an authorized return."

"No, I suppose it isn't. I'm here to see the abbot."

"The abbot?"

"Yes. The bartender at the inn told me the abbot was the man I wanted to see."

A worried look crept onto the monk's face. He

164

nodded. He turned and Paul followed him along a dark hallway lit by torches to a massive wooden portal.

The monk lifted an iron knocker, clanked it two times, then pushed open the door.

"Monsieur DuMond has arrived, Abbot." The little monk bowed and left the room. The door closed with a loud click of the lock.

Paul stood in a huge gallery of tapestries, some more than 30 feet high, which appeared to be scenes from Greek mythology. He looked up at a vaulted ceiling, then down at a simple wooden table ten feet in front of him. His pulse began to race. The man standing behind it was at least six feet five inches tall, completely bald, with a pallid complexion that seemed all the more so because of his white, bushy eyebrows. Yet he looked somehow familiar, something in his face. There seemed to be a family resemblance, as though perhaps this abbot were an uncle or a second cousin. Paul couldn't put his finger on it.

The man pointed to a straight back wooden chair and spoke with a booming voice. "Have a seat, please." The word "please" reverberated off the walls. He sat and folded his hands in front of him. "So you're back. Early, aren't you?"

"Excuse me, Sir. With all due respect, everyone keeps saying that, and frankly, I don't know what they're talking about."

"No, of course not. Because you aren't due back for quite some time. When you're on the other side you forget. Technically, you're still on the other side."

"Forget what?" Paul said.

"That you left here with a mission."

"Left here?"

"I am your Higher Self, Paul. We're working toward perfection in this place. You agreed to play a part. You were sent on a mission. Now it seems you've come back early."

"But I don't recall . . . "

"Work on remembering, Paul. It will come to you."

"Yes, Sir, I will. But the reason I'm back, it's

important."

"You've given the matter careful consideration?"

"Of course."

"I see. Well, then, let's get on with it."

"It's about Angelique."

The abbot nodded and opened a book. He ran his finger down a page, looked up. "What about Jean-Luc Gaulois? Isn't he in St. Pierre, too, on the day in question?"

"I guess he is."

The abbot turned the page, scanned the text. "My, my." He clicked his tongue. "You've built up a sizable debt."

"I suppose I have," Paul said. "That's going to count against me, isn't it?"

"You'll regret it eventually. Unless you straighten things out." The abbot shrugged. "Jean-Luc saved your life, and you haven't bothered to repay him. You're responsible for another man's death--the night watchman. You set a trap for Bébé."

"Yes--but. But Bébé had it coming."

The abbot shook his head again. "When will we ever learn not to take matters into our own hands?"

"Are--are you saying I don't deserve to live my life with Angelique?"

The abbot closed the book and leaned forward. "No one here expects you to be perfect, Paul. That's why Christ was sent into the world--to atone for your shortcomings. You'd do well to remember that when you get back."

"There must be some solution," Paul said. "Some way Angelique and I can be together."

The abbot brought the tips of his fingers together. "What you need to understand, Paul, is that we're all one big happy family of humanity--of life. Unfortunately, when we go to live on the earth plane we often lose sight of that, think we're separate, that it's every man for himself. As Christ says, love your neighbors, love your enemies, love everyone as yourself and you can't go wrong. Because we are all ourself. It's a shame so few people listen, because if a person continually flits off on ego trips, if all one thinks about is one's own selfish pleasure and one's own selfish gratification, we'll never get anywhere, never arrive at our destination of perfection." He paused. "So now, you're here to ask to be together with the love of your life, Angelique. Given what I've said, it's a rather selfish request, wouldn't you agree? Where is your love for fellow man?"

Paul considered and said, "Earlier, you asked about Jean-Luc Gaulois. I take it you think I should be concerned about him?"

The abbot's brow furrowed. "Aren't you? He saved your life."

"Suppose I were to ask for him and Angelique to be saved?"

The abbot looked at the ceiling. "Try again."

Paul took a stab. "Jean-Luc and Bébé?"

The abbot leaned forward, a smile broke on his face. He pointed a finger in the air. "Now we're getting somewhere."

"Okay, I want to make up for the error of my ways. I want Jean-Luc and Bébé to be saved from the Mt. Pelée eruption."

The abbot picked up a gavel and slammed it down hard. "Done!"

"Wait a minute," Paul said. "Don't I get something in return?"

The abbot put down the gavel. "Certainly. You get the slate wiped clean."

"But, but--what about Angelique?"

"You can't have everything, Paul. To paraphrase the Buddha, 'Life is difficult.'" He paused--seemed to reconsider. "On the other hand, mercy may be called for in this instance. Tell you what. You will join her in 50 years. Precisely 50 years from this moment you will be together once again. That will give you time for penitence."

Minutes later, Paul descended the hill from the

abbey. As he placed one foot in front of the other, the abbot's words echoed in his mind.

Fifty years . . . precisely from this moment. What did it mean?

Why, it must mean that Angelique was killed, killed in the eruption . . . that he'd have to live his life without her, that he'd have to wait to join her in the afterlife.

He was going to die on May 8, 1952, at seven o'clock in the morning. Dear God.

He passed through the portal in the wall of the town and stepped onto the path that led to the place where he had entered this land. He'd return to the cave of the *quimboiseur,* and from there go immediately to Grande-Riviére and take the first boat.

There was an empty feeling inside him, a longing for his love, the part that now was missing. He was doomed to live his life without Angelique, must live another 50 years, years in which he must learn the importance of love for his fellow man. Fifty years. It was impossible to imagine, it almost seemed forever, but at least he knew the two of them would be together eventually, in the hereafter, for eternity. He told himself he should be glad of that, thankful, even though it seemed such a long, long time to wait.

10

As Paul started down the path I lifted out of his mind, floated above him in a disembodied state and watched. Then I had the sensation of being in motion, of moving along so rapidly my surroundings became blurred. Within a matter of perhaps 30 or 40 seconds I found myself in another place, a dark place that also felt like the interior of someone's mind, though very different from the one in which I'd spent the last two days.

It occurred to me that a mind has a feel to it in the same way a room in a house had a feel--a living room or a den or a bedroom. Each says a lot about its owner. Whereas Paul's mind seemed masculine and irascible, this one felt soft, gentle. Just shy of feminine. Whomever it belonged to was asleep, dreaming a peaceful dream of flying above the clouds. This caused me to remember the trip I'd taken to get to Martinique, the plane ride to Atlanta, to Miami and island hopping down the archipelago. Now I was 2,000 miles away from home, and a whole year before the Wright Brothers took their first flight.

That's when my mind began to work.

I'd been gone for two days so no way was I going to get back in time to save my father. By now it must be Wednesday, my father thought he was going to die on Thursday. The trip took almost two days. Good Lord, Jeff must be frantic because surely he had tried to wake me up and I was still here--at least my mind was--so my body must still be zoned out in the same sleep-like state as when I'd last seen it.

Then a thought struck which undulated through what would have been my intestine if I'd had one. *Maybe my body had died.* Maybe I'd traveled so far into such a distant and remote dimension and stayed so long that the cord which had connected me to my body had become disconnected. Maybe I now was doomed to exist in this disembodied state forever, hopping around from one mind to another for eternity, a silent observer of events in the lives of people 50 years ago. Dear God, I hoped it wasn't so. But whoever heard of someone sleeping for two whole days?

Maybe Jeff had carried my body down the mountain and taken it to a hospital. Doctors and nurses could be standing around it right now, scratching their heads and wondering what was causing my coma. Maybe they were feeding me intravenously, the way they were feeding Papa. Maybe when I got out of this, I'd wake up in the hospital.

Maybe Jeff had taken my comatose body and a bottle of glucose and put me on a plane. Maybe I'd wake up in a hospital in Richmond--maybe in the room next to my father. Then I'd be able to save him, except I still didn't know how I was going to do that even if I did wake up in the next room. The abbot had said Papa and Angelique would be reunited in 50 years. If it were true and she were dead, the only way the two of them were going to be reunited was for Papa to die, just as he had thought.

Then it occurred to me, since Papa was also

comatose, maybe his mind was already knocking around somewhere in this dimension. Would I meet up with him?

The more I thought about it, the more unlikely it seemed that Jeff would try to cart my comatose body back to Richmond. It would take almost two days and about four changes of planes--not an undertaking he was likely to begin without exhausting every possible effort to bring me out of it. No, it was more likely I was still sacked out in the cave of the *quimboiseur* or that he'd gotten me to a hospital in Fort de France.

It did cross my mind that it might only *seem* to me that I'd been gone for two days. Maybe time traveled at different speeds depending on where you were. Didn't Einstein say time was a dimension, too, and therefore it was relative? Maybe in this realm you could travel backward and forward along the strand of it. In an attempt to explain Einstein's theories, someone had once told me that time was like a river. We're like passengers in a boat. From where we sit, there's only the present moment, the place we are now. Though we can remember where we've been, we can't see where we're headed. If we could get a different perspective on the river, could rise above it in a helicopter or an airplane, we would see both the past and the future clearly.

These thoughts swirled in my mind as a beam of light from the morning sun shot through the window and landed squarely on the closed eyelids of the person I inhabited. He rolled over and buried his face in the pillow, but could not return to the dream of flying high over the sea and above the mountains, up through the clouds. He was awake now. The dream was over, a fading memory of heavenly bliss.

He rubbed the sleep from his eyes, threw his legs over the side of the bed and slid his feet into the slippers waiting there. It was Thursday, May 8, and a day to be joyful--the celebration of the Ascension into heaven of our Lord Christ, Jesus of Nazareth. These thoughts made me think it must be Jean-Luc. They were certainly foreign to any Paul would have had.

He crossed the room to the small wood stove, lifted the top, scraped a match on the metal and held the flame to crumpled paper. It ignited and engulfed a small, carefully arranged pile of kindling. He replaced the top and put a coffee pot on the precise spot he knew would soon be hotter than any other on the surface of the stove. His thoughts told me it was his custom to prepare the coffee and set the fire before he retired in the evening.

He went to his washstand, began his morning toilet. My suspicion was confirmed. It was Jean-Luc. He looked at his bony body in the mirror and told himself he must remember to eat more. He'd lost weight since moving to St. Pierre and no longer had his sisters and his mother around constantly pushing food his way and beseeching him to eat. For the last few days, he'd skipped dinner completely because his aunt, a widow who owned the house where he now lived, had gone to Fort de France to stay with relatives while the volcano belched and fumed. Normally she invited him for the evening meal.

He dressed, made the bed, walked out the door onto the balcony and breathed in the sweet, spicy smell of hibiscus. The terrible rain of the night before had washed away the volcanic ash which had covered everything, so that he could once more see the cobbles of the street down below and the red tile of the roofs of buildings across the way and up the hill. For the first time in days the air was free of the stench of sulfur.

The morning sun broke free from the jagged, mountainous horizon. Rays of amber light fanned out from it. He leaned on the banister rail next to the post where the purple bougainvillea climbed and gazed toward the sunrise. Pink girded the undersides of high clouds, as they scattered rapidly in the wind revealing bright blue sky. Jean-Luc said his morning prayers, feeling drawn into this great miracle of God--before him, around him, above him, below him.

Then something happened which I knew went far beyond his normal daily communion. From nowhere in particular and from everywhere at once--the blue, white, pink and amber of the sky, clouds and sparkling sun--the entire scene became bathed in the most amazing light. Something about it was unfamiliar. I recognized it instantly as the same incredible light I'd seen at the end of the tunnel, yet so intense now it almost obliterated everything. Jean-Luc continued to pray, to thank God for giving him this time on earth, for the beauty of creation and for the wonderment of nature. His words came as in a chant, spontaneous, without premeditation. As they did, his being began to meld with the light, to blend with the land, the sun, the sky--with all that now radiated with the vibrant glow--the bougainvillea and sweet hibiscus flowers, the soaring gulls.

He felt that if he were to let go completely, stop chanting--relax and surrender--he would lose himself completely. Cease to exist as a separate entity. He'd become one with the light and all that was. By continuing to chant this prayer, he could remain in this condition of being almost there, but not quite there--he could know God, remain in His loving presence, ecstatic, on the very edge of complete unification with Him and nature. And so chant is what Jean-Luc did, and did, and did.

He had no idea how long he spent in this ecstacy. Neither did I. At some point his consciousness directed itself inwardly, away from the sun and the sky--away from God. Instead latched onto mudane thoughts. Questions filled his mind having to do with whether the coffee might be boiling over and where Paul had been for the last day and a half. One by one they intruded on his state of bliss, gradually pulling him away from the edge of unification. The light began to fade. The scene before him returned to softer shades of blue, pink, white, and amber as he emerged into full, awakened consciousness. A thought struck him with a sense of absolute and unquestionable fact: The city of St. Pierre and all the people were going to be destroyed--completely wiped out. He must leave now or die.

How this could be, he wondered? How was it possible?

173

Then he remembered Mt. Pelée and her behavior over the last month. He could feel, inexplicably, the pressure building up inside her. Those who had insisted she were about to erupt were correct. His heart began to pound. A sense of impending doom took hold, the realization time was short. He must leave, get away from the city--as far as possible, as quickly as possible.

Inside his apartment Jean-Luc removed the coffee pot from the heat. He threw the few things he owned into a satchel. In no more than three minutes walked out the door, down the steps and into the empty street. His footsteps echoed off the sides of buildings as he hurried west.

He calculated the quickest way out of town, *Victor Hugo* to *Rue de Marseilles,* then remembered his good friend Paul.

He must not leave without him.

The police had come looking for Paul, yesterday, to question him in connection with an incident on a French freighter. Apparently, a young woman who fit Angelique's description and a young man the police suspected might be Paul had forced their way on board and started a fire which had killed one of the ship's crew. It sounded extremely far-fetched to Jean-Luc that Paul was in any way involved. What reason would he have had?

Jean-Luc was certain very little time was left--that the hour glass on St. Pierre was running out. He hurried up one of the stone stairways, nervously assuring himself that it would take only a few minutes longer to leave town by way of Paul's apartment.

Dear, dear Paul. He was the reason Jean-Luc was pulled to God.

Jean-Luc's sisters and his mother had always pampered him, catered to him and paid him homage. Although Jean-Luc appreciated and valued their affection, he felt smothered by it. His father, on the other hand, never had time for him. Jean-Luc's heart ached relentlessly for want of his father's attention and affection.

"Maman, where is father?"

"He is in Fort de France, my son, on important business."

"When will he return, Maman?"

"In a few weeks, my dear."

"Then will he teach me how to ride?"

"Perhaps, my son. You know how busy your father always is."

No doubt the women of the family saw Jean-Luc's pain--his longing for the father who was never there. They tried to compensate for it by making him the center of attention. These good intentions served only to push Jean-Luc away. He sought solitude in his room with his books and his thoughts. Then one summer he became obsessed with Paul DuMond.

Jean-Luc reached *Rue Victor Hugo* and turned in the direction of Paul's apartment, his satchel in his hand. The sky was bright blue above him, the clouds completely dissipated. He picked up the pace. He could feel the pressure from Pelée continuing to build.

Paul lived on the next plantation. Jean-Luc had known him, if only casually, all his life. It was the summer Paul's father locked him in the smokehouse that Jean-Luc became enraptured. Perhaps it was Paul's physical appearance. He was such a fine specimen of a man--tall, blond, muscular, with piercing blue eyes. By contrast, Jean-Luc was short, skinny, weak, with dark hair, and ears that protruded at right angles from his head. Paul hardly knew that Jean-Luc was alive--but Jean-Luc was well aware of Paul--secretly came to worship him and to think of him constantly in ways Jean-Luc now pushed out of his mind. He believed them to be sinful.

When he heard that Paul's father, the blow-hard of a drunkard, had locked Paul in the smokehouse and left him there to die, Jean-Luc took a hacksaw from the shed, filled an old wine bottle with water and stole across the harvested fields of sugar cane.

He crawled on his belly the last hundred yards to the smokehouse to insure he would not be seen--although he knew it was likely the elder DuMond was passed out

175

from drink by that time in the evening. He sawed through the lock as quietly as possible. He pushed the door open carefully. It creaked.

"Quiet," he said in a coarse whisper. Then he felt stupid for having spoken to an inanimate object.

As his eyes adjusted, Jean-Luc saw Paul in the shadows, chained to the wall--half dead. His heart went out to him. He touched a finger to his lips to tell Paul not to speak, then sawed through the shackles on his wrists.

"It is impossible to believe a Frenchman could do this to his son," he said.

Paul's magnificent body collapsed on the dirt floor, practically lifeless. Jean-Luc reached under Paul's arms, felt the firmness of his muscles as he dragged him outside. He cradled Paul's head in his lap, caressed his brow, wished desperately to kiss him passionately, but held back. "Here, drink," he said.

Paul swallowed, haltingly at first--then gulped the water down.

"How shall I ever repay you?" Paul said.

Just be my friend--stay close to me, Jean-Luc had thought.

Now it was only a few more blocks to Paul's apartment and the urges Jean-Luc had felt then still pushed him forward now, although it seemed clear Jean-Luc had never and would never act upon them. As far as Jean-Luc was concerned, life was a test, not unlike Christ's 40 days in the wilderness or Buddha's temptation under the fig tree. Although joy broke through the hardship of it now and then, he viewed the time spent on earth as a necessary journey on the way to a paradise with God. It was a test full of obligations and sacrifices--one of which was to maintain sexual purity.

Jean-Luc arrived at the building that housed Paul's apartment, shot down the alley at a sprint and stopped at the door. His heart pounded as he knocked.

No answer.

He knocked harder, so hard his knuckles hurt.

"Paul, Paul, wake up!"

176

He grabbed the doorknob, shook it, peered through the louvered shutters of the window, cupping his hands around his eyes.

The bed was empty.

Where could Paul be? With Angelique?

That must be it. Paul must be with her, probably the two of them were fornicating at this very moment, Jean-Luc thought. He felt his face flush. A dark cloud of jealously mixed with disgust descended over him. Angelique would be Paul's downfall as he had predicted.

He must not judge. The Scriptures were clear on this. He must do his best to save Paul--except, how could he now? Angelique's apartment was in the opposite direction. He had no time to double back.

Jean-Luc shook his head and hurried in the direction of the hills. The Lord would forgive him for leaving Paul behind. His will would be done. Christ himself had spoken directly to Jean-Luc about the impending doom of St. Pierre. If Christ wanted Paul saved, He would surely do it Himself.

As Jean-Luc headed toward Morne Rouge--as the buildings and harbor of St. Pierre receded behind him in the distance--he came to a profound decision. As one who was blessed, as one who was personally chosen by God, he must spend his life in God's service. He believed he had been called to do so, and he certainly must not disobey so clear a beckoning from the Divinity. Jean-Luc saw his future at the instant I lifted from his mind.

In what seemed less than two seconds I was high above St. Pierre, moving so fast everything was a blur. Over the buildings I soared, down to the boulangerie and through the walls to a bedroom at the rear of the shop. I saw Angelique asleep in bed. Then I was inside her mind.

I was settling in, getting used to the fully feminine feel of this space, more feminine I judged than my own mind, when Angelique thought she heard a door creak far away. A cool, foul current of fear crept over her. A faceless brute had entered the house and appeared suddenly, a large club in his hand. She backed away, lifting her hands and arms in a feeble attempt to protect herself. He swung at her--missed--hit a stack of dishes that crashed to the floor--kept coming at her, his fangs bared, his lips curled to reveal the vicious teeth of a rabid dog. They snapped at her and she could not escape, was boxed into a corner.

Wait, a window, she thought. It was a long way to jump but her only chance.

"Angelique?"

Someone called for her to leap.

"Angelique."

"Yes--what?"

Angelique opened her eyes. It was Madame Dupont, the woman who worked in the boulangerie and the ethereal being of light who had greeted me at the end of the long dark tunnel.

"You asked me to wake you." She knelt by the bed and took Angelique's hand. "You were twisting, turning. It must have been a dream, poor dear."

"Yes," Angelique said. "A bad one."

Madame Dupont stood. "I must apologize for the noise--the pots and pans I knocked over."

"Oh . . . yes. Think nothing of it. Thank you, thank you so very, very much for allowing me to stay--"

"It is the least I could do. Men are such beasts." She shook her head. "To think what they tried to do, almost did."

Angelique sat up. "My father--has he returned?"

"I do not think so. Excuse me, dear, but I must attend to the bread." Madame Dupont turned to leave.

"I shall return to say good-bye," Angelique called after her, then threw her legs over the side and slipped into her shoes.

She made the bed carefully, washed, dressed and went quietly through the back door and up the stairs to the apartment. She prayed to Jesus her father would not be home.

Silently, she opened the door and stepped inside,

crept to his bedroom and saw that the bed was rumpled, but empty. Where he was, was anyone's guess. Anyway, it didn't matter--not as long as he did not return while she was there. She'd take her things and go up into the mountains to the cave of her half brother, the *quimboiseur*, and into Paul's arms. Together they would leave this place, this island, this life--if one could call it that. They would begin anew in a different land.

Angelique hesitated when she reached the door of her own small room, stood for a few seconds taking in the four whitewashed walls, the simple dresser, her bed and the crucifix over the headboard. This was her port in the storm.

She went to the window, her window on the world, and looked out--first at the cobbled alley, then to the red-tile roofs of adjacent buildings, and over them to pale yellow walls and light blue shutters of house after house-- one row after the other all the way up the hill. Finally, her gaze rested on Mt. Pelée, far on the horizon. Nothing arose from the mountain, no smoke, no ash, no orange glow. She listened. No voodoo drums. It was quiet for the first time in what seemed weeks.

She turned back to the room and saw that everything was as she left it two days before, her bed carefully made, the doll in Normandy costume arranged on the pillow. She recalled the time long ago when her father had brought it to her from St. Barthélémy. She picked it up and fluffed the ruffles around the outside of the white cap that covered the doll's ears and was tied under its chin. This gift was evidence of a time when her father was not an evil man.

An image of him--drunk, staggering--flashed in her mind. She fought to push it away, but it was no use. He reared back, a hairy bellowing ape, "Women are made for one thing--to give pleasure to men." His hand came at her and she ducked.

She shivered. She must force herself to focus on the job she needed to do, to gather her things and run to Paul as quickly as possible.

She opened the dresser and shoved clothes into a shopping basket. She took a silver mirror and comb from the top drawer--treasures--gifts that brought better times to mind. When she had almost finished arranging her belongings, she opened a music box on top of the dresser. A ballerina twirled to the melody of Tchaikovsky's Nutcracker Suite. As she watched it for the ten-thousandth time, she prayed to heaven her life with Paul would be different from what her mother had known--that it was possible for the love between a man and a woman to be sustained for a lifetime.

She closed the music box, wrapped it in a towel, bent down and tucked it under the clothes folded in the basket. Then she stood and looked around the room one last time--at the simple, whitewashed walls, at her window on the world. She wasn't sorry to leave her father but she was sad to leave this room.

She walked out the door onto the landing and looked up at the sky, just beginning now to clear. Martinique was in for a beautiful day--a wonderful day for a walk in the mountains high above Basse Pointe. A good day to start a new life. She must go now to say good-bye to Madame Dupont.

As she went down the steps, she heard footsteps in the alley.

Papa?

Yes, they were his. What should she do? Run? But where? She was cornered.

She hurried up the steps and through the door into the apartment.

She must hide. Where?

No use. He would surely find her.

She went to the kitchen, dropped the basket, took a long knife from a rack. She backed against the wall beside the passageway to the other room.

The door opened.

"Angelique?"

It closed.

"Angelique? Where are you?"

180

Footsteps headed to her bedroom, then to the kitchen.

He came through the door, his back to her.

She lifted the knife.

Do it, do it now, she told herself.

He turned, his eyes grew wide, his jaw dropped. "Angelique, no."

She held the knife above her head.

"I'm leaving, Papa. I'm going with Paul. Don't make me hurt you. Step back."

The muscles in his face relaxed and he held out his hand. "Give me the knife."

His lips twisted into a wry smile and he moved closer.

"Don't touch me, don't come near, I swear by the Holy Virgin I will cut you, Papa."

He took another step. "The knife," he said. "Give it to me."

She jabbed at him. He stepped back. "You wouldn't dare," he said. "You haven't got it in you."

Tears welled up.

"Don't force me, Papa."

"You're coming with me," he said. "I've got you matched with a nice man who'll take good care of you."

He stepped closer, grabbed for the knife, but missed.

"No, Papa, no! I don't--I don't want to, Papa."

"Give it to me. Give me the knife, now. Make it easy on yourself."

He lunged.

She came down hard. He drew back. Dark red liquid filled a gash in his arm.

"You little wench!"

She darted through the kitchen door, into the living room, scrambled for the door to the outside.

He came after her. "Don't you dare defy me, Angelique. I know what's best for you."

She reached the door, pulled on the knob as his arm came over her and slammed it shut. He grabbed her arm

181

and she turned, swung the knife with everything she had. The point plunged into his neck. His eyes bulged. He screamed, grasping the knife.

She lifted it and stabbed again.

Blood spurted from the wounds and he staggered backward, his hands clutching his throat, blood gushing out between his fingers.

She ran into the kitchen, dropped the knife and grabbed the basket with her belongings.

When she reached the outside door and opened it, she looked at him sprawled on the sofa--twisting, turning--his hands around his neck, blood running out between his fingers and down his arms. He gasped for air.

"I'm sorry, Papa. I didn't want to hurt you. I will pray to Jesus to forgive me for what I've done, and I will pray to Him for your eternal soul."

An hour and a half later the sky above Angelique was bright blue, the air clear, and the foliage still smelled damp from the rain of the night before. She walked along the old Carib Indian path that wound through the tropical forest. It was almost as if she were in a trough of greenery that rose high into the air. She touched a large chestnut tree as she passed. A mountain palm brushed against her face. It occurred to her that she was halfway to Morne Rouge.

Suddenly the ground began to undulate.

She wondered if it were an earthquake.

She heard a deafening clap followed by another. She was thrown to the ground, which shook and shimmied and rolled.

When it finally stopped, she sprang to her feet and spun around in the direction of St. Pierre. Foliage blocked her view. She stood on tiptoe and saw a great cloud of smoke in the sky in the direction of Mt. Pelée, billowing upward.

Then she realized it was an eruption. Yes, the eruption of Mt. Pelée had come to pass as some had said it would. Her heart began to pound.

Where is Paul?

Was he still in St. Pierre? Or would he be waiting for her at the cave?

She clutched the basket to her chest and ran and ran a hundred meters at least, as the underbrush scratched and pulled and tugged at her clothes. Then she tripped and tumbled to the ground. Her belongings fell from the basket.

She gathered them hurriedly, then thought what was the use of running? Even if she were able to keep up the pace all the way to her half brother's cave, it would still be hours before she arrived. She had planned to be there at noon, and noon it would have to be. If Paul were still alive, he would be waiting for her.

She trudged forward and was praying for him when I lifted out of her mind and moved straight up away from her, now an invisible point of consciousness with no body to envelope me and no one's mind to inhabit but my own.

As I ascended, my first thought was that Angelique had not died in the eruption. I wondered if she were still alive and living somewhere in Martinique.

My second was that I needed to get back to my body, back to the cave of the *quimboiseur* or to the hospital if that's where Jeff had taken me. But how? I didn't know the way, or even where to begin the journey. Madame Dupont, the lady from the boulangerie who had greeted me, had said there were many rooms in her father's house. I was in one that was 50 years in the past. Would it be necessary to pass through other rooms on the way to the present? How did one navigate the dark tunnel in the opposite direction? Where did one find the entrance to it?

Maybe I should head over to the other side of the island toward Basse Pointe and try to locate the cave. But even if I was able to find it I would still be in the past. My body certainly wouldn't be there. I hadn't even been born.

Maybe that was what I should do, though. Perhaps I could find Paul and tell him Angelique was still alive and he should wait for her rather than go to Grande

Riviére to take a boat.

But *how* was I going to tell him? I had no body, no form whatsoever. As far as I could tell I was invisible. He would never even see me, but if he could, would telling him mean he would never meet and marry my mother? And if he never met my mother, would I never be born? Would I disappear in a puff of nothingness upon telling him to wait for Angelique?

I decided I'd better not try to change the past. The thing to do was to get back to the present. But how? How did one travel from the past to the present?

I was beginning to despair, not only because I had no idea how to get back to my body but because I was now high in the sky, perhaps 10,000 feet in the air above the erupting Mt. Pelée and what only minutes before had been the city of St. Pierre. The gray-black cloud continued to grow as I imagined a cloud from an atom bomb would hurl itself outward and upward in immense upheaval. Then all at once I saw the same heavenly light in the sky Jean-Luc had seen in his state of meditation, the same light I had headed to at the end of the tunnel of darkness.

At first I thought it resembled a gigantic luminous ball in the sky. Then I realized it permeated everything, that everything glowed with it as though the vibrations of this light and everything it touched--the billowing cloud of the eruption, the earth, the sea, the sky--all were in harmony. Rather than hot light as from an incandescent source, it seemed somehow pleasantly cool and serene and welcoming--the very essence of love and unity.

As I watched in awe, I saw beings of light emerge from it, ethereal beings such as Madame DuPont had been. First I saw hundreds, then thousands. I forgot my own predicament as I watched them hover above. Their faces were so kind and gentle and understanding it is difficult to find words to describe them. All were turned in the same direction, all gazed toward the cloud of the eruption and the place where the city of St. Pierre had been. As I looked down I soon knew why they had come. People were emerging from the inferno and the ethereal beings were going out to meet them.

As I focused in, I saw that not everyone who emerged from the volcanic cloud was having an easy time of it. Almost all at first were encased in what I will describe as a sort of form-fitting elastic garment, although it wasn't really a garment at all. Without anyone telling me I knew, in the same way one remembers something long forgotten, that this garment was the last vestige of each person's physical body, the last vestige of life on the physical plane. I also somehow knew that each individual must make an effort to throw it off if he or she were to make a successful return to the nonphysical world. I use the word "return" not only because of what I had learned from Paul's visit to the Abbey, but because those who threw off the garment with relative ease immediately embraced one or more of the beings in waiting as though they were returning from a long journey. They seemed delighted to be home at last and together again with long-lost friends and loved ones from whom they had been separated.

Others had a difficult time shedding the garment but were coached out of it by ethereal beings. Still others refused to listen and remained inside the vestige of the physical plane. Some appeared to be in a kind of stupor, others seemed in torment. I wondered if the dark tunnel weren't a tunnel at all, but rather this thing I've labeled a garment. I recalled having sensed other beings in the tunnel who seemed lost and unable to see the light. I remembered they seemed to be trying to hold on, to remain where they were rather than to venture forward. In other cases it appeared that demons of their own minds were after them.

As this scene played out before me, I learned one reason why some might wish to remain attached to the physical plane. After one was greeted, embraced by an ethereal being and welcomed back with love, he or she was given what I will describe as a review of her life on earth, a panorama which played out rapidly before her in much the same way one's life is said to flash before when she faces death. In this instance, however, the ramifications of each decision made and each deed done on the physical plane became known to the individual--acts of kindness as well as acts of selfishness or cruelty. Not only did the person *see* the results of her decisions and actions, but she *felt* them as well, experiencing the precise emotions of joy, sorrow, anger or hate which had been felt by each person who had been affected. It is not difficult to see why someone who was cruel or spiteful or bigoted--whether toward another person, race or sex--had a particularly rough time of it. I wondered at the incalculable horror monsters such as Stalin or Hitler would confront. Perhaps they were among the lost souls who refused to throw off their earthly garments, knowing what was in store, preferring instead to be taunted by demons of their minds.

It was during this panoramic review as well that a person learned how successful she had been in accomplishing the tasks she had chosen to undertake on earth. Needless to say, those who had paid attention and accomplished what they set out to were ecstatic. Others regretfully resolved to pay closer attention and to apply more effort if they were ever fortunate enough to have another opportunity.

Prior to this I'd thought that life was unfair for many--that the whim of fate had dealt many bad hands. Those born into St. Pierre, for example, only to be blown to bits on May 8, 1902. But I saw now they each had chosen their place and time, that each had reasons for their choice. These reasons weren't clear to me but were to them.

I thought of myself and wondered if my purpose on earth were to save my father. Then I realized that a person has different tasks to perform at different stages of her life. Saving my father was one of mine. Another was to expand the place of women in society beyond the role of homemaker, even if only in a small way. The hostility I'd felt toward the situation at the newspaper evaporated as though a weight were lifted. I'd taken on the challenge freely, had not been thrust into a situation I didn't choose. Rather than continue in the role of martyr, I resolved that if I were able to return to my body and to the present, I'd resume the task of breaking down the sex barrier not only with enthusiasm but also with a sense of humor rather than of rancor.

It also occurred to me that before I departed earth I was expected to share the insight and the knowledge I had gained on this journey to those on the other side. Those who were ready would accept it. Those who were not would reject it as a flight of fancy--pure, unadulterated fiction.

But how was I going to get back? Was I like Dorothy in the Land of Oz? All I had to do was tap together my ruby red slippers? I didn't think so. I didn't even have feet. Then I saw that one of the beings whose life was being reviewed was Madame DuPont of the boulangerie. I hovered nearby. When she was fully integrated into the heavenly domain, she turned and came toward me, a smile on her face.

She didn't speak, not words, but I understood that she had expected to see me. Apparently, the plan always had been to meet me here when my education about what had happened so long ago was complete. Then she would guide me back to the cave above Basse Pointe in 1952.

I took Madame Dupont's hands and we began to move together, traveling faster and faster until our surroundings became blurred from the speed. We passed through many rooms or lands or realms on our way. None of these words describes them very well because it wasn't like being in a house where a person moves from one room to another by passing through a door, not the same as taking a trip in the physical dimension where one moves along and the scenery gradually changes. It was more as if one place *dissolved* into another the way the scene of a movie fades out and another appears.

I recall her telling me that many were the provinces of different souls, as had been the land where my father had gone to meet his Higher Self. This caused me to wonder about my own Higher Self and the land that She inhabited, but I soon suspected I would not arrive there until the end of my life on earth. Perhaps Madame

DuPont would be the one to greet me there.

Unfortunately, we passed through each land so quickly I was scarcely able to take them in. I do remember one that resembled a quaint European village. Another gave the feeling of wide open space with breathtaking views of snow-capped mountains, lush valleys and endless evergreen forest. Another had a lake so wide I couldn't see across. In this land the sun was soft and golden and the sky an incredibly rich baby blue with small white clouds drifting by. One resembled a futuristic city with glass and chrome towers which reminded me of the Emerald City from *The Wizard of Oz*. We passed through others where nothing tangible appeared to exist. I discovered these were similar to libraries because they contained knowledge. Instead of having to look the knowledge up in a book, all I had to do was think of a subject and the information came flooding in.

I asked Madame Dupont why I hadn't seen all this when she first led me to the St. Pierre of 1902. She told me it had not been appropriate then. Now she was taking me this way so I could sample what existed here. Even so, my tour would be limited because the nonphysical side was as vast and infinite and varied as the physical.

Finally, we arrived in a forest. A giant redwood came into view. We headed directly for it, toward the large hole in the trunk. Madame Dupont smiled and said, "Good-bye--until we meet again."

I closed my eyes and held my breath as I plunged inside. When I opened them I was standing in ankle-deep mist.

May, 1952

11

Far away, I could hear the chant--as though in some corner of my mind. "Come back now . . . through hole in hollow tree, come back now . . . through hole in hollow tree--"

Gradually the tapping of the tambourine became clearer, more distinctive. "Look in fire and awake . . . look in fire and awake--"

I opened my eyes and watched the flames. They pulsated and curled, wrapped themselves around the sticks, flickered. White vapor rose from red hot coals and disappeared into the air.

Soon the *quimboiseur's* voice and the tapping seemed next to me. I turned in the direction of the sound and opened my eyes. He was there with his tambourine.

"You are back now . . . back from long journey." He gave the tambourine a final thump and grinned.

I rolled my head in the other direction. Jeff studied me.

"Welcome back," he said. "How was it?"

"You can't imagine," I said. "I don't know where

190

to begin. I actually was able to experience everything as though I were inside people's minds--Angelique's, Jean-Luc's, Papa's." I stretched. "Man oh man. At least my body still works. I can tell you, I was almost certain you'd have moved me to a hospital. Weren't you worried?"

"Why should I be worried? I told you I'd look out for you. I was here the entire time."

"For two days?" I said.

"Two days? Please." He looked at his watch. "Twenty minutes."

"But I was gone two days. It was morning when I got to St. Pierre and I spent two nights."

Jeff tapped his temple with a finger. "In your mind."

"But I could touch, feel, smell, Jeff. I wasn't dreaming."

He shrugged. "It's your mind that makes things real--made them real to you, makes them real to you now. For example, at this moment what you see is reflected light that's passed through the lenses of your eyes to strike the retinae, which have translated the light into impulses which are sent by the optic nerve to your brain."

"Uh-huh, I get it. You're telling me even though what I think I see is you in need of a haircut, it's really unscrambled nerve impulses."

"Your mind does the unscrambling and makes them into a picture that looks real. The other senses are unscrambled impulses, too. The bottom line is, your brain manufactured the whole thing."

"Maybe the time difference between what you experienced here and what I experienced there has something to do with Einstein's theory of relativity," I said.

Jeff raised an eyebrow. "Really, Claire. We've all had dreams that seemed to go on for days."

He wasn't going to believe me and there was no use in trying. I took his hand and squeezed it. "Speaking of nerve impulses, I don't want to pass up this opportunity to comment on the ones we had, let's see--last night for

191

you, three nights ago for me." I smiled. "Real humdingers, weren't they? We had those nerve endings working overtime."

He closed his eyes. His neck and face flushed as he shook his head.

"Sorry. Couldn't resist," I said.

Jeff rocked forward. "Maybe we should wait until we're alone. Then we can make sure the equipment that carries the impulses still works." He offered me his hand. "Did you find out anything in this dream of yours that will help us save your dad?"

"What we *need* is to find Angelique. She didn't die in the eruption."

The *quimboiseur* tapped my arm.

"She in Morne Rouge. That day, after your Papa left, I tell her of prophecy."

"Why didn't you just tell me where she was in the first place?" I said.

"It better for you to see for self." His eyes sparkled.

"Maybe so," I said. "It has changed my outlook."

Jeff stared at me, clearly puzzled.

"Where in Morne Rouge?" I said. "Which house?"

"Next to tobacco shop." Quimbo pointed a finger into the air. "Must be careful on way down mountain. Bébé use. Grow coca and hemp. Must pass house on path."

Jeff's brow furrowed. "Bébé, the gangster? The guy whose henchmen chased us into this cave?"

"Same one," Quimbo said.

"I'll bet that's why they were headed this way last night and saw us on the bike," I said.

Jeff looked into the darkness of the cave. "We can't go back through there."

Quimbo pointed the other way. "One path down mountain. Must pass house of Bébé."

"Once we get by him," I said, "how far is it to Morne Rouge?"

"It on other side of mountain pass. Ten

kilometers."

"Then another 20 kilometers to Fort de France," Jeff
said. "That's a total of 18 or 20 miles." He looked at his
watch. "It'll take six hours--unless we find
transportation."

"My goodness, Jeff. You don't think we're going to
walk? Not when saving Papa's life depends on our
making it to the plane on time."

I suppose I should have been worried about meeting
up with Bébé Dominique and his band of thugs but was
too excited about what I'd experienced. We walked
downhill on the path, a deep sliver cut in the foliage of the
rain forest. Within 15 minutes I'd given Jeff a synopsis of
what he refused to accept as anything more than a dream.
I decided it didn't matter what Jeff or anyone else thought
and turned my attention instead to the display of nature
all around. A remnant of the glow of the light from the
other side still must have been with me because I felt in
awe as I took in the scene. Passing giant bamboo,
mountain palms, chestnut and mahogany trees, we were
almost engulfed by foliage. It was hot, bugs swarmed.
Normally I'd have felt uncomfortable because of the
temperature and the insects and the humidity or perhaps
even frightened by what I would have seen before as an
alien environment. Instead, I had the sensation of being
part of it, of being one with it, the same feeling I'd had
when I viewed the sunset from the motorcycle. The life
force was expressing herself and I was seeing the outside
of what was inside, the physical manifestation of the
invisible: one thing, completely and utterly connected.

Then it came to me with the same unequivocal
sense of knowing that Jean-Luc had experienced during his
revelation. I'd learned the secret of life. Of course, I
thought, why hadn't I grasped it before? It is *the urge to
become* I'd sensed in myself for as long as I could remember.
I now realized this was the light's desire to express and
experience itself. A vision flashed in my mind of a cave, a
cavern like we have in the Blue Ridge Mountains of Virginia

with millions of stalactites and stalagmites forming intricate and wondrous patterns glistening with tiny droplets of water. The whole was nature and each stalactite or stalagmite a separate soul, or species of plant or animal. Each had its own identity but was also part of the larger formation of rock. Every drop of water was a current life leaving in its path a tiny deposit which helped shape the species, or in the case of humans--the soul. At that moment I understood that the realm of my father's Higher Self was a metaphor his mind had created just as mine had created this cavern, and that his life, my life and your life are like those water droplets. They are expressions of the light and cause something larger to grow, a universe that is becoming. They are sent forth as knights were sent forth to the Crusades.

I pushed by leaves and branches savoring the sensation, but after a while it dissipated. I noticed Jeff's shirt was dark with sweat between his shoulder blades. I wiped perspiration from my brow with the back of my hand.

"It was a whole lot cooler in that cave," I said.

"And a lot safer, if your dream is true of Bébé's vow to cut off the private parts of anyone connected with your father. Keep an eye out for hemp or coca. That's how we'll know we're getting close."

I dodged a palm leaf. "Not sure I'd know either one if they slapped me in the face."

"You know, Claire, I've been thinking. I always try to keep an open mind, but I'm certain most people don't. If I were you, I don't think I'd say anything to anyone about this dream of yours."

"You don't think there's even a tiny chance it really happened, do you Jeff?"

"I told you, I'm trying to keep an open mind. Maybe there is some truth to it. You did know about Angelique being alive, and apparently how this Bébé fellow survived. I can't explain that. But even if what you think you experienced really happened just as you said, I'd keep it to myself."

"Or risk being turned over to the men in white coats?"

"Something like that."

Jeff dodged a branch. I thought about his advice. He was right, of course. Besides, how did I know for certain it really had happened? In a way it did seem like a dream. There wasn't tangible proof.

"You know, Jeff, I can't stop thinking about something the abbot said."

"What's that?"

"He said Buddha said that life is difficult."

"I believe the translation is closer to 'suffering.'"

"He did say he was paraphrasing. Anyway, I've never thought of life that way before, but now that I have, it seems maybe the suffering isn't quite so bad."

"You mean, if you *expect* life to be difficult, then it doesn't seem so difficult?"

"Exactly," I said. "And besides, if everyone chooses his or her particular mission, they choose their brand of suffering so to speak. So why complain?"

"Overcoming obstacles, difficulties, is how we learn," Jeff said. "Only, I don't remember choosing mine. Do you?"

"I doubt anyone does. You have to listen to the small voice inside."

"Whose? Jiminy Cricket?"

"Difficulty is the catalyst of evolution," I said. "I hadn't thought of it that way."

Jeff stopped and took hold of a plant growing by the path. "Say, look at this." He broke off a piece. "See. It's made of five small leaves. Kind of like a hand with three fingers and two thumbs."

I took it from him; looked at it.

"So?"

He spoke softly now. "So it's hemp, *Cannabis sativa*, commonly known on the streets of New York City as marijuana. The stuff they make reefers out of."

I looked down the path at hemp ten feet high on either side. "So here we are. What do we do now,

Keemowsabbe?"

"We proceed, very carefully." Jeff motioned for me to follow. "Hopefully we'll come to a place where things open up a bit and we can get a look at what's ahead."

I crept along behind him, placing my feet, careful not to step on anything that would make a sound as I looked from one side to the other and back to Jeff's sweat-drenched khaki shirt.

After 25 yards or so, the path curved to the left and the ground on the right fell away. Jeff crouched low and came to a stop, put his hand behind him and patted the air. He looked over the hemp. "How are we going to get by that?"

I scooted beside him and saw that the path wound downhill and became wide enough for a car. A hundred yards ahead on the left was an outbuilding of some sort, a shack with a pickup truck next to it. Two men were unloading boxes.

On the right, farther down, was a house where three cars were parked. One was a black Peugeot, which looked like the car that had chased us the night before. There was also a green Plymouth coupe, and one of those funny little French cars that look like a bathtub turned upside down. Straight ahead, between us and the house, was a platform on stilts. A man on it sat in a chair, his back to us, a rifle across his lap.

"A lookout," I said softly.

"Uh-huh. At least he's turned the other way," Jeff said. "They're not expecting anyone to approach from this direction, except the *quimboiseur*, and I imagine they think he's harmless." He nodded toward the shack. "They're unloading dynamite. Must use it to clear the jungle."

"How are we going to get past them? If we crawl through the field under the cover of the hemp, the lookout will see it moving."

"There must be a way," Jeff said. "It'd be easy if we could wait until dark, but we'd miss the plane."

I sat with my back to the hemp. A hollow place formed in my gut. "I was just beginning to believe in some

196

master plan I'm part of--that I was somehow destined to come to Martinique, learn about my father, and bring the episode that began before the Mt. Pelée eruption to a conclusion--a happy conclusion." I shook my head. "Now this."

Jeff sat beside me, touched my thigh. "If there's such a thing as destiny, Claire, it's on our side. Think of it, Angelique still alive--the abbot's prophecy. Maybe you did travel to the spirit world."

He looked over the hemp. "Hey, the men who were unloading that truck are walking to the house."

I scooted beside him. Sure enough, the two men were walking along the road, halfway there. "All that leaves is a lookout with a high-powered rifle," I said.

"At least his back is turned. You know, Claire, we could take the path almost all the way to the dynamite shack. The hemp is so high he wouldn't see us even if he did look this way."

"We'll never get by the house," I said. "It's downhill from the lookout, and the area around the house is wide open."

Jeff motioned for me to sit again. "Here's the plan. We'll get as close as we can without being seen. You'll wait, I'll go into the shack, rig up a plunger to a detonator and a carton of dynamite--which I'll put on the back of the truck. I'll pull the plunger and lay it against the cab with the carton behind it so when I roll the truck down the hill and it hits the house, the carton will be pushed forward and set off the charge. The explosion will create one helluva diversion. Then we'll make a dash for it."

I waved my hand in front of his face. "Wait a minute, you've forgotten, this is my gig--remember?"

"What?"

"*I'll* go into the shack and rig the dynamite."

Jeff shook his head. "No, no, no."

"Look, Jeff, I got us into this. I'll get us out."

"Claire, this is no time to prove you're every bit the man I am."

My face flushed. "That's low, Jeff, really low. And

incredibly condescending."

"Be reasonable, Claire. How many dynamite charges have you set?"

"None, but--"

"I'm an archaeologist, Claire. In my business you have to move earth and stone. I've set hundreds."

I folded my arms across my chest. "So tell me how to do it. I'm a quick learner."

Jeff pried loose a hand and squeezed it. "Claire, I know you're brave. I've seen you in action. But whoever rigs this dynamite had better know what he's doing, and be quick about it." He kissed my hand. "I love you, Claire. I won't let anything happen to me, or to you--we've got too good a thing going."

I pulled his hand to me and kissed it.

Crouching, I moved silently down the path behind Jeff until we were within 20 yards of the dynamite shack. Then I climbed into the hemp, taking care not to move a twig.

I held my breath as Jeff continued on, until he slipped inside the shed. I sat, watched, wiped sweat from my eyes and forehead, felt it run down my back into my trousers as I inhaled the pungent sweet odor of cannabis and prayed that Jeff was right about destiny being on our side.

I waited as I felt my pulse thump and recalled the day eight years before when I opened the front door to find Billy Hanover's father standing there with his hat in his hands, pulling the brim through his fingers, pain contorting his face.

"We got a telegram today from the War Department, Claire. Didn't want to tell you on the phone. Billy's missing in action--feared dead."

I shivered in spite of the heat. Billy's mission must have been to die on a beach in Normandy.

What was Jeff's? To die on a marijuana farm in Martinique? God, I didn't want him to leave me now.

Please, Lord, keep Jeff safe.

Slowly, the door to the shack opened. I held my breath as Jeff tiptoed out with a carton of dynamite in his arms, a plunger on top. After a few steps he reached the pickup, lifted the deadly load over the side and spent several seconds fiddling with it. Then he looked in my direction and held up a hand--his index finger and thumb touching each other.

My pulse was off to the races. I got into position to run.

Jeff put his hand on the door to the cab. It creaked. Not a small creak that might be mistaken for a bird. No. It was a loud, long creak, impossible to ignore.

"Stop right there!" the lookout shouted in French. A shot rang out.

Jeff stepped out of the cab with his hands in the air.

In less than a minute the lookout arrived, his rifle pointed at Jeff. He said something I couldn't make out and motioned for Jeff to start toward the house. The two of them walked out of my line of vision. I listened to the sound of their footsteps until nothing was left but silence.

Think, Claire, think, I told myself. *Now's not the time to fall to pieces. Jeff isn't dead, only captured. Luck hasn't run out yet.*

They didn't know about me, that I was hiding in the hemp, and Jeff certainly wouldn't tell them. He'd pretend to be alone--a drifter, perhaps--interested in stealing their truck. In a moment, they'd all be inside, gathered around him, questioning him.

Torturing him?

There was no lookout now. No one could see me. The truck was rigged with a charge of dynamite, waiting.

I scrambled out of the hemp and ran to it, climbed in, spotted the keys and looked through the windshield at the house. I had a clear shot.

But wait a minute. Jeff was in there.

I looked to the right, then to the left--the Peugeot, the funny French car and the black Plymouth.

Yes!

199

I twisted the key. The engine turned over once, twice.

Come on, baby! Come on!

It roared to life.

I found the emergency brake, released it, pushed in the clutch, pulled the gearshift into first, stepped on the accelerator and let out the clutch. I was rolling--bouncing toward the house and the cars, the door of the cab still open, swinging wildly. I held tight to the steering wheel. It was as though I were on a bucking horse and unable to grasp him with my knees. Somehow, incredibly, I kept my foot on the gas. The engine wound up tight. I turned the wheel, pointed the hood ornament squarely at the black Plymouth, clenched my teeth. The eyes of two men grew wide and their mouths fell open. They were inside the car I was heading for.

Okay, you turkeys, here it comes!

I flipped the gearshift into neutral and dove from the pickup, floating through the air in slow motion, watched the ground rise up to meet me, hit, felt the air pushed from my lungs, saw stars spin around me as I turned through a double somersault--the earth, the sky, the earth--and skidded to a stop. I got up and ran, hit the ground again as the pickup rammed the Plymouth, buckled and exploded. Smoke, flames, debris mushroomed out, obliterated the car and the truck. I covered my head, the noise punishing my ears. I got to my feet, ran to the house and crouched, my heart pounding, sweat dripping from me. I gasped for air.

Seconds later two men charged out of the house, pistols drawn, shouting in French, running toward the flaming wreckage. One was an older man--a mulatto with gray hair. The other wore a black shirt.

I entered the house and found myself in a front hallway. Jeff sat in a chair at the far end beyond an open door, his feet bound and his hands tied behind his back.

I ran to him.

"Man, am I ever glad to see you," he said.

"Don't ask me what we're gonna do next." I untied

his feet and hands.

"Get the hell out of here, that's what," he said.

I followed him down the hall, stayed behind him as he opened the front door an inch.

"Uh-oh." Jeff nodded to a door a few feet away. "In there," he said.

I stepped into a butler's pantry and pulled the door almost shut, leaving it cracked slightly so I could see out, my hand on the knob. Jeff stepped behind the front door, his back flat against the wall.

Black Shirt burst in, flung open the door, blocking his view of Jeff, who shoved the door hard into his back, knocking him down. Jeff dove on top of him, and they rolled--once, twice. Jeff grabbed the hand with the pistol and knocked it hard against the frame of a door as I pushed my way out of the pantry. The gun went careening across the floor and I dove for it, scooped it up, felt my finger on the trigger and pointed the barrel at Black Shirt's head. He rolled, which brought Jeff in the way, so I pulled up. The gun went off with such a jerk it almost jumped out of my hand. Thank God I missed him, I thought, as I tried in desperation to draw another bead.

What followed was one helluva fight. Jeff's nostrils flared and Black Shirt's face was red and contorted as they struggled, kicked and squeezed. Jeff pushed a finger into Black Shirt's eye and twisted, but Black Shirt wiggled free and lunged on top of him.

A clear shot!

But if I missed, oh God if I missed. I crouched to find an angle.

They rolled again. I saw Black Shirt had a knife. Where had that come from?

Jeff grabbed his wrist in an effort to push the knife away, but Black Shirt pushed even harder, moving the blade closer and closer to Jeff's throat.

Jeff brought a knee into Black Shirt's solar plexus. The air in him exited with a hiss. He staggered back, raising the knife high over his head.

I pointed and squeezed--crack! crack! crack!

201

The first shot hit him in the stomach, the second in his chest, the third missed him, but the force of the first two lifted Black Shirt off his feet. I will never forget the startled look in his eyes. He was pushed back as though a rope were attached to him and it was yanked by a truck.

He landed on the floor in a heap.

Slowly, cautiously, I approached, pointed the gun at him. The startled look was still there, but something was missing. His eyes were glassy like a fish on ice. I knew that at that moment he was headed to the light. Or perhaps he would remain in the tunnel rather than experience the self-judgment that surely would be in store.

And what about Bébé?

I turned around. Jeff stood to one side of the door, the Plymouth and the pickup still blazing in the background. I saw the black Peugeot pull away and head downhill.

"Definitely an old version of the Bébé you described," Jeff said.

"Black Shirt is dead," I said.

Jeff leaned out the front door and looked from side to side. "Where are the two guys who were loading the dynamite?"

I pointed to the flaming wreck.

"In the Plymouth? Really?"

I sat on the floor; put down the gun. "Three people are dead."

"Yep. Come on, Claire, let's get the hell out of here." He offered me a hand.

"Three." I felt my stomach heave and a salty taste in my mouth. Bile rose in my throat. I tried to swallow.

"No time to hang around, Claire. We've got to go-- before Bébé comes back with reinforcements."

"I can't, Jeff. I'm gonna be sick. They're dead. All three are dead because of me."

"Let's think about that later, okay? That is, unless you want to join them--want both of us to."

I looked up, took his hand, swallowed again.

"We may need this," Jeff said. He scooped up the

gun and was out the door.

I followed him to the funny French car.

"Hey, we're in luck." Jeff pointed to the key and climbed in.

I took a seat on the passenger's side. The engine came to life. Jeff grabbed a gearshift that stuck out of the dash and rammed it forward. We were off, bouncing across the field toward the road.

"Had one of these in Egypt," Jeff said. "Not much power, but they're sturdy little buggers."

"How can you be so cavalier?" I said. "Three men are dead."

He shrugged. "They had it coming."

"It's because *I* did it, isn't it? You didn't kill anyone."

"Claire . . . "

"If there is such a thing as cause and effect like Papa was thinking about on his way up the mountain, I'm in one helluva mess."

"Look, Claire, I think the law of self defense applies even at the cosmic level. Besides, look at it this way--you proved you can take care of yourself and me all at the same time."

"That's not the way I intended to do it."

We reached the paved road at the base of the mountain and turned in the direction of Morne Rouge.

"You were really something, you know," Jeff said. "Imagine, driving a pickup loaded with enough dynamite to blow up an army, and ramming it into a car."

I shifted in my seat and felt a sharp pain in my side. "Can't wait to see the scrapes and bruises I'll have to show for it."

I leaned back in the seat. The little car bounced along, whirring like a big lawn mower. Thick vegetation whizzed by on both sides, a warm breeze fanned the perspiration on my face and neck. I almost felt cool for the first time since we left the cave. But I also felt tired--completely, utterly drained, and like sobbing--sobbing over the deaths of those three men.

We started up hill, past a sign that said it was seven kilometers to Morne Rouge, around smooth curves, hairpin turns, back and forth, higher and higher. Jeff downshifted the little car into second. It struggled onward, upward.

He pointed. "That's where we went off the road last night."

I rolled my head and looked through bleary eyes, inhaling the rank odor of rotting vegetation. Sure enough, I saw the flattened foliage. I fought to keep bile from rising in my throat. The name the thugs had used for me came to mind.

At last we reached the top of the mountain. I looked out over green valleys and mountains to a bluish-purple peak on the horizon which towered over the others: Mt. Pelée.

Jeff said, "If Angelique's in Morne Rouge, and if she's willing to drop everything and come with us, we'll make it to the airport with time to spare. It's downhill all the way. That next range is nothing compared to what we just climbed."

Then he looked in the rearview mirror and said, "Uh-oh."

I turned.

A black Peugeot was on our bumper. It lunged forward, bumped us. The little car rocked and skidded.

"Hold on," Jeff said.

He shifted into high and mashed the gas. The car accelerated into a curve and the rear tires skidded, but Jeff turned the wheel and it straightened up with a wobble. In seconds we were into another curve, tires screaming. I looked over a cliff to rocks hundreds of feet below and felt a familiar lurch.

Jeff glanced into the rearview mirror. "Damn. He's right on our butt."

We went around a blind curve well on the left side. I grimaced and braced myself for the inevitable crash-- which thank God didn't come.

"Where's the gun?" I said.

Jeff pointed to the seat, then turned the wheel and I was thrown against the door.

We were on a straight stretch now and I grabbed the pistol and leaned out the window. It was difficult to take aim on this side of the car because I was right-handed. Then we went around a left-hand curve and I had to press my knees into the door to keep from falling out. For a second I thought I might pull the car over on top of me. The pavement rushed by below.

We slammed into a right-hand turn and I was thrown backward away from the window. I struggled to get my head and my arms out. I had a shot, pulled the trigger twice--crack! crack!

"Get back inside, Claire! Oh no!"

I flopped back on the seat just as we left the road.

Slowly, it seemed, the car tilted forward and we were floating--I felt a queasy lift as we turned and headed backwards. We hit, skidded, the car turned sideways and I was thrown against the door.

Silence.

I opened my eyes, struggled to orient myself, looked at the gun in my hand. How many bullets did this thing hold?

"You okay?" Jeff said.

"I think so--where's Bébé?" I looked out and saw leaves and branches everywhere, pushed open the door and squeezed out. The little car had cut a tunnel through the ferns and mountain palms. I struggled toward it.

Jeff was waiting.

"Careful," he said. "He's sure to be armed."

I offered him the gun.

"No, no. Keep it. You're pretty handy with that thing."

We reached the edge of the road. Jeff peered out--looked first one way, then the other.

"Don't see him." He motioned. "Come on."

We stepped onto the pavement.

"What do we do now? Walk?" I said.

"Till we can catch a ride. Better stick close to the

edge, though, in case we have to dive back into the bushes."

"Don't know if my body can handle that again."

Halfway around the next bend I touched Jeff's arm. "Look." I pointed.

Skid marks went straight where the road turned and led to the mangled wreckage of the Peugeot--its front end folded like an accordion against a stone embankment.

I approached the car cautiously, the pistol ready, crept along side, looked in the driver's window and pointed the barrel in the face of Bébé Dominique.

He looked at me with tired eyes, blood seeping from one corner of his mouth. "So," he said. "It ends like this." He coughed more blood.

"Don't worry." I lowered the gun. "I'm not going to shoot a defenseless man."

"Who would have thought?" he said. "The daughter of Paul DuMond." He chuckled, but his smile quickly turned to a frown.

Sure he was a villain. But he was an old man, too, and suffering. Anyway, it wasn't my place to judge him. He'd get that soon enough. He'd be the one to judge himself.

I tried the door. It was jammed.

He lifted his hand. "Do something for me," he said in a coarse whisper.

I leaned closer.

"Tell your father he gave me 50 years."

"What? I don't understand."

"Your father. He set a trap. But he gave me 50 years." Bébé chuckled. "I like having the last laugh." Then he was still. His eyes glazed over.

I reached through the window of the Peugeot, found his wrist. I dropped it and turned to Jeff. "He's dead."

"Couldn't happen to a nicer fellow," Jeff said. "Come on, we've got a walk ahead of us." He paused, and held out his hand. "May I see the gun?"

I handed it to him. "You're a pretty heartless fellow, you know that?"

Jeff pulled the breech. "Empty, but I'm not surprised. Thought I counted six."

I rested my knuckles on my hips. "You're really something, Jeffrey McDannon."

"I've learned that a fellow's got to be tough if he's going to hang around with Claire DuMond." He wiped the gun on his sweaty shirt, held it gingerly, no fingers touching where they might leave prints, and tossed it in Bébé's car.

Jeff looked at his watch as we started down the mountain.

"Better hurry," he said. "There still may be time to make that plane provided we find Angelique, and transportation, in Morne Rouge."

12

I had hoped we would catch a ride, but no cars or trucks drove in our direction while Jeff and I walked from Bébé's car, almost at the crest of the mountain pass, down the curving, winding road, back and forth from one hairpin turn to another, into the town of Morne Rouge. At least it was all downhill. The trees and foliage formed steep walls which made it seem we were walking in a gorge, blue sky above, the sun straight overhead, the temperature well into the nineties. It was humid and the vegetation on each side was green and lush and it held moisture--creating a haven for insects which buzzed and whirred around my ears. Even after my revelation about the unity of life I didn't want to be dinner for them so I fanned them away and slapped at the little buggers, missing more often than not, hitting myself instead.

I felt sweat running down my back as we reached the turn and walked toward the spot where Jeff had run into the chicken. The bird's relatives were out in force--fully recovered from the tragedy. A cock tilted his head and eyeballed us. He guarded hens that scratched and pecked in the dirt between the road and the houses and shops that formed the main street of the town. Palms leaned across like long curved swords.

"There." Jeff pointed. "That red cylinder that bulges in the middle. That's the French symbol for a tobacco shop."

The words on the sign of the shop next door read, "Fragrances and Potions of the World." There was an illustration of a woman's hand holding an ornate bottle.

"What do you know?" I said more to myself than to Jeff.

"Better hope she's here," he said. "If there's any chance we're going to make that plane."

"Yes. It's just that . . . after being inside her mind, and my father's mind when the two of them were together. It's a bit much, that's all."

"Uh-huh." Jeff looked up and scratched his head. "I don't get it. A perfume shop?"

"I'll explain later." I reached into the pocket of my tattered safari pants and felt the locket. I opened the door. A bell rang.

"One minute, please," came a female voice in French.

The door at the back of the shop opened. An old woman appeared. She had deep creases in the tan skin of her face and straight white hair that fell below her shoulders. As I studied her, recognition unfolded in her eyes.

"You are the daughter of Paul DuMond," she said.

"And you are the mother of Angelique," I said. "So you too survived the Mt. Pelée eruption."

"Predicting the future has served me well in this lifetime, although I must admit, I was not prepared for this particular moment."

"We've come for Angelique," I said. "We wish to bring events full circle, but we must hurry. My father is two days journey by air."

"Angelique has gone."

"What?" I said. "But Quimbo said she would be

209

expecting--expecting to be reunited . . . "

The old woman pursed her lips. "To be reunited with Paul DuMond? Yes, she was expecting this."

"Then, why?--"

"The priest came--the priest who was Jean-Luc. He told Angelique that Paul DuMond was in Richmond, in Virginia. That *you* were in Fort de France."

"Oh, Lord," Jeff said.

"Where is she?" I said.

"She has gone to Fort de France to find you."

I grabbed Jeff's wrist and looked at his watch. "We must find her quickly. We haven't much time."

"Where can we get transportation?" Jeff said.

"Sometimes there is a taxi parked by the café."

We said good-bye and went out the front door. Across the street parked by the café was a black Citroen with the little white sign of a taxi on the roof. As we ran toward it, I noticed the rear windshield was missing.

"Jeff, do you see what I see?"

Toussaint was behind the wheel. He looked up at Jeff, then at me, rolled his eyes and shook his head.

"We need to go to Fort de France," Jeff said.

"Apologies, monsieur, but I am not sure this taxi is free. Those soldiers kept me in interrogation for three long hours, an experience I do not wish to repeat."

I slid in back. "You must take us, Toussaint. A man's life depends on it."

"A man's life?"

Jeff got in next to me and pulled the door shut. Toussaint sat with a frown on his face, looking at me in the rearview mirror.

"I thought we were friends, Toussaint," I said.

"You are *sympathique*, mademoiselle. I like you, but I do *not* like being shot at by gangsters. I do *not* like being chased. I do *not* like having my rear windshield broken by flying bullets."

"You don't have to worry about gangsters anymore--not now," Jeff said. "I can guarantee you that."

"No gangsters?"

"I promise you, Bébé and his men will never bother you or anyone else again," I said.

Toussaint turned the key, pulled the gearshift. We crept away from the curb as though we had all the time in the world.

"There is one thing," I said.

"What is that?"

"You're gonna have to step on it."

"Step on it?"

"As in--get the lead out. We're in a hurry, got a plane to catch," I said. "A man's life, remember?"

"There is the matter of a gratuity," Toussaint said. "I do not believe what I received on Sunday was fully commensurate with the loss of revenue which may have resulted from the three hours I was out of business due to the rather unpleasant grilling I received at the hands of the legionnaires."

"I see," I said.

"A bribe?" Jeff said.

"Not a bribe, monsieur. I am a humble businessman who attempts only to make a living."

I looked out the window. Thick green vegetation moseyed by. If we were lucky, we were going 25 miles an hour.

"Toussaint, my friend," I said. "I am a great believer in the profit motive. You will be paid 200 francs if you bring this boat to flank speed--and I mean put the pedal to the metal. You will receive 300 if we make our plane with Angelique Dubois in tow."

He looked over the seat at me. A grin showed white teeth. "Now you are speaking my language."

He pressed the gas, hunched over the wheel and air began blowing in through the window. It brought welcome relief from the heat.

"Someday, Toussaint, you will come to recognize the significance of this," I said.

"The significance of what, mademoiselle?"

"Giving us this ride and the other one when you outran those gangsters. Picking me up at the airport in the middle of the night. Helping us was one of your missions in this life. So far you've accomplished it beautifully."

He looked at me in the mirror, deep wrinkles in the normally smooth skin of his brow.

I turned to Jeff. "Where do you think we should go?"

"She's looking for us, right? Where would she go to do that?"

"Let's see. If it were me I'd try the hotels, of course. Toussaint, our first stop is *La Residence de la Port.*" I looked at Jeff's watch. "An hour and ten minutes to flight time, and it's the last plane out today. We've got to be on it."

Twenty-five minutes later we came to a stop in front of the hotel.

"Jeff, if you'll get our bags, I'll check with the desk clerk."

I hurried into the lobby, past ladies and gentlemen in tropical attire, and was suddenly aware of my own appearance. I hadn't washed or changed clothes since I crawled through a cave, swam an underground lake, hiked a jungle, blew up a Plymouth and was in a wreck. I hadn't even combed my hair.

The clerk glanced up from a pile of paper work, spectacles perched on the end of his nose. His eyes grew round.

"Yes, mademoiselle?"

"I'm Claire DuMond. I checked out on Sunday. Has anyone come by asking for me?"

"Why, yes, mademoiselle."

"Was it a Mademoiselle Dubois? She would be in her sixties."

"Mademoiselle Dubois--that is correct. But I would have thought certainly she was much younger."

"Where is she? It is imperative that I find her."

"Why, she has gone. When she learned that you had checked out, that you left with no forwarding address."

212

"Oh no, no, no." I exhaled. "Did she say where she was going?"

"She did not, mademoiselle. I presume she went home. I believe she said she was from the village of Morne Rouge. It is 20 kilometers by car."

"Thank you," I said. I turned away, a sick feeling in my stomach.

Though bleary eyes I saw Jeff close the trunk of the taxi.

"Did you find her?" he asked.

"She's gone. Oh Jeff, after all we've been through. The desk clerk thinks she went back to Morne Rouge."

"Oh no." Jeff looked at his watch. "Less than 45 minutes to flight time. There's just no way to go there and get to the plane in time."

"Then we have to take the plane. We have no other choice." I opened the door to the taxi.

"But your father . . . "

I slipped into the back seat. Jeff sat beside me and closed the door.

"The airport, Toussaint," I said.

"This is awful, Claire. I feel terrible."

"We'll have to move to plan B," I said. "I've got the locket. I'll put the old snapshot I have of Papa in it, and I'll dangle it in front of him--talk to him, pretend I'm Angelique--use what I've learned about their life together-- the days before the eruption. When he comes to--oh God, I hope he does come to--I'll explain that Angelique really is alive, but he'll have to come here to be reunited with her."

Jeff nodded. "Good plan. Might work, actually. That is, if your dream was accurate."

"It's the only chance we've got, and anyway, he's going to be awfully disappointed if he dies and finds out Angelique isn't there to meet him." I sighed and leaned back in the seat. "I'll tell you one thing. When we get to St. Maarten, I'm going to take such a long hot shower it may cause a water shortage on that island."

Toussaint glanced back at me. "You were speaking in English, mademoiselle. I did not understand all of it.

213

Does this mean that Mademoiselle Dubois will not be joining us?"

"Apparently not, Toussaint," I said. "But don't worry, you've done all that you could do. You've earned your 300 francs."

"Thank you, mademoiselle, thank you very much. My wife and children thank you, too."

"I did not know you were married, Toussaint."

"I am not, but when I am, they certainly will want to thank you."

The flight to St. Maarten was uneventful. Once we were in the Phillipsburg airport, I did as I had said I would. I took a long, hot shower, changed into fresh clothes, applied lotions to my skin and potions to my bumps and bruises. Then I brushed my teeth three times. When I finally walked back into the crowded waiting room, I still had aches and pains but at least felt clean. Even so, I was drained emotionally.

I spotted Jeff--showered and shaved, but needing a haircut now more than ever--and sat down beside him.

"If I keep telling myself I feel better, maybe I will feel better," I said. "And if I keep telling myself plan B is going to work, maybe it will. Anyway, no matter what happens, I think I can take it now because of what I've learned. It never really sank in before, but now I know there is so much more to everything than what we can see in this physical world--things we can't possibly understand but which fit together in a way that's somehow meant to be. It's changed the way I look at life. Death isn't the end I thought it was. We've got eternity for things to work out, and all we can do in any given moment is try our best."

"Maybe so," Jeff said. "But I thought it was going to work out now. I mean, I was really starting to believe in destiny, maybe even that you did go on this trip into the minds of others. What I don't understand is, if the non-physical realm exists, and the past and future exist there, too, how could the abbot be wrong? He said they would

214

be reunited in *exactly* 50 years."

"Maybe it was just Papa's imagination."

"More likely the whole thing was a dream, as I said before."

"Pardon me," a woman said with a French accent. "I am very sorry to interrupt. Are you Claire DuMond?"

A handsome, exotic-looking middle-aged woman stood before me. She was well-groomed, refined, with smooth, tanned skin. Salt and pepper gray hair framed her face, and she had high cheekbones and dark, penetrating eyes.

I jumped up. "Angelique?"

Angelique put down a leather valise and extended a delicate hand.

"Yes," she said. "So good to meet you."

"How can it be?" I said. "We thought . . . you came to our hotel, and we had checked out, and you . . . "

"Yes, and so I decided I must go to Richmond in Virginia by myself. That somehow I would find Paul. I must have been on the plane that left Martinique before yours. We are no doubt leaving here, however, on the same plane."

"Ah-hem," Jeff said.

"Oh yes, excuse me," I said. "Angelique Dubois, meet Jeff McDannon."

Angelique offered her hand.

Jeff took it and bowed in the European way, brought her hand to his lips and clicked his heels. "I believe destiny has led us to this meeting."

"Indeed," she said. "Indeed it has."

Forty hours later the car I was riding in slowed and came to a stop next to the curb. I opened my door, stepped onto the sidewalk and gazed at J. E. B. Stuart on his prancing horse. It seemed a long time since I'd last seen him. Even the azaleas and dogwoods along Monument Avenue had lost most of their blooms.

I took a breath and looked up into a sky that was predawn pink. Birds in huge oak trees lining the grass

215

median chirped a noisy medley, coaxing the arrival of the sun. All indications were that it would be a lovely day.

I watched while Jeff opened the door for Angelique. She stepped beside him. He glanced at his watch. "Made it. Almost half an hour to spare."

"No matter what happens," I said, "I'm going to bed for 24 hours when this is over. Thank goodness I finished the feature story for O'Malley on the plane."

We walked through the front door of the hospital and into the lobby where Dr. Martin sat in a chair. He stood.

"Claire--Jeff. I rushed over as soon as I got your call from the airport."

"Thank you, Doctor," I said. I introduced Angelique, then asked, "How is Papa?"

We moved toward the elevator.

"No change," Dr. Martin said. "Still catatonic."

"I believe this is going to work, Doctor," I said. "But it's difficult to tell you why without going into a long, involved explanation."

We stepped onto the elevator.

"Third floor," Dr. Martin said. The operator closed the door. "Claire, we've run every test known to man. At this point I'm willing to try anything."

"Something happened 50 years ago." I touched Jeff's wrist, turned it and looked at his watch. "Almost exactly 50 years ago only minutes from now, that I think is responsible for his condition. He's convinced he's going to die at seven o'clock this morning." I let my hand slide into Jeff's and squeezed it. "I believe Angelique is going to head that off."

We stepped off the elevator and started down the hall.

"You have my full support, Claire," Dr. Martin said. "I wouldn't tell my colleagues this, but I've been at this doctoring business long enough to know that the mind and body are inexplicably connected."

We reached Papa's room. I took a breath, looked first at Dr. Martin, then at Jeff. "I think it would be best if

216

Angelique and I went in alone."

Both men nodded.

Jeff said, "There's a waiting room at the end of the hall. That's where I'll be."

"Just have me paged when you need me, Claire," Dr. Martin said.

I turned the knob and gently pushed the door open. The room was dark, but I could see my father lying on the bed, neatly tucked in with his arms out, folded across his chest. His eyes were the same as before, open and empty, staring at the ceiling.

I held the door for Angelique, then closed it gently so the lock didn't click. Angelique tiptoed across the room, slid open the drapes and turned the Venetian blinds until the sun came pouring through.

She came to the edge of the bed, her back to the light, her body a silhouette.

"Paul, Paul, c'est moi, Paul."

An area on his cheek below his eye began to twitch.

Angelique put her hand in the pocket of her skirt and withdrew two gold lockets.

"Paul, it is I, Angelique. I am by you, here in this room. I have been by you all these years--you just could not see before, but I am here. All you have to do is look."

His head rolled her way. He blinked. A hint of recognition.

"That night, Paul, that night--in the back of my mother's shop. Just the two of us. I said we would have it always. It has sustained me these many years.

"The abbot, Paul, he said we would be reunited--his words were we would be rejoined in 50 years. What the abbot didn't tell you is we have been together always--will always be together in spirit.

"It is not time for you to die. . . . Not now. You do not have to die to be with me."

She lifted the lockets and held them for him to see.

"Remember, Paul. That night, that last night, we exchanged these? I have kept mine close to my heart all these many years. Now the two lockets are once again united."

She opened one to reveal a photograph of him when he was young.

He blinked.

"Look, Paul. See how handsome you were. You are handsome now, of course. In many ways--more handsome. But you were young and blond and strong. What we felt for one another, Paul, do you remember? You must remember."

His eyes were clearer and his lips moved, but still no sound came out.

"Quimbo said much damage could be done by interfering with the wheel of life. But, Paul, you didn't interfere. By your response to the abbot, you wiped the slate clean. There is no need now for you to die. I am here, we are together. The circle is complete."

He blinked, squeezed his eyes together, opened them.

"Yes, Paul, it *is* me. I'm right here--you can see me can't you?"

Was I imagining it, or did Papa's eyes seem to focus?

"I am older now, Paul," Angelique said. "We are both older now. Gray hair, some wrinkles. But we're still the same, the same inside--aren't we, Paul?"

He blinked again, as if he could not believe his eyes. He moved his head from side to side.

"I want to be together with you, Paul. Is it possible to begin again after so many years?"

His lips moved. "But . . . how can this be?" he said. "You died--I *thought* you died--in the eruption. That *I* would have to die to be with you."

Angelique threw her arms around him. "Oh, Paul, I have waited so long--we have waited so long--so long to be together once again. Now it is true. We are together at last, at last."

He put his hands on the bed and pushed in an effort to sit up. "But how can it be? Surely you were dead. Is it reincarnation? The locket? Where did you get it? The abbot? How did you know?"

Angelique sat on the bed beside him, took his hand and squeezed. "Quimbo--Quimbo told me about the abbot, about his prophecy. I have known all along, all these years, we would be together once again--precisely at this moment. And together we will be, from this moment on."

As I watched, joy welled up. Angelique held Papa's hand, brushed the white hair from his forehead, wiped away his tears. The two of them looked into one another's eyes for what seemed a long, long time. A peace settled over them.

At last, when it seemed appropriate, I circled to the foot of the bed, gently turned the crank. The head of the bed began to rise. "In a few days, Papa, when you're strong again, I'll tell you about what happened. Right now, though, it's enough to say that it was destiny, Papa. Providence. Some things are meant to be. It was the way for everything to unfold for you, for me, for Angelique. It was the way for everything to come full circle."

"Yes, but you must tell me some of it now."

"I went to Martinique," I said. "I met Jean-Luc, the *quimboiseur*, I even met Bébé--who thanked you, by the way, for the 50 years you gave him."

He chuckled, shook his head.

I went to the telephone by Papa's bed, picked it up and dialed the operator. "Would you page Dr. Martin, please? Tell him Paul DuMond is awake and ready to see him."

As I watched Papa and Angelique become engrossed in conversation it occurred to me that I never would have guessed that the quest I'd started would end this way. I remembered what Jean-Luc had said when Jeff and I were sitting in his office at the Church of the Sacred Heart. He had said it is dangerous--futile--for mortal man to predict the will of God. What I had just been through was testimony to that.

As I looked back at all that had happened and mulled things over, I concluded that the best course in life is to follow one's conscience, do the wisest one can in each and every circumstance, and trust that she's involved in a plan which is unfolding, becoming. That events which may be painful will eventually lead to things working out for the best--whether it takes 50 years or several lifetimes.

The following Monday morning, I stepped off the elevator and turned down the hallway to the newsroom, only to look up and see Alexander O'Malley standing in my way, his feet shoulder width and his hand palm out like a traffic cop.

"That was some boondoggle you took to Martinique, DuMond. I just had a look at your expense report. Two pairs of safari pants? Three-hundred francs for a taxi?"

I lifted my jaw with the back of my hand.

O'Malley's expression transformed from a scowl to a grin and he pointed at me and laughed. "Got you that time, DuMond. You should have seen your face."

"You got me all right, Mr. O'Malley."

He went over to a stack of papers on a rack, pulled out a section and gave it a tap. "Heck of a piece, DuMond. Makes me glad I had the foresight to send you down to Martinique because you really did a number-- especially the stuff on the jailbird who became the dope kingpin. Oh, and I almost cried when I read about the old fellow who left St. Pierre the day before his wedding. I'd say you're ready for more big assignments, wouldn't you?" He nodded. "Yep. This may win a Pulitzer."

"I'm ready, Mr. O'Malley. And as for a Pulitzer-- maybe it will. I suppose it is interesting," I said. For a second I considered telling him the story might have been even more interesting, but the world wasn't ready. Instead, I found another section of the same paper, opened it and folded back a page for him to see.

"Here's a piece you may have missed," I said. "I wrote this one, too. It's also pretty good, don't you think?" I pointed to my photograph on the engagement and wedding announcements page.

O'Malley took it from me and studied the text, one eyebrow cocked. "Uh-oh. Does this mean I'll have to stop calling you DuMond?"

"McDannon, Mr. O'Malley. Call me McDannon. As an Irishman, that should roll right off your tongue."

AFTERWORD

The woman I've called Claire DuMond had stopped talking but her eyes still held mine. I gave myself a little shake and looked at my watch. Incredible how time had passed. The fire was almost out. I got up and put on another log, thinking my wife and daughter would be back soon if they weren't stuck in traffic.

I returned to my seat.

"The urge to become?" I said. "That's the secret?"

"The urge to become."

"And we're all one thing? The light?"

"All is one," she said. "Any modern-day physicist will back me up--quantum mechanics. What seems solid are vibrations. Physical reality is ethereal stuff arranged in wavelengths. Things only look separate because they're vibrating at different frequencies."

"Sounds as though you've studied up," I said.

"Wouldn't you, if you'd been through what I have?"

I hit the stop button and punched rewind. "Why do I feel as though I'm separate, that my consciousness is mine alone?"

"Because you have a body and an ego which have been built up since birth. You have memories. Experiences. A mother and wife and children. But behind all that is your true consciousness. If you could peel the built up part away you'd come to it. That's why some people drink themselves into oblivion or take drugs, and others lose themselves in meditation. They want to reach the eternal Self."

"Like a newborn in its crib," I said. "Still, it's difficult to grasp."

"It will come to you a little at a time," she said. "In fact, I believe you'll write a book about it."

"Really? Beyond the one of your story?"

"It'll get under your skin. And that's how it will come out."

"Why didn't you write this book?" I asked.

222

"The timing. Anyway, I had other fish to fry."

The tape recorder clicked and I reached for it. "What happened after O'Malley took you off the Woman's Page?"

"The name McDannon rolled off his tongue daily for the next five years. I became an editor." She smiled. "Then I retired to have babies."

I felt my eyebrows lift.

"That surprises you?"

"You were such a--"

"Feminist? We each have missions, our need to unfold and become and in so doing to bring forth a higher unfolding. Often a mission takes the form of a hero's journey. We venture into the unknown to return wiser and more fully developed than we left. I was fortunate to have had one to Martinique and another into what was then a man's world of journalism. But now I believe the most fulfilling journey a human can take isn't available to the male of the species."

I put the cassette in its box. "The one that lasts nine months?"

"Yes, and miraculously out comes another knight on his way to the Holy Land. I wouldn't trade the experience for anything, nor can I imagine life without my children and grandchildren."

"What happened to your Papa?"

"He and Angelique spent 25 years together, happy as newlyweds. They departed this life within three minutes of one another at just after seven o'clock on the morning of May 8, 1977, seventy-five years from the eruption of Mt. Pelée."

Call 1-800-879-4214 to Order These Titles:

Under a Lemon Moon

By David N. Martin, this mystery novel reveals true metaphysical insights in a haunting story of murder and revenge that will take you on a spine-tingling karmic journey from Mexico's Sierra Madre mountains to Atlanta's Chattahoochee river . . . and from the valleys of human existence to the heights of uncharted dimensions. A quality paperback, 288 pages. $12.95. ISBN 0-9646601-7-2.

Beyond Skepticism, All the Way to Enlightenment

In the modern world we are trained to focus on what we can touch and see. But so much more surrounds us. Stephen Hawley Martin gives readers a vision of the nonphysical reality that supports and informs the physical, then tells how the theory can be laboratory tested and challenges scientists to prove or disprove it. Perhaps most compelling, however, he explains how readers can harness the forces that create their lives and provides techniques to get in touch with their higher selves, find their purpose and be guided by a higher intelligence which will lead them to enlightenment. A quality paperback. $11.95. ISBN 0-9646601-4-8

The Enlightened Companion

A 90 minute audio cassette tape performed by Stephen Hawley Martin. Side one covers key ideas contained in his book, *Beyond Skepticism.* Side two will guide you on a meditation designed to help you overcome buried fears, find your purpose and get in touch with higher guidance. $11.95. ISBN 0-9646601-5-6.

The Search for Nina Fletcher

Raised a Virginia aristocrat by a grandmother who kept hidden the truth about the mother she never knew, Rebecca Fletcher must find her mother or lose all hope of keeping the beloved family estate, Live Oaks, from the hands of sinister developers. Swept up by events, she travels to the Mediterranean island of Corsica and into a nonphysical dimension where the truths of human existence are revealed and she learns purpose of her life. By Stephen Hawley Martin. A quality paperback, 288 pages. $12.95. Available in August, 1995. ISBN 0-9646601-3-X.